W9-BCP-268

BOOKS BY JAMES PATTERSON

The Confessions Novels

Confessions of a Murder Suspect (with Maxine Paetro)
Confessions: The Private School Murders (with Maxine Paetro)
Confessions: The Paris Mysteries (with Maxine Paetro)
Confessions: The Murder of an Angel (with Maxine Paetro)

A complete list of books by James Patterson is at the back of this book.
For previews of upcoming books and information about the author,
visit JamesPatterson.com or find him on Facebook.

CONFESSIONS
THE
MURDER
OF AN ANGEL

JAMES PATTERSON
AND MAXINE PAETRO

VISION

NEW YORK   BOSTON

Copyright © 2015 by James Patterson
The Trial © copyright 2016 by James Patterson

Vision
Hachette Book Group
1290 Avenue of the Americas, New York, NY 10104
grandcentralpublishing.com
twitter.com/grandcentralpub

Originally published in hardcover and ebook by Little, Brown and Company in October 2015
First mass market edition: April 2017

Vision is an imprint of Grand Central Publishing. The Vision name and logo are trademarks of Hachette Book Group, Inc.

The publisher is not responsible for websites (or their content) that are not owned by the publisher.

The Hachette Speakers Bureau provides a wide range of authors for speaking events. To find out more, go to hachettespeakersbureau.com or call (866) 376-6591.

ISBNs: 978-1-4555-6859-8 (mass market), 978-0-316-30112-1 (ebook)

Printed in the United States of America

OPM

10 9 8 7 6 5 4 3

CONFESSIONS
THE
MURDER
OF AN ANGEL

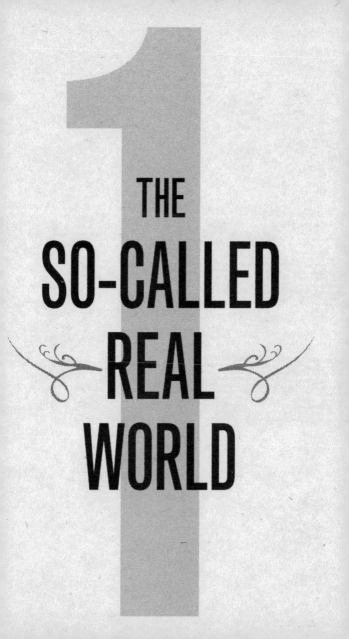

1

THE
SO-CALLED
REAL
WORLD

Hello, friend.

I have a lot to tell you . . . good and bad.

Today was *huge*.

It's been three months since I checked myself into Waterside, an exclusive rehab facility for those who are psychologically on the edge—or *were*, like me. By the time I got dressed this morning, my discharge papers were already signed and I was more or less ready to leave the loony bin and reenter the "real world."

It was early yet, about eight fifteen on a cold winter morning. I was relaxing on a fancy teak bench outside Waterside's grand pillared entrance overlooking the Hudson River in northern Manhattan, waiting for my three brothers and uncle to pick me up. I had dressed appropriately in all black: a Hervé Léger hooded coat, a turtleneck sweater, stretch wool pants, and flat-heeled Louboutin boots. I even wore lipstick and a silver headband in my dark hair, which had grown almost to my jawline in the three months since the three-alarm fire, the fatal car crash, and the total destruction of my innocence. More on that later.

My therapist, Dr. Robosson, had told me after our final morning session, "You sound very good, Tandy. Once you're back in school and settled in your new home, the routines of your New York life will reassert themselves and you'll be better than ever. Let's set up an outpatient schedule soon. I'm here for you, always."

She walked me outside and gave me a pillowy, perfumed hug, a kiss on the cheek, and a card with her cell phone number. My eyes got teary, but I was glad to say good-bye to this place.

When I had first checked myself into Waterside, Dr. Robosson had said to me, "Tandy, you've lived through fire and rain, and weathered more storms in the last year than most people have even heard about in their entire lives. If all that's happened hadn't devastated you, I'd really worry. You've been badly hurt, even if the scars don't show. You just need to talk and heal. Get a good amount of the three Rs: rest, relaxation, and reality check. Am I right?"

She had been indisputably right.

My parents were dead. I'd been accused of killing

them, viciously attacked by the press, and even jailed. I'd beaten back the forces of bad, worse, and criminally heinous. I'd solved crimes: my parents' deaths to start with, and then the murders of friends and strangers. All while uncovering mysteries, long-held secrets, and epic lives of blood relatives that surely had a profound and sometimes damaging impact on mine.

Before the events of this year, I had been known as a brainiac, a nerd with a gift for sharp analysis and first-class problem solving. I was completely unemotional, and therefore absolutely clearheaded. Those are the skills that made me a natural detective.

But by the time I turned myself over to the professional care of Waterside's psychiatric staff, I had changed. I felt everything. I cared too much. I was sleepless, jumpy, emotionally ravaged: a ragged tangle of nerves.

Now, after the intense psychotherapeutic intervention that included marathon talk therapy, meditation, steam baths, comfort foods, and dreamless sleep, I had metamorphosed from a traumatized teenager who'd been repeatedly subjected to mortal danger and shocking betrayal into a traumatized teenager who finally understood the truth.

And what was the truth? The truth was that I'd been deceived by so many people I loved, I no longer trusted *anyone*. It wasn't my fault. I'd been naïve. Accordingly, I'd been crushed but not broken. I was still emotional, but the Sullivanians, Freudians, Jungians, Skinnerians, and Far Eastern disciples among the Waterside staff all agreed. I wasn't insane.

I was *mad*.

Madder than hell.

2

My anger was real and justified. But would anger cure me...or destroy me?

That was the question.

The longer I sat on the bench in front of Waterside, staring at the river and the droning highway below, the more agitated I became.

I already regretted tearing myself from my lounge chair in the quiet, fern-filled solarium where my to-do list never had more than two items: Sip tea and listen to good music.

Instead, I was dressed for my first day of school, and despite assurances from the shrinks, my sudden flashes of anger troubled me. I wondered if I was really ready to take on the outside world, which could be crazier than I ever was.

My uncle Jacob had wanted me to check out of Waterside last week and come home to our new apartment for a few days so that I could get my bearings before starting school.

But I hadn't been ready to leave the warm embrace of Waterside, the spa days, the luxury of being treated like a fragile baby chick.

I had put off leaving until the last minute—which was now. I was rubbing my arms against the cold breeze coming off the river when I heard the crunch of tires on gravel and turned to see a long black limo with tinted glass pulling into the semicircular driveway.

A driver got out of the car. He was six feet tall, muscle-bound in black livery. He wore a black driver's hat and had tattoos on his knuckles.

He said, "Ms. Angel? I'm Leo Peavey. I work for your family."

Unsmiling, he picked up my backpack and opened the back door for me. I looked inside, expecting to see my brothers and my uncle Jacob, but only Hugo, my youngest bro, an eleven-year-old master of trouble-making, was there.

"Where is everyone?" I said to Hugo.

"*I'm* here. Sorry to disappoint."

I opened my arms to the little monster who had been coming to visit me just about every week since my admission to Waterside.

He spoke with his face pressed into my coat. "Have fun at Waterside Penitentiary?"

"Of course," I said, kissing his head. "It was like Christmas and the Cherry Blossom Festival all rolled into one."

"Ha. What did they do to you, Tandy?"

"They forced me to sleep late, drink peppermint tea, read *Harry Potter*, and listen to Chopin. All at the same time."

"Sounds horrible," Hugo said. He meant it.

I cracked up.

My little bro went on. "Uncle Jake and Matty are setting up your computer. Harry had early practice this morning. I hope we get there in time."

Getting there in time meant arriving at school before the window for enrollment in the second term closed. I couldn't miss that.

Leo had just negotiated the curving on-ramp to the Henry Hudson when, without warning, our wheels failed to grip the slippery highway and we went into a long, slow sideways skid on the ice. I gripped Hugo's hand as we slewed across the lanes. And then I saw a dark SUV behind us, bearing down on us at high speed as we spun around.

Time slowed, and I saw exactly how our car would get T-boned at sixty miles an hour. I was already hearing our screams and the ripping, screeching sound of metal on metal.

I remembered how a black Escalade chased my

car not too long ago...and how that pursuit ended in many horrifying deaths.

I grabbed Hugo and braced for the crash.

The last thing I saw was the SUV—windshield tinted impenetrably black—before squeezing my eyes shut, waiting for the inevitable.

3

Car horns began to blare.

I opened my eyes. Just in time to see the SUV shooting past our still-spinning car, skimming a guardrail, then getting traction and speeding off.

Our driver wrenched back control of the limo, and his eyes shot to the rearview mirror as he shouted, "You kids all right?"

Hugo was as pale as milk, and my heart was still flailing in terror. I exhaled shakily and said, "We're good," but the shock of the narrowly missed accident wouldn't fade.

I was lucky to be alive.

As the limo sped along the highway, I tried to put the accident out of my mind for my sake and Hugo's, and ready myself for the looming reality of high school.

I had always been regarded by my peers as odd, weird, and, at the very least, a peculiar girl. But as odd, weird, and peculiar as I was, my three brothers belonged in the square-peg-round-hole category just as much as me.

There was a reason for this.

I thought back on my session with Dr. Robosson less than an hour ago. We were sitting in her office, wrapping up before my departure from Waterside.

She said, "Tandy, I know how you feel about medication, but I've written you a prescription for a mild tranquilizer. You can take one in the morning before school, and one before bed, if you feel too agitated to sleep. They're very safe."

She tore the prescription from the pad, but I was already shaking my head *No, no, no*.

"No more pills, Dr. Robosson. I'm done with them, forever."

I was remembering other pills that had brought me and my siblings to this place and time.

Our overachieving parents, Maud and Malcolm Angel, had set impossibly high standards of performance for us. And to help us reach those standards, we were all given a daily regimen of pills produced by the family business, Angel Pharmaceuticals.

We were told the pretty, colorful pills were vitamins. In fact, they were drugs designed to boost certain talents many times over while completely repressing our emotions—which Malcolm and Maud believed are detrimental to success.

Because of the pills, Hugo has the strength of an adult male athlete. Our older brother, Matthew, is a Heisman Trophy–winning football player for the New York Giants.

Their nuclear tempers are also legendary. When Matty or Hugo gets mad, *run*. Run fast.

My twin brother, Harry, is an artistic and musical genius, but withdrawn and socially inept. I'm also very awkward around people, but like my father, I have a highly scientific mind. I have the ability to look at disparate parts and intuit what the whole will look like. I'm nearly always right.

But until last year when I stopped taking the pills, I had no feelings, no messy emotions, and, like Matty, had been called a sociopath more than once. I had the perfect personality for a corporate CEO, and my parents hoped I would head up the family business one day.

Even then, I thought I'd rather be dead.

The full truth about how the pills changed the regular-smart Angel kids into high-achieving, sociophobic *freaks* didn't come out until after our parents were gone. But charts of our progress, memos about the experiments, and the pills themselves remained.

The evidence was undeniable.

Maud, Malcolm, and our uncle Peter had willfully experimented on us and on other human lab animals before we were born. Some of those people—a lot of them just *kids*—had died.

And still, to this day, Angel Pharmaceuticals produces "the pills." Because they are called vitamins, they are not under the purview of the FDA. Our despicable uncle Peter, currently the sole proprietor of the company, is cagey enough not to sell the pills in the United States. Instead, he ships them overseas.

I've grown up fast in the last few months, and I'm still working things out. I don't yet know how, but I'm sure of at least this much: As soon as possible, I'm going to bring Angel Pharmaceuticals down—board up the headquarters, sue the hell out of my uncle Peter, and burn the factory to the ground.

~ CONFESSION ~

I hated my parents.

But I loved them, too.

Malcolm and Maud were ruthless, never allowing me or my brothers to accept failure or even second best. When we did excel, it was always expected and rarely celebrated. Punishments were severe, involving anything from copying whole books—in perfect calligraphy—to military boot camps. Displays of emotion were strictly forbidden.

Can you imagine being a little kid in that kind of environment? No wonder we all turned out so...peculiar.

But then, there were the other times. I remember snuggling between them in their enormous bed, being read to from gorgeous picture books in Urdu or Japanese. Playing dress-up in Maud's closet, tripping in her stilettos and dragging her furs around the room like a Hollywood star. Watching Malcolm experimenting with a new recipe in the kitchen, taste-testing his always delicious gourmet dishes.

When I found out about the pills and how our parents used us as their personal guinea pigs, I was enraged—but not really surprised.

After all, if the drugs were able to turn people into superhuman genius prodigies, Malcolm and Maud were going to make sure that their children would be *first in line* to take them.

Side effects be damned.

4

I watched the highway roll past the car windows. Twenty minutes after leaving Waterside, Leo slowed to approach the old spired church with stained-glass windows on the corner of Seventy-Seventh and Columbus.

This church had been repurposed as All Saints Academy, and during the school year, it was like an old-fashioned one-room schoolhouse where students of all grades took their classes together. But far from having lessons in a rickety building on the prairie, we were tutored under the vaulted ceiling of a Gothic cathedral on a beautiful New York City avenue.

Up ahead, I saw a dozen kids I knew sitting together on the wide church steps, kidding one another and laughing.

"We made it," Hugo said to me. "We beat the bell."

Before the car had fully stopped, Hugo bolted out right into traffic. I yelled and Leo braked hard. He ejected himself from the driver's seat, and with horns blowing behind us, he ran around the nose of the limo, grabbed Hugo by the arm, and hoisted him onto the sidewalk.

"You want to get killed, Mr. Hugo? Why? You're the boy with everything."

As I got out on the sidewalk, Leo handed me my book bag—a python Proenza Schouler satchel—and his card, saying, "If you need me, just call."

Then Leo Peavey sped off and disappeared into the morning rush hour traffic.

Standing in front of All Saints, my school since kindergarten, I had a flash of first-day-of-school excitement. I wished Harry was here with me, but he was off at an intensive music workshop that got him permission to be out of All Saints this first week.

Then I heard a familiar voice calling, "Hey, crazy."

I turned and saw C.P.—my former best friend and current worst nightmare—with her hands on her hips and a nasty grin on her face, showing she wasn't kidding. She was taunting me for real.

Memories of the last time I'd seen C.P. hit me with the force of a tsunami. On that unthinkable day, the traitor had been standing in her lacy lingerie, clinging possessively to James, the boy I had loved with my whole heart.

Of course, that meant that he'd betrayed me, too.

5

When I met Claudia Portman, aka C.P., she was an outcast, like me. She could be bitchy or funny, depending on how you took it. She had her own witchy fashion style, which she mostly pulled off. After her former friends abandoned her for behavior unbefitting a bestie, she and I quickly joined forces as a bonded pair of inseparable oddballs.

But last year, C.P. had deceived me unforgivably by hooking up with James. Even though she apologized way after the fact, saying, "I just couldn't help myself, Tandy," her matter-of-fact apology was so transparently false, I could never trust her again.

There were three sides to this story: hers, his, and mine. But who cares about theirs? My side had been vetted and psychiatrically approved. I was doubly wronged by any standard, and I didn't have the time or grace within me to forgive or forget either one of them.

I understand that if you can't forgive, anger takes over you. And I say, "Bring it on." Remembering pain is how you learn never to let the cause of it happen again.

Now, standing in front of the school, with her taunt still hanging in the air, I faced C.P. head-on.

She looked different now.

She had extensions, good ones that made a cascade of honeyed brunette waves down to her shoulders. She was wearing a tiny Nicole Miller skirt and a tight top with sheer netting from shoulder to shoulder, something I would never dare to wear to school. This was the high-priced-hooker look favored by private school girls, but it really begged the question of who here was the crazy one.

Her insult hung between us like a freeze-frame of a tennis serve. Then the action resumed.

"So the nutcase returns," she said. "Did you escape? Hey, everyone, the House of Psychosis is missing a lunatic."

I took aim at my former friend, shouting, "I could vomit up alphabet soup and make more sense than you."

She said, "Really? I'm right here, psycho. Dazzle me with your wit. If they didn't electroshock it out of you, that is."

With that, Hugo jumped between the two of us, pointed his phone at C.P., and snapped a picture. He examined it and said, "C.P., you ugly."

"Shut up, you little tapeworm," she snarled. Then other voices cut in with more insults, calling me a lunatic, a nutjob, batshit crazy.

C.P. was taunting me again: "Are those your *dead mother*'s clothes, Tandy? I just *love* the boots."

Instead of walking past her, or laughing in her face, I shot back, "I got them in Paris. Where'd you get *your* outfit, C.P.? Sluts R Us?"

"Oh, too funny, Tandoori. Look, why don't you just go back to Water-Fried until you're normal? Which will be…oh, exactly *never*."

I was gathering myself for a sharp comeback when Hugo stepped up to C.P., pulled back his arm, and, before I even had a chance to freak, punched her right in the gut.

This was no joke. Thanks to the pills, Hugo was *strong*. I saw C.P.'s feet lift off the ground as she fell backward onto the sidewalk and let out a stunned grunt.

Another girl sputtered at Hugo, "You *psycho*. You can't hit girls!"

Hugo said, "What *girl*? All I see is a pathetic bitch who asked for what I gave her. Actually, she demanded it."

A whistle blew sharply, and we all turned to see a florid man with flyaway hair and a small mouth that was pinched around a whistle. His little black eyes were like bullets behind his glasses.

He shouted, "Everyone freeze!"

Friend, all this happened within the first ten minutes of my return to All Saints Academy.

6

Our former headmaster, Mr. Thibodaux, had been a tough disciplinarian, but very caring. It seems that he had left during my absence from All Saints, and his replacement was barring our path to the school.

He introduced himself haughtily. "I'm Dr. Felix Oppenheimer. Who are you?"

"That's Tandoori Angel," said one of C.P.'s posse before I could respond.

"Hugo's sister? I should have guessed."

C.P. was on her feet by then, her eyes watering with either pain or humiliation, but she was standing—which meant that Hugo had held back with his punch. Thank God. He could have killed her.

"Are you all right?" the headmaster asked C.P.

"He *hit* me," she said, pointing to Hugo, "really

hard. Christ, I might not be able to have babies because of him."

"Claudia, skip the blasphemy and go see the nurse," said the headmaster. "You two," he said, pointing at Hugo and me. "Stay right here. Everyone else, go inside—*now*."

He got on his phone and made a couple of phone calls with his back to us. Then he waited on the sidewalk until Leo reappeared with the car.

Our driver was still applying the brakes when Dr. Oppenheimer delivered both a threat and the biggest insult of all.

"Hugo, the next time you use physical violence, I'll call the police. Effective tomorrow, you will write a letter of apology to Ms. Portman and you will read it out loud in assembly or you will not be allowed to attend All Saints this term. I've been in touch with your guardian.

"Tandoori, because of this ruckus, you've missed your deadline for admission. I'm sorry for you. But you didn't plan appropriately. Right now, both of you must leave."

Hugo sputtered. He was about to launch a retort, but I put my hand on his shoulder and told Dr. Oppenheimer we were both sorry for our behavior.

Hugo wriggled under my hand, but he didn't say a word.

When my brother and I were in the car, the registrar, Mrs. Benardete, bent to the car window and said to me, "You can fill out the registration form online, Tandy. I'll work on the headmaster, but you must send me the paperwork today."

I nodded, then sank so low into the backseat that I was practically lying down. Hugo threw his arms around me and started crying. Despite his strength, he was still just a little kid, and I was the only mom he had. I patted his back and said, "It's okay. Don't cry." But I was scared for him.

I hadn't started this fight with C.P. I hadn't started *any* of the fights with C.P. But if there had been any question in my mind before, there was none now.

This was *war*.

7

The car was silent, a swift projectile, impervious to outside forces, and Leo was taking us "home" to a place that didn't feel like it yet.

Let me explain.

After my mother's hedge fund went bust, she was sued into the next century. She owed fifty million dollars to creditors, which was more than we had or could borrow.

The bankruptcy of Leading Hedge forced the sale of our incredible co-op in the legendary Dakota apartment building. But days before we were to be turned out on the street, Uncle Jacob took me and my brothers to Paris.

This voyage and our time in Paris was a lifeline of the most magnificent kind. Our uncle, whom we had only known for a short time, had pulled some very old strings, and we learned that we were heirs to a large inheritance. Our benefactor was Hilda Angel, our father's glamorous mother, who had died before any of her grandchildren had been born.

But she had planned for us.

Gram Hilda's bequests had conditions and a team of stuffy legal advisors attached. But for the present, her estate paid each of us a generous monthly allowance and bought us a new home in the San Remo Apartments.

The San Remo is a grande dame of an apartment building that was built in 1930. Like the Dakota, the building takes up an entire block on Central Park West. One of the San Remo's unique features is that above the eighteenth floor, the building is topped by two ten-story towers.

We were closing in on Seventy-Fifth Street when Hugo sat up and said, "See that, Tandy? Our apartment, way up on the sixteenth and seventeenth floors, just under the north tower—guess how long it takes for an orange juice balloon to hit the sidewalk from way up there."

"Hugo!"

"Kidding. Just *kidding*."

A few minutes later, Leo cruised up to the curb and braked the car outside the stupendous building.

I drifted through the doorman-flanked entrance behind Hugo, passed the elegant common rooms, and stepped into an elevator. After a long upward whoosh, the doors opened inside the only apartment on the sixteenth floor—a duplex, and it was ours.

Uncle Jacob was standing in the foyer, waiting. The look on his face showed a colorful range of feelings: relief, dismay, and pure cold anger.

"Oppenheimer called," he said. "How could all this happen before the bell? I'm getting flashbacks to all the other beyond unpleasant phone calls I've had to field because of you children."

I said under my breath, "We'll always have Paris."

"What was that, Tandy?"

I never got a chance to answer.

8

Uncle Jacob, my father's oldest brother, is a former Israeli commando. He may be old—approaching fifty—but he's a proven killer. And he'd sacrificed his good life in Israel to be our guardian.

He had saved my life several times in the first three months that he lived with us—one of the many ways he'd shown that he loved us.

But Uncle Jake was no pushover. Hugo was about to run past him, but Jacob put out his arm and stopped him cold.

"Hugo. What is this crap?" he asked as I floated past them, taking in the sights of our childhood, wide-eyed with appreciation for the artifacts we were able to salvage and trying to move beyond their argument.

Hanging in the foyer was the UFO chandelier from

my childhood. Wired to the doorbell, it was a silver saucer-shaped disc with lights that blinked in time to the theme song from the movie *Close Encounters of the Third Kind*, which it played when the bell rang.

Beyond the foyer was an unbelievably spacious living room with a marble fireplace, casement windows on three sides, and a terrace with a panoramic view of Central Park.

Inside the living room was the eccentric collection of hyperrealistic objets d'art my mother had loved to collect: Robert, the lifelike sculpture of a man drinking beer while watching TV in a recliner; Pegasus, a winged, white-lacquered piano that was Harry's own instrument, on which he practiced and played; and Mercurio, a merman hanging by his tail from the second-floor ceiling within the coil of the spiral staircase. Even the lipstick-red leather sofa and the Pork Chair, which had pig's feet and snorted when sat upon, were here.

I teared up for the second time today.

I knew that our attorney, Philippe Montaigne, had bought back these items when we came into our inheritance, but I hadn't seen them in so long, it was as if old deceased relatives had come back from the dead.

As I gawked, Jacob was having strong words with Hugo.

"Do you understand that you could be charged with assault, Hugo?"

"A misdemeanor," said Hugo. "Plus, I'm a minor."

Jacob went on. "If you've hurt C.P., you could be tried in juvenile court. Her parents have vast resources, and you, Hugo, are part of a family with what are called deep pockets. I hope I don't need to explain again that you could lose your inheritance."

Uncle Jake was referring to Gram Hilda's main condition for our inheritance, that we would lose it all if we "disgraced the family name."

"C.P. was verbally abusing Tandy," Hugo shot back.

Jacob said, "Violence is the last resort of cowards."

Hugo looked up at him, mouth opened. "But you're a soldier!"

The corners of Jacob's mouth turned up for a second. "Good job standing up for your sister," he said. "But no more violence, agreed?" Our uncle stretched out his hand.

Hugo grinned and shook hands with Jacob.

Which, when Hugo was involved, was not a promise of anything.

9

Jacob put his arm around my shoulders and walked with me into the living room. He was looking at my face, but his sleeves were rolled up and I was looking at his scarred forearms, a permanent reminder of the black night when he carried me out of Gram Hilda's burning house. My uncle Hero.

"Are you okay?"

"Never better," I chirped.

It was our private joke, and he laughed. It was a good laugh, hearty and masculine. I loved him. On the other hand—and there was always another hand—six months ago, I'd never heard of him. It was our loathsome uncle *Peter* who had introduced my sibs and me to Jacob and turned over our guardianship to him.

"The rest of the day is all about you," Jacob said. "After that, it's back to swimming with the sharks."

"Fantastic," I said. "I can swim with the best of them."

"Quite true," he said. "Take a look at your room while Hugo and I go out for groceries. Here's your elevator key." He pulled it from the pocket of his khakis. "But stay here. Get to know your new phone. Change your passwords. Read a book. There are sandwich ingredients in the fridge."

I hugged my uncle, and when he said, "That way," I headed to the spiral staircase. We'd had just such a staircase in our old apartment. I whispered hey to Mercurio as I passed him, and when I got to the landing, I saw four open doors. Jacob's bedroom, Hugo's, Harry's, and the fourth was painted my color, firmament blue. That room was mine.

I clapped my hands over my mouth, walked through the doorway, and just stood there, taking in the open sky through the windows, the four-poster bed, the desk with a laptop in the center, and the bookshelves all around, holding my books and my specimens of branched coral.

On a dress form in the corner was my mother's jacket, the one Madonna had worn in the movie *Desperately Seeking Susan*. It was a metallic greenish color with embroidery on the back, showing a pyramid with an eye on top, like the artwork on a dollar bill. I loved that jacket. It reminded me of the rarely seen, fun-loving parts of my mom's personality.

I went to the desk and opened my laptop. The software said, "Hi, Tandy."

Without even thinking, I opened my in-box, which was stuffed with hundreds of e-mails. I'm not going to lie to you, friend. I skimmed the list, my heart beating hard in my throat, looking for a message from James.

Partially relieved, but freshly disappointed, I found nothing that would jar my heart or wrack me with waves of pain and fury. I deleted huge blocks of out-of-date newsletters, sales pitches, and spam. And when I was done, I changed my password and installed the new encryption program Jacob had left for me.

After that, I uploaded Harry's music playlist and checked out my new iPhone and iPad.

When I heard the UFO toot its announcement that someone was at the door, I ran downstairs to greet my family. After some happy screams and dancing around on the beautiful parquet floors, dinner preparation commenced.

Harry and I had some quiet time as we figured out how to make crepes without a crepe pan.

He said to me, "You feeling okay?"

"Meaning?"

"Have you had a chance to process, uh, everything that's happened?"

"Everything? Sure, but I wouldn't say I'm cured."

An hour later, my older brother, Matty, arrived with his dreads tied back with a cord, his laser-blue eyes sparkling, and wearing his own New York Giants jersey under his jacket.

He held out a huge bunch of paper-wrapped roses. "Happy birthday, little sister," he said.

"It's not my birthday."

"Well, yeah, it is."

Crap. I'd forgotten my birthday. And Harry's!

10

"I told you I could surprise her," Matty said to Uncle Jake. He tossed the roses down, picked me up, and twirled me around like I was five.

I laughed and beat his shoulders with little-girl fists. Finally, he put me back on my feet.

"Well, in my own defense," I said, resetting my hairband and smoothing my hair, "I haven't as much as seen a calendar in months. Or a clock, for that matter."

Everyone laughed at me, and Hugo said, "Welcome back to Planet Real Life, Tandy."

While I was being twirled and danced around and Harry came out of his room, Hugo had brought in a wooden crate marked SPECIAL DELIVERY, which he opened with a pry bar. Inside were wigs and masks, and we all grabbed for something outrageous. I'd always wanted to see what I looked like as a blonde—and from what I could see in the mirror over the sofa, I didn't look at all bad! And Jacob looked hilarious with a ponytail.

Over a very unusual dinner that included our favorite dishes from restaurants all over the city—tandoori prawns from the Indian restaurant on Columbus for me, smoked hot dogs from Hugo's favorite deli, and Szechuan alligator tail from Shun Lee West for Harry—we reminisced about other birthdays and I told tales about the real psych ward on the top floors of Waterside.

After dinner, we went back to the living room. Matty dragged Robert over to join us, saying, "No TV for a few minutes, okay, bro?"

Hugo took possession of the Pork Chair, and Harry and I sat on the floor and opened jokey presents: latex claws, big yellow teeth, and hot chili candy. Jacob brought in a chocolate cheesecake and set it down on the coffee table, and Harry and I blew out the seventeen candles together.

But the frosting on top was when my brilliant, talented, musical twin went to his Pegasus piano. He pushed up his sleeves, wiggled his fingers dramatically, and then sang a "Happy Birthday" song in a voice that reminded me of Willie Nelson.

Well, we're havin' a happy birthday.
Happy birthday to me and you.

I believe it's our seventeenth birthday.
You know it's come at last, you do.
And when you're havin' a happy birthday,
there ain't no time for feelin' blue.

We laughed, we applauded, and Matty popped the cork on a lovely Dom Pérignon. I've never had a birthday half as good. Ever.

It was a beyond-fabulous evening in the Angel household.

I knew I had to cherish it because history had taught me that life could turn completely upside down in the time it took to say "Man, it's really good to be home."

11

Our school bell is a real bell—and it was tolling.

The kids hanging out on the front steps, the knots of girls gathered in the little courtyard between the school and the apartment house next door, and the bunch of boys sitting on the stairs to the rectory, all got to their feet and streamed into All Saints Academy. Thanks to Mrs. Benardete, I joined them.

Footsteps echoed between the stone walls, backpacks thudded to the floor, and chatter bounced around the twelve rows of pews in the nave. I went to the front row, taking my seat on the aisle behind the railing on the right. A second later, I noticed that my dearest enemy, C.P., was sitting across the aisle, with a few kids between us on my left.

Feeling a wave of revulsion at the sight of her, I looked straight ahead and thought about Hugo.

In just a few minutes, my little brother would have to make his public apology to C.P. for punching her. I had told Hugo I would sit directly in his line of vision, and that anytime he looked at me, I would be smiling and giving him a thumbs-up.

He'd said, "If I were you, Tandy, I'd sit in the back so you can make a fast escape."

I couldn't tell if he was joking.

Dr. Oppenheimer came up the right-hand aisle and stood in front of the pulpit, his gaze settling on me for an instant before moving away. He cleared his throat and said, "All right now, everyone. Settle down. This morning, we will hear from Mr. Hugo Angel. He has something he wishes to say."

Heads swiveled to watch Hugo come up the center aisle. He usually wears his hair in a long, rusty mop of curls. But for today, Harry had trimmed Hugo's hair and combed it back.

Hugo had also put aside his daily uniform of jeans and a Giants T-shirt and instead wore a white dress shirt and a pair of blue slacks.

He looked adorably mature.

As he passed my seat on the aisle, I tried to read his expression, but he was giving nothing away. He climbed the steps and took the pulpit, but given his four-foot-ten-inch height, he didn't exactly tower over it. Still, he had presence.

Oppenheimer said, "Please give Hugo your attention."

Blood rushed to my face. I was anxious for my little brother. Would he embarrass himself? It didn't matter. I would love him no matter what.

Hugo said, "Good morning, God and Dr. Oppenheimer and Claudia and everyone.

"I have something to say. I know it's not right to get physical when all that's happening is name-calling. So, Claudia, I apologize for hitting you yesterday. That was wrong. I lost my temper, and I won't do it again.

"But what *you* did was also wrong. You attacked my sister without provocation. Through no fault of her own, Tandy has been through the seven circles of hell. Our parents recently died, our brother was accused of murder, and it was Tandy who found out the truth and saved us from a lifetime in prison. And, C.P., as her best friend, you know what Tandy has suffered more than anyone. But as a friend who then betrayed my sister in the cruelest way possible, know that one of her circles of hell is entirely inhabited by *you*. Just when you should have been the most supportive, you did everything you could to make Tandy suffer even more. Judging by your behavior yesterday, you're continuing your sick little games even now. For that, you deserve every ounce of her pain, times ten. And I hope you get it.

"So I want to finish by saying please accept my apology for hitting you, C.P. I mean that sincerely.

But until you apologize to my sister, I advise you to stay out of the Angels' way. If you see us in the hallway, keep your eyes off us. If you see us in class, don't speak to us. And if we're coming up the stairs, I strongly suggest that you *don't come down*.

"May God bless all the students and faculty of this great school and all the people they love and who love them. Amen."

"Amen" in unison rolled forward from all the rows behind me. And then the most remarkable thing happened. Almost everyone jumped to their feet and applauded, and some even whistled and stamped as Hugo came down from the pulpit.

I grabbed his arm and squeezed it. He grinned and continued up the aisle. I almost expected him to start slapping hands, for people to throw flowers.

It was a true triumph. My little brother, a super kid in every way, had defended my honor and his.

Instinctively, I turned toward C.P. She stood there, glaring, still as a stone, her expression a combination of rage and disbelief. And then I lost sight of her as the boisterous kids spilled out into the aisle.

But I saw enough to know that she was mad, all right. And knowing her as I do, I could tell she wouldn't let this public takedown go unanswered.

Not a chance.

12

After the dismissal bell rang, I took a cab to a gray stone building on William Street in downtown Manhattan where our family friend and lawyer, Philippe Montaigne, has his office.

Phil is one of the good guys, but he is also Uncle Peter's lawyer, and so not above suspicion.

I took the elevator to his suite on the twentieth floor and announced myself to the young woman at the desk. She phoned Phil, and within ninety seconds, he came through the inner door and held out his arms to me.

Phil is a very handsome man. He always looks crisp and smooth in dark suits, his thinning hair shaved short and his skin a warm Caribbean bronze.

Philippe filled a mug for me at the coffee urn and took me into his airy modern office. I sat down in a chair across from his desk, dropped my bag to the floor, and turned my fierce attention on him.

"What's so urgent, Tandy?" he said, getting right to it.

"I have to talk with you about Angel Pharma."

"Okay. I'm listening."

"I saw things when I was in France that prove Angel Pharmaceuticals is a criminal enterprise."

"That's quite an assertion, Tandy. What happened in France?" Phil asked me.

I told our dear family friend the parts of the Paris sojourn that had to do with Angel Pharma. I briefed him about my grandmother's scientific mind, and that she had arrived at formulas to boost intelligence and strength. "But she abandoned these recipes when the animal trials showed her that the effects could be remarkable—but fatal," I explained.

I named names. I cited examples. I told Phil that I had found documents that linked my father and my uncle Peter to the recovery of these formulas for "smart" drugs that had carried lethal side effects. I knew of three boys in France who had died from taking the pills, and I didn't doubt there were countless others.

"You have the documents proving this?"

And that was when my agitation overwhelmed my happiness at seeing Phil. He was only asking me a simple question, but it felt like a challenge. I hesitated before speaking again, using a moment to collect my thoughts and calm myself a little.

I took a breath before saying, "The documents were destroyed when Gram Hilda's house was set on fire. But I have anecdotal evidence. *Good* evidence.

"Phil, my brothers and I took these drugs our whole lives. You might say we benefited from them; it's true that we test very high in intelligence and physical skills. But based on what happened to other test subjects, we could be *dying*.

"Meanwhile, Peter Angel is still exporting pretty pills with poetic names as candied vitamins. It's immoral, unethical, and has got to be illegal. Phil, you believe me, don't you?"

My anger had been surging as I spoke. I hadn't quite managed to keep it out of my voice.

"Tandy, Tandy, please calm down," said Phil. I saw concern in his face, and I trusted his sincerity. But I couldn't calm down. I felt frantic and frustrated and afraid that he wouldn't take me seriously.

"Your doctors have given you full batteries of tests, and you're in the top one percent of perfect health," he said.

My God, I wanted to scream bloody hell. I clenched my fists and bit my lip, and I felt sweat dripping into my eyes.

Phil said reasonably, "And to your main point, Tandy, you understand, you can't close down a corporation with undocumented anecdotes that are legally ancient and took place in another country."

Lights flashed in front of my eyes, and I found it hard to breathe. I grabbed the edge of the desk and tried to plant my suddenly weightless feet on the floor.

What was wrong with me?

Was it my newfound righteous anger blazing along my neural pathways that was making me feel this light-headed? Was my anger actually running the rest of me?

Or was I having symptoms of an early, pill-induced fatal illness? I tried to swallow. I licked my dry lips, and I stood up straight.

"I don't care about what we can't do, dammit!" I shouted, leaning over the desk to get right in his face. "Do not try to pacify me. No one is tracking these drugs. No one knows what is becoming of the people taking them. I can't sit by and let this happen.

"And neither should you."

I smiled into his shocked face and sat down. "Now, where do we begin?"

~ CONFESSION ~

At night, when I'm alone in bed and I finally allow the cold loneliness to steal over me, my thoughts always, *always* turn to James.

Our feelings had been so strong, they had broken through my pill-induced emotional coma and had overcome the unbelievable obstacles our parents had piled between us.

It was just a few months ago that I had reunited with James in, appropriately, the most romantic city in the world. We'd spent a magical evening exploring Paris together, giddily drunk on wine and love. Later, in a tiny and shabby Parisian hotel, James and I had finally, fully, become one. It was the most incredible night of my life.

The next day would be the most devastating.

By the time I woke up, James was gone. His cowardly good-bye note made me question everything and answered nothing. And the next time I saw James, he had just slept with my best friend.

Less than an hour after I had bitch-slapped C.P. and slammed the door in James's face, his horrible and extremely powerful father was dead, just after he had shot my driver in the head. His car had crashed into a tree while trying to run mine off the road.

Soon after Royal Rampling's death, my uncle Peter bought back the controlling shares of Angel Pharmaceuticals from Rampling's estate. I knew it had to have been done with James's blessing. He had hated his father but had already admitted that he had no intention of giving up his father's money, even for me.

When I think about that, my brain seizes up in a blind, wordless *fury*.

But despite all the ways that James had used and betrayed me, I confess that a loathsome little part of my heart wouldn't stop longing for him.

I daydreamed about his smile. The way he loved to stroke my hair. His casual references to our future together. Every single time he told me he loved me.

And in the safety of darkness, like now, I can't stop myself from recalling—in excruciating detail—everything we had done that night in Paris.

And despising myself for every aching thrill I felt.

I coped with my first chaotic week at school, avoiding C.P. by keeping to the outer passageways of the school between classes and studying in the isolated choir loft. I even got praise from Dr. Oppenheimer for a succinct description of chaos theory.

But underneath the appearance of normality, I hadn't forgotten my new mission in life.

I *burned* with it.

On Friday, the school day ended at last, and Leo was waiting for me at the curb. I got into the car and turned my thoughts to the meeting ahead, and after fifteen minutes of stop-and-go traffic on Forty-Second Street, Leo dropped me off in front of the iconic Chrysler Building.

By then, my mind was totally focused. I went through

a revolving door that released me into the building's marbled lobby and found Philippe Montaigne staring up at the gorgeous Art Deco murals on the thirty-foot ceilings.

I tapped my lawyer on the shoulder. We hugged, then grabbed an open elevator. As the car rose toward the nineteenth floor, Phil said, "Let me do the talking."

"I'll do my best, but I'm under a lot of pressure, Phil," I said. "You could say that my purpose in life is about to culminate here and now."

"Please, for your own sake, keep your expectations in check, Tandy."

Before I could say, "Me? Never," the elevator doors slid open into a spacious reception area and we were shown to a glassed-in conference room, where six gray-haired, gray-suited lawyers and my paunchy, ginger-haired uncle Peter sat around a marble conference table.

I could see Peter's pink little eyes behind his glasses. Because of his porky looks, we kids had called him Uncle Pig most of our lives.

Maybe that was one of the reasons he hated us. But it wasn't the only one. Once, when I was younger, I had even asked him.

"Because the whole snotty pack of you are revolting. Especially you."

Now he smiled broadly upon seeing me. He was putting on a show. "How are we feeling, Tandoori?

All better now? All your marbles accounted for? Got new bulbs in your chandelier?"

"I'm fine, Uncle Peter. And how is your worldwide reputation for limitless corruption and deplorable greed faring?" I smiled venomously as I took the seat opposite my uncle, with Phil to my right.

Peter sarcastically introduced me around as his brother Malcolm's daughter. "Tandoori is named for an Indian cooking oven."

When the snickers and introductions had ceased, Phil said, "My client is the victim of Angel Pharmaceuticals products. We're here to serve notice that if your vitamin division is not voluntarily closed down until independent scientists can study your product line, we will notify the FDA, the FBI, the IRS, and Interpol regarding the questionable ingredients in those so-called vitamins."

There was a moment of stunned silence, which I enjoyed. We'd caught Angel Pharma napping. I was prepared for anything, or so I thought, until all the lawyers started barking like hyenas.

"If I may address my niece," said Uncle Pig.

Phil said, "Address *me*, Peter."

Ignoring him, Peter stood up, walked around to my side of the table, and stabbed the air with his forefinger, *this close* to my nose.

Reflexively, I rolled my chair back.

Peter's spittle sprayed my face as he hissed. "Because of those pills, you're as healthy as a cow and more intelligent than you were ever meant to be. And in all these years, you've never shown a smidgen of gratitude for your extraordinary life, you little *shit*."

From the murderous look in his eyes, it was clear he was more than willing to end my extraordinary life right then and there.

14

I was stunned by Peter's vehemence and audacity. It was as if he had actually taken a sledgehammer to my heart.

I fumbled for a comeback and was coming up with nothing when luckily Phil picked up where Peter had left me for dead.

Phil said, "We can prove that children who were given those so-called vitamins aged rapidly and died before their twentieth birthdays. My client is seventeen."

"Please provide evidence of this fairy tale," Peter said. "I wager that you cannot, because it is one hundred percent pure bull crap, not to mention outrageously libelous. Allow me to confer with my lawyers."

The hyenas barked some more, saying sarcastically how scared they were of what I could do to the company. They thought they were hilarious but obviously were not funny at all.

Phil went on, "As I was saying, Peter, we can do this the easy way. You agree to discontinue all shipments of your products until independent scientists we approve have analyzed the ingredients. Or we will notify the agencies I mentioned, and my client and her brothers will sue for damages. They will sue *you*, Peter, personally."

"We're not discontinuing a damned thing, so do your worst," Peter spat. "In fact, we have a boatload heading for Shanghai tomorrow morning. As for you, you little snot," he said, turning to me, "you've got nothing on me. I can't wait to wipe the courtroom floor with your nasty little face."

I'd been seething since Uncle Pig became my guardian. I'd kept myself under control for most of the last year, but now the dam that had been holding back my fury burst wide open.

I stood up with my backpack and unzipped it. A flood of candy-colored pills poured out across the conference table, causing the lawyers to recoil in surprise.

The pills were beautiful, not just because they were of every shape and color. They were beautiful because they were evidence, and because every single one of them was stamped with the name and logo of Angel Pharmaceuticals.

"I've got nothing on you?" I said into Peter's startled face. "I've got *everything*, Uncle. I can't wait to bring this evidence to court so the whole world will know that you're a soulless maniac who has caused irreparable damage to your own flesh and blood.

"You had full knowledge that these pills are dangerous and even lethal but freely gave them to us anyway. For all I know, you may have already killed us."

15

Pills continued to cascade off the long marble table and onto the floor as I walked briskly out of the conference room with Philippe right behind me. I fixed my expression into a mask of supreme indifference. But in truth, I was scared and furious. My heart was like a fire hose pumping hot, adrenalized blood through my veins.

Phil pushed the button for the elevator and said, "Think about this carefully, Tandy. Going head-to-head with Peter when he is fighting for his life is going to be a nuclear war. *Everyone* is going to get dragged through the mud. Are you sure you want me to proceed with this action?"

Phil looked very concerned. And I understood what he was telling me. Before the case was over, injuries would be inflicted on both sides, and not just to me. My brothers would go through the grinder as well.

But I had a firm belief that right was might and that we would beat Peter and shut down his corrupt, child-killing drug factory. It was a fight worth fighting.

"The company may try to negotiate," Phil told me as Leo opened the car door for me. "He doesn't want the FDA poking into his laboratory, that's for sure."

"You know Peter. You think he'll negotiate?"

"Not a chance," he admitted.

"He may try to shut me up permanently," I said. "There have been several attempts on my life in the last year, like the fire that torched Gram Hilda's house in Paris. But I'm willing to risk everything to have Angel Pharma shut down, so help me God."

"A good reason to keep your head down. On the other hand, you could win tens of millions in damages."

I barely heard what he was telling me. I said, "Phil, I'm officially authorizing you to file a complaint against Angel Pharmaceuticals. As soon as possible."

As we left the building, I said good-bye to my lawyer and put on my shades. After Leo locked me inside our bulletproof car, we headed uptown, and I thought about the elements of our case.

Charts had once existed of the Angel kids' drug protocols. There were memos and documents and reports, cartons of them. And there were inquiries from other governments that saw the military potential of Angel Pharma's products, thanks to the mind-boggling results from physical examinations done on Matty and Hugo.

Unfortunately, this rich stash of incriminating evidence had burned up in the fire in Paris, but Hugo, Harry, Matty, and I were alive. And we could testify to the effects of Angel Pharma's so-called vitamins on us—if we lived that long.

I was abruptly brought back into the moment when the car stopped in the familiar semicircular driveway.

I asked, "Leo, do you have a license to carry?"

"Yes. I'm armed at all times: gun, knife, and hands. I'm a master of MMA."

"Good."

"I also have eyes in the back of my head."

He took off his cap, and two piercing blue eyes that were tattooed on the back of his shaved scalp stared me down.

Leo's reflection winked at me in the rearview mirror. I laughed and said, "I'll be down in forty-five minutes."

Leo opened the car door for me, and I marched up the steps and through the front doors of Waterside.

16

I took a chair in the anteroom of Dr. Robosson's office. I crossed my legs and pulled on my hair as the standard "Be Happy" music played through the speakers and the familiar fragrances of lilac and lemon balm came through the ventilators. Nothing had changed a bit in the week since I'd left Waterside.

But *I* felt different.

I no longer resided here and was neither confined nor protected by the high granite walls and the hundreds of caregivers at this place.

I was thinking of my lounge chair in the solarium overlooking the river when voices came through the door: Dr. Robosson's warm tones, interspersed with a man's gravelly "Good-bye. See you tomorrow, Doctor R."

The door swung open. A hunched, barefoot man in a terry-cloth robe shuffled out, and Dr. Robosson invited me in.

She was wearing a rosy pink suit and smiled broadly as I went to the chair across from her larger one. She closed the door, and when she was seated, she gave me a long look—what I call an eyeball diagnosis. Then she said, "How have you been, Tandy?"

I burst into tears.

Oh, man, I was not ready for that.

Dr. Robosson looked terribly worried as she passed me the tissue box. I pulled out a wad and sobbed into them. When I'd pretty much cried myself out, Dr. Robosson said, "Tandy? What's happened? What's hurting you?"

For some reason, I found this hilarious, and so a couple more of my precious forty-five minutes were spent dissolved in hysterical laughter. Oh my God. It felt so good to laugh.

Dr. Robosson waited me out, and when I was truly ready to begin my session, I said, "Nothing is hurting me, Dr. Robosson. It's just that I'm so relieved to see you."

Her face relaxed. She smiled and leaned back in her chair. "I missed you, too."

I laughed again. Look, I know I was somewhat hysterical. And then I blurted, "Dr. Robosson, the new apartment is wonderful. I have a beautiful room, and our lawyer tracked down a lot of our old furniture and bought it back for us."

"That must feel pretty good," said my doctor.

I nodded, and she asked me what else was on my mind. It felt great just sitting across from her familiar face and nurturing presence.

I said, "That first morning, when I went back to school, C.P. was on the front steps, almost like she was waiting for me to show up."

"I see. Tell me more about that."

"It was horrible. She attacked me from the first word, as if *she* was the one who was betrayed. I stood up for myself, believe me, but it was a ridiculous fight. And then Hugo punched C.P. in the stomach."

"*Oh*. What happened then?"

"The headmaster stepped in and told Hugo he had to apologize to C.P. in front of the whole student body."

"Oh, wow. How did that go?"

"Amazing. He made his apology and then absolutely tore her down, and got everyone in the school on his side in the process. He finished to standing applause. For an apology!"

Dr. Robosson laughed appreciatively and said, "You seem very proud of him."

"I am. I love my little brother so much, and I'm even a little jealous of how he takes on a world in which he can hardly control a thing. And he just kills it."

Dr. Robosson smiled. "It's safe to say your days of having the emotional range of a robot are over."

I grinned.

Dr. Robosson shot a glance at the little red clock on her side table and said, "Our session is almost up. Shall we meet again, same time next week?"

"Oh, Dr. Robosson, I have to tell you this one more thing. I went to Angel Pharmaceuticals with my lawyer today. And we stood up to my uncle Peter and his gang of legal thugs. We said either he had to stop shipping the pills or I'd sue him for the damages. Big-time."

"Tandy. You waited until this minute to tell me that?"

"I'm wondering if my parents would be furious with me. Or if they'd be proud," I said.

She said, "They'd be proud. But those are both big subjects. Let's spend some time on this next week, okay? And try to remember your dreams."

I found Leo watching birds with a pair of binoculars. He opened the car door, and I got into the backseat knowing that my frontal attack on Angel Pharma was all I'd be thinking about until I saw Dr. Robosson again.

When I walked into the apartment that late afternoon, it was as though I had stepped into the path of a cyclone, one of those twisters that sound like a runaway freight train headed right at you.

It was *insane.*

Everyone was in the living room. Even my mother's prized sculpture, Robert, had been pulled with his recliner up to the television.

Matthew was lying on the sofa, feet pointed at the football game. He had jacked up the sound to headache-loud. Judging by the number of bottle caps on the coffee table and beer bottles on the floor, Matty and Robert had been partying for a long while.

Jacob was yelling something to Matthew that I couldn't make out.

Hugo was curled up in the Pork Chair, hugging his knees, and from the way his chest was heaving, I knew he was crying his heart out.

Harry was twenty feet away, playing his piano as if he was the only one in the room. I didn't recognize the tune, but it was something military, with menacing thrumming and sharp notes cutting through the sound of cheering fans from the TV.

I yelled, "What's going on?"

Uncle Jacob held up a newspaper, one of the New York City daily tabloids. The headline took up half the page.

ANGEL IS DEVIL IN DISGUISE

"Have you seen this?" Jacob shouted. He shook the paper, and the inside pages broke loose and fluttered onto the floor—all but the front page, which Jacob gripped tightly in both hands.

I said, "No, what is it?"

I eased the front page out of Jacob's grasp and scrutinized the photo. It was Matty's Tesla, and it looked like it had rear-ended a van. Matty was being helped out of his car by two uniformed cops. Blood was running down his face.

Now I looked at Matty in the flesh. Both of his eyes were black and blue, and some of his hair had been shaved, with stitches visible in his scalp.

There was pounding on the ceiling: our upstairs neighbor registering a complaint. By then, Jacob had clearly overshot his limit. He bellowed at my twin, "*Stop!*"

The piano cut out instantly.

Jacob found the remote under the pile of Cheetos bags and switched off the TV.

"Sit up," he said to Matthew. "Right now."

"Christ," said Matty. "I'm watching the game."

And now we were all watching *him*. He had a ferocious "don't even *think* of messing with me" look on his face that I'd seen many times before—usually when he was running with a ball under his arm and was returning a kickoff through enemy lines.

But that expression crumpled as Matty sat up abruptly and put his feet on the floor.

"I got cut from the team, all right? I'm out of a job. I didn't want to tell anyone until I got a new deal."

Hugo got out of the chair, climbed onto the couch, and threw his arms around Matty's neck.

"They're crazy!" Hugo cried. "They can't fire you, Matty. They need you."

Matthew said, "Sorry, buddy. I violated my contract. People get cut from ball clubs all the time. It's just the first time for me." He lowered his eyes to the floor. His wretched form radiated shame and misery.

Would our family's pain ever stop?

18

The sudden silence seemed to have a vibration of its own. Since I'd walked into the apartment, the sun had dropped below the horizon. Without the TV on, the apartment was nearly dark. And now the vignette on the red sofa had the look of a surrealist painting.

The three of them were a study in pain.

Hugo stood on the sofa, bouncing with a nervous energy and listening intently. Jacob sat in the chair, leaning toward Matty. He still held the paper in his hand.

Jake said, "Matthew, don't you think you owe us an explanation?"

Matty's voice cracked when he said, "There's no one to blame but me."

He dropped his head into his hands and began to

cry. This was freaking heartrending. Matty hadn't cried when our parents died. He hadn't cried when his girlfriend was horribly killed or when he was charged with her murder.

I don't remember *ever* seeing Matthew cry.

Jacob went over to the sofa and put his arm around Matty's shoulder. He said, "Take it easy. Just talk to us."

"Don't be nice to me, okay?" Matty said.

He broke into a new round of sobbing, and then, when he'd caught his breath, he said, "What happened was—I got loaded. I was leaving a club in Brooklyn. There were girls. They're always around me, you know, Jake? They climbed into the car without asking, and sure, I thought, why the hell not?

"And then one of them was kissing my ear, and the music was blasting and I was drinking Stoli out of the bottle and I lost control of the car and I ran into a parked van.

"It added up to nothing. *Nothing.* No one was hurt. Not badly. One of the girls has a broken arm. She's seventeen. I didn't check her ID when she got into my car, you know?

"I bailed myself out this morning and then...and then I got cut from the team, and because of that, my reality show was canceled. And so that you know *everything*, I also lost my savings," he said. "All of it. I made a risky investment. That's why I got loaded in the first place."

I expected Jacob to ask about the injured girl, to say something about the DWI or the legal implications of the accident, but he said, "You mean you're broke?"

"Yeah. Except for the pittance from Gram Hilda's estate. I can't live on that—I'm officially busted."

"You can forget that 'pittance,' too, now," Jacob said in disgust. "There was *one* condition on your inheritance. One. 'Don't disgrace the family name.' And here it all is. Drunk driving, teenage girl injured, fired from the team, and who knows what kind of lawsuits are coming.

"This whole mess is now global entertainment news. TMZ to the moon. You'll be getting a notice from the trustee, if you haven't already. Check your e-mail."

"I lost my phone."

Harry laughed at that one. He'd lost a lot of phones himself. But Hugo, Jacob, and I stared at Matthew in disbelief. I was shocked that his fantastic, enviable life had fallen apart in just one day. What had made him so reckless? I'd already surmised that his anger problem was caused by the drugs, but maybe they'd affected his judgment in the long term, too. How would we ever know?

Jacob had worked himself into a fury all over again.

Standing over my oldest brother, he said, "Okay, Matthew. I want you to listen carefully. Unlike your siblings, you're an adult. You're going to have to pull yourself out of this mess. It's the only way you'll recover your reputation and self-esteem. There will be no freeloading; you'll find no safety net here."

Hugo got between Matthew and Jacob and shouted at Jacob. "He's our brother first, last, and always, Jake! Don't you dare talk to him that way or I'll punch you in the nose."

Matthew stood up and, looking more like a homeless man than a celebrated all-star athlete, headed to the doorway.

"There won't be any more trouble, Jake," he said. "Bye, kids."

Hugo cried out, "Matty, don't go!"

But the door closed, leaving only the memories of the terrible scene still hanging in the air around us.

"He's family," Harry said to Jacob. "We take care of our own." I agreed with Harry and Hugo.

Jacob said, "He's been looking for a way to crash, and now he's done it in every sense of the word. I won't have him bringing down the three of you."

"We can take care of ourselves," I spat.

"When you're twenty-one, you can take care of yourself. For now, you have me," Jacob returned.

I tossed my head as if I still had long hair, then spun around and headed up the stairs to my room with Hugo on my heels. Harry went back to the piano and ran the scales listlessly in the dark.

So much for a pleasant family evening.

I wondered if there would ever be peace and harmony in the house of Angels again.

About an hour after Matthew left our apartment, Jacob knocked on our bedroom doors and summoned us to dinner.

It was a tense, overcooked meal of chicken, string beans, and potatoes that was interrupted several times by texts and phone calls to Jacob, which he took out of earshot.

"Hey," said Hugo as Jacob began clearing the table. "I'm not done with my pudding."

"Sorry," said Jacob. "And I'm sorry I yelled, but Matthew is almost twenty-five. He must account for his actions. And he will. The girl in the car with him, Sandra Rendell, is filing a lawsuit. He has a DWI, and it's not his first. Matthew's insurance will pay for the cars, but not for the fear and emotional trauma he caused a number of people, some of whom are opportunists. And since Matthew is broke, I honestly don't know what he's going to do."

My heart was banging almost louder than the dishes and cutlery Jacob was taking to the kitchen. I wished I could close my eyes, click my heels, and go back to our wonderful homecoming birthday party with cake and gag gifts and singing.

Nice thought, but no. I was still at the horrid dinner table. Sometimes there's nothing you can do about timing.

"Jacob, I need to have a family discussion on a different subject entirely."

Jacob sat back down at the dining table, which had been bought new and had no memories attached. But I would say there were enough memories among those of us at the table to populate a war museum.

My brothers and Jacob turned to me, and out came my opening line.

"I hired Philippe to represent me against Angel Pharmaceuticals and Uncle Peter, personally, for damages because of the pills. Me and anyone else in this family who wants to join me."

"I'll back you up," said Harry. "I don't know if I'm damaged, but I'm not what anyone calls normal."

"Sign me up, too," said Hugo uneasily. "I know I'm a little messed up in my head."

That broke my heart.

"Phil says you have a case?" Jacob asked me.

"He does."

I sounded completely sane to my own ears when I said, "I've always known I was meant to do something important with my life, and now I know what it is. I have to put Angel Pharmaceuticals out of business.

"And you, Uncle Jake, more than anyone else, know why."

20

I was in my new room, which reminded me so much of the old one. Same blue walls, my desk under the window, and lights from the city and the traffic below casting rays and moving shadows on the ceiling.

I should have felt comforted by the familiarity and safety of home, but I couldn't sleep.

I thought of the elderly couple Jacob had taken me to meet in France, sweet people whose children had taken Angel Pharma pills at the behest of my uncle Peter.

I remembered the photo of the three boys, who had been cheerful and ordinary in the best possible way, until their parents had been seduced by promises that their children could be extraordinary—talented, brilliant, athletic geniuses. All they had to do was take the pills, keep records, and send the reports to Peter Angel.

That was ten years ago. Those boys were long dead.

But I knew their names.

I knew how to find their parents again.

I thought about the time my brothers and I had gone to see Peter at the factory in Hell's Kitchen. We had seen forklifts moving wooden crates into position for shipping. We had read the names stenciled on the crates: STRONG AS OX. MORE BEAUTIFUL THAN PEONY. VERY SMART CHILDREN. NO WORRIES.

These were the same pills we had taken, but they had been renamed for the Chinese markets.

The memory of that enormous warehouse filled with millions of pills sent rage ripping through me again. If I didn't stop Peter, I was as complicit and as responsible as he was.

I was so fiercely engaged in my own thoughts that my phone buzzed several times before I realized it.

I grabbed my phone and said hello.

"Tandy. It's Katherine."

My God. My God.

Hearing her voice was so shocking, but also delicious and amazing. It was as if I had stepped out of my body into lightness and something like hope. For so long, I'd thought Katherine was dead. Then, only three months ago, she had astonishingly found me in Paris.

How had she come back to life? It was impossible—and yet it was true. It was her voice, her face, and she was completely material. My sister, Katherine, who had been dead for six years, was *alive*.

The experience of walking with her for an unforgettable hour had been surreal. I couldn't stop staring at her. I had known all the details of her death, and I had mourned her for so long that of course I doubted my sanity.

But I wasn't crazy. Katherine, my wonderful big sister, hadn't come out of the shadows just to say hello. She had come to warn me that my life and the lives of our brothers were in danger. And she had made me promise to forget about her, saying, "Your safety and mine depend on keeping our meeting a secret."

Still, I'd told Harry. I'd told Jacob.

And then I'd tried to forget my only sister.

That had been excruciating, but never mind. She was calling me. I screamed her name, then belatedly covered my mouth. It was a big apartment, but it wasn't soundproof.

"Tandy, Tandy, how are you?"

"No, you first," I said. "Tell me about you!"

"I suppose that's fair, Tandoo. After all, I'm calling you. But I can only say that I am happy. So please tell me about you. I'm dying to hear some news."

I told Katherine I had checked out of Waterside, and, ignoring the C.P. drama, I gave her some of the brighter notes of my return to big-city life. But in the end, my new lifetime occupation jumped out of my mouth.

"I'm taking Peter to court. I'm going to stop him from pushing the damned pills, Katherine. I'm going to shut him down. And I'm going to make him pay."

There was a long silence. I could almost hear her thoughts wafting toward me over thousands of miles of ocean, though I had no idea where she really lived.

"Katherine?"

"Tandy. I'm here."

Her voice had lost its shimmer. I held the phone with both hands.

"What's wrong, Kath? You agree, don't you? In fact, I was thinking maybe you could give a deposition."

"Tandy, no. You have to stop. Did you forget everything I told you? You don't want to go against Peter. It's dangerous for every single one of us."

There was a crackle on the line, and then a beep that told me we had been disconnected. Fear for her safety swamped me. I did every kind of search and operator-assisted redial, and when I couldn't reach Katherine, I put my phone on my chest and turned off the lights.

When I woke up in the morning, I hadn't moved at all. The phone was exactly where I had placed it.

Katherine hadn't called me back.

CONFESSION

When I was little, I adored my sister, Katherine, more than anyone else in the world. She was gentle and kind—two qualities sorely lacking in my parents—and she was the one I ran to when I needed comforting. I wanted to be just like her, in every way.

Then we found out she'd been killed in an accident abroad.

And it was all because of Peter.

He was our uncle, older than our father. But somehow, he had developed a sick obsession with my sister—his *niece*—when she was just a child. He had openly hated the rest of us but indulged Katherine by buying her gifts, taking her out for treats, making her sit on his lap. God knows what else.

In the basement of Gram Hilda's house, I discovered repulsive love letters my uncle had written to my sister when she was still a teenager. I imagine she felt helpless to stop him, with our parents not exactly being the supportive type.

So when the opportunity presented itself, she took the only way out.

When Katherine was sixteen, my parents gave her a trip to South Africa as a special reward for being accepted at MIT. Ever the genius, she successfully faked her own death and went into hiding, never making it known to us that she was still alive for fear that Peter would find her. Even now, years later, she couldn't reveal herself because she was terrified of what he would do to her.

My beautiful, smart, promising sister—now a refugee from her own family.

So if you want to know the real reason for my crusade to burn Angel Pharma to the ground, it's simple.

Peter Angel.

I want to destroy him for what he did to my sister, my family. Without the money and the prestige that the company affords him, he would be less than nothing. Financially, socially, and professionally, he might as well be dead.

Speaking of dead, you might be wondering why I need to go through the trouble of annihilating Peter through his company, when, for a certain sum of money, I could go the more direct route.

Believe me, friend. It's under careful consideration.

AGAINST
ALL
ODDS

2

21

The Supreme Court of New York is in a 1920s granite-faced, classical-Roman-style building with a carved pediment and soaring columns standing in the heart of lower Manhattan.

At almost nine o'clock on a Monday morning, as light snow fluttered down on Centre Street, Philippe and his second chair, Drake DiBella, along with my brothers and me, climbed the wide steps to the entrance of the courthouse building.

It was, in the truest sense of the word, *awesome.*

It would be an enormous thing for four kids to take on their parents in a court of law, but this was way more than that. We were taking on our uncle and, by extension, a major corporation. My brothers and I were ready.

I missed Jacob's strong presence, but he was in Paris, fighting to retain Matty's inheritance. Despite our uncle's absence, I felt good. My righteous anger warmed me with steady heat. I was ready for vindication and justice at last.

We climbed an impressive marble staircase to a hallway where uniformed officers opened the doors to courtroom 928. The room where so much would be decided today was imposing and austere. It was paneled in dark wood to shoulder height, with stark, white-painted plaster above the panels, tall windows on one wall, and pendant lights hanging from the ceiling like frozen teardrops.

Only a few dozen people sat in the gallery. The six of us walked up the aisle and through the gate. Chairs scraped as we took our seats at the plaintiff's counsel table.

We had just taken our places when laughter and loud talking rolled up from the back of the room. I recognized Uncle Pig's grunts and the responding barks and yaps of his legal team.

Team Pig went to the counsel table across the aisle from ours. They couldn't have appeared more self-assured. It was as if once this bothersome little proceeding was over they would each get into their private jets and take off to Saint Thomas or Ibiza.

Actually, I might have looked a little smug myself.

We were in the right. We had been criminally used without our knowledge or consent in order to test drugs for commercial purposes. These drugs had altered our brains and actually turned us into freaks.

Since our meeting with Peter's lawyers two weeks ago, Philippe had filed a complaint with the courts and Peter's horrid legal team had moved to dismiss it.

Now the judge would make his decision.

I'd done some research, of course. Judge George Campbell had a reputation for fairness, but that meant he was also known to deep-six frivolous lawsuits. I hoped when he'd listened to both sides, he would do the right thing.

As if the judge had heard my thoughts, he came through a narrow door right behind his bench. He was tall, lanky, and in his midsixties. He had a bit of a smile as he sat down and rolled his chair into position.

The bailiff called the court to order and announced that this was the case of Matthew, Tandoori, Harrison, and Hugo Angel versus Peter Angel and Angel Pharmaceuticals.

Judge Campbell looked down at the papers in front of him, and then he looked up at us. The room seemed to swim as the judge's warm brown eyes connected with mine. I suddenly worried that our claim of abuse might have suffered when translated into legalese.

The judge adjusted his glasses and said, "I've read the complaint filed by the plaintiffs and the motion to dismiss made by the defendants. The court understands that the plaintiffs are aggrieved that their permission wasn't sought before ingesting these performance-enhancing drugs. They were children, and all but one are still children. It would have been prudent and morally correct to wait until they were old enough to agree to take nonessential supplements."

I relaxed my jaw muscles and unclenched my fists. The judge understood how we'd been betrayed and harmed and that Angel Pharmaceuticals had to be stopped.

He turned back to the document in front of him.

"The court finds, however," said the judge, "that even assuming that all the allegations made by the plaintiffs are true, they have not suffered any damages. I'm looking here at four remarkable young people, all of whom are A-plus students, creative in their endeavors and exceedingly capable intellectually. One, in fact, is a celebrated athlete, while another is an acclaimed musical prodigy. I find no scientific evidence to support their claims."

What? What was he saying? It felt as if the floor had tipped sideways, that I was about to pass out.

I grabbed Harry's arm. And although the judge's voice sounded warped and muffled, I forced myself to hear.

Judge Campbell said, "For that reason, the defendant's motion to dismiss is granted—with prejudice."

He removed his glasses and looked straight at me, the warmth gone from his eyes. "That means, children, that you are barred from refiling your claim against the defendants. *Permanently.*"

22

I was in complete shock.

I wasn't even sure I'd really heard what Judge Campbell had said. Did he say we had lost and Peter had won? It was inconceivable.

The judge stood up and headed toward the door behind the bench. He was leaving?

No. This was not happening.

I shot to my feet and called out, "Judge Campbell, please. You're missing the point, Your Honor. Those pills were not approved by the Food and Drug Administration. The pills turned us into *freaks*!"

The judge half turned toward me, and he was scowling.

"You've had your day in court, young lady. I've

made a decision. If you don't understand, ask your lawyer to explain. Good-bye. And good luck."

Hugo was trapped between the counsel table and the bar behind him. He picked up his chair and hurled it so that he could get out, screaming, "Judge, listen to her!"

But the judge had slipped through his back door and was gone. I stared for an interminable minute at his empty chair. Then I turned to Phil and shouted at him, "What happened? What the hell just happened?"

Phil put one hand on my shoulder and the other on Hugo's head and said, "It was a summary judgment, Tandoori. It's final. Do you understand the term *with prejudice*? It means we are prohibited from refiling the claim, as he said."

I shouted, "Then you have to file a different complaint! Or come at it from another angle. We can't just let this go."

"We lost, Tandy," Phil said. "This was always going to be down to either a yes or a no. Win or lose. We gave it our best, and the evidence was insufficient. We're done."

I was shaking my head *No, no, no.* I had risked so much by going up against Peter, and I had been so sure that the judge would see how my brothers and I had been used and abused. I just couldn't accept the finality of the judge's decision.

But there was no doubt in Uncle Peter's mind.

He crossed the aisle in two steps and leaned across

Philippe to say to me, "Happy now, snot-face? Case closed. You can't win them all, Philippe."

Peter strode up the aisle with his entourage in tow, the sound of his laughter echoing throughout the chamber. I was awash in humiliation.

Why didn't the judge understand what had been done to us?

And then Matty's gigantic face was in front of me.

Matty said, "Sorry, kiddo. We all feel as bad as you do, but it's time to go home."

Harry was urging me to move and Phil was holding out his hand to me, but I snapped again.

I screamed at Phil, "This is *wrong*! The judge made his decision, and he can unmake it."

Police officers were heading toward us. This was more humiliation than even I could stand. I followed Phil up the aisle, through the double courtroom doors, and across the wide mezzanine to the stairs.

Phil's long legs were carrying him quickly down the staircase, and I kept calling him as I trotted to keep up.

He stopped short when we reached the ground level. Now that I was looking directly into his face, I saw how upset he was. It finally hit me that he'd just lost a case, and he cared about that. And he cared about *me*.

Crowds of people streamed around us as we stood on the center medallion in the vast marble floor. Phil said, "There are thousands of lawyers in New York who are looking for work, Tandy, and you can hire any one of them. But I'm telling you that this horse is dead. It doesn't matter how much you beat it, or yell at me.

"If you were my daughter, I would tell you the same thing. It's time to quit. I know it hurts—"

"You think?"

"—but we didn't have a provable case."

He went for the courthouse's main doors with the pack of us following behind him. Outside, snow was falling more thickly than before, and it had a crazy effect on me, like static in my mind.

I watched Phil and his deputy walk swiftly toward a pearl-gray town car. They looked like people in a 1940s black-and-white film. All that was missing were umbrellas turning inside out and hats blowing down the street.

I heard Matty calling me, and I turned to see that my brothers were at the car and Leo was holding open the back door. I must have looked wild.

"You having a heart attack, Ms. Tandy?" Leo asked me.

"No. But thanks for asking."

I flung myself into the car, and my brothers piled in after me. Matty took the jump seat facing us.

I'm sure they all saw the blood in my eyes when I said, "This isn't over. Whatever Phil says, whatever the courts decide, I *will* make Peter pay."

23

I sat between Hugo and Harry in the back of our bulletproof car. Harry was plugged into his music, Hugo was telling Matty how many pounds he could press, and I was mulling over the bloody beating we'd just taken in courtroom 928.

I wasn't raised to lose.

Maud and Malcolm Angel were parental terrorists. They rewarded success with fantastic gifts called Grande Gongos and penalized failure with memorable punishments known as Big Chops.

None of us had been spared, and none of us had been told that we were loved. Ever.

Why were we such remarkably unusual children?

Was it nature, nurture, or pharmaceutical enhancement?

The answer is yes. All three.

What made our parents different from other tiger moms and dads was that they practiced what they preached. Malcolm excelled at one thing—running Angel Pharmaceuticals, which he did all night and all day. Maud walked the razor's edge of high finance, and that stressful work made her largely unforgiving. Her motto was "I'll sleep when I'm dead."

If my parents had still been alive and we'd lost a case of this import, we would all have been Chopped. Big-time.

Trust me, it would have been bad.

I was very quiet as we drove uptown. I was a product of my parents after all. I was coming up with an action plan.

24

Once home, I nuked a burrito and took it upstairs, where I locked myself into the sanctuary of my soft blue bedroom and settled myself down to do research of an urgent kind.

First, I made a list of all the important news outlets and created a spreadsheet with phone numbers and e-mail addresses. I ranked each name on my list according to how willing they might be to run with a juicy scandal.

When my list was solid, I composed a press release that I could personalize to individuals but that was universal enough to go to all the journalists and pundits on my list. It was a script I could read, and I could also send it by e-mail.

This is what I wrote to Dr. Norton Abel, senior science reporter at the *New York Times*.

Dear Dr. Abel:

I have read your articles on psychotropic drugs, and I believe you will be interested in my firsthand account of abuses by a major pharmaceutical company that manufactures powerful drugs disguised as "vitamins."

These drugs were designed to turn ordinary children into geniuses with superior strength and exceptional intellect, but under some circumstances, these pills have caused mental defects and even premature death.

Since this pharmaceutical giant cannot get approval from the FDA, they are marketing these pills overseas, where they are allowed to promote these drugs for use by children without restriction.

Dr. Abel, this is not a joke. I have taken these pills most of my life, and so have my siblings. I've met parents whose children have taken the same pills and have died.

You know of me and my family and our relationship to this corrupt corporation. Please contact me at your earliest convenience so that I may tell you the whole wretched story.

Yours truly,
Tandoori Angel

I called Dr. Abel at the *Times*, and when his assistant said he was out of town, I sent him the e-mail.

Then I rewrote the opening and contacted renowned TV doctors Sanjay Gupta, Nancy Snyderman, and Mehmet Oz.

So far, no one had taken my calls, but it was still early in the day. I rewrote the pitch, underscoring the criminal child abuse that my brothers and I had been subjected to, and I called Nancy Grace at HLN.

Child abuse usually made her furious, but again, I was told she wasn't available. I sent her an e-mail, and then I had a brainstorm. I phoned Chloe Rhodes, a reporter at the New York *Daily News*, who had just written that horrible story about Matty's car accident.

Surely she would want an inside scoop on the Angels.

I called. She picked up, and after one full hour on the phone, we were like friends. Rhodes said she'd call me back in an hour—and she did.

"I'm sorry," she said. "I couldn't sell the story to my editor. Without documentation, we could be sued, Tandy."

It was a huge setback, but I didn't have time to whine. I sent a flight of personalized e-mails to West Coast entertainment shows and gossip magazines.

To my profound disbelief, no news service or supermarket tabloid responded. Not one soul in the entire media world even wanted to *interview* me. How could this be true?

Then I finally got it.

Anyone who called Peter Angel to confirm my

story and get his side of it was told that I was insane, that I had been institutionalized and defeated in court.

Oh my God. What had I done?

I had been so confident that the truth would win out that I had missed one point entirely. The pundits and reporters I had called had smelled blood, all right. *My blood.*

Why go against the gigantic Angel Pharmaceuticals with only my unsubstantiated word, when they could write about my mental breakdown—which was demonstrably a fact? I'd killed my own credibility. No one would believe anything I said ever again. Anything *any* of us said again.

That hurt too much.

I went down to the kitchen and drank probably too much of a bottle of merlot while standing at the sink. After that, I staggered up the spiral staircase to my room. I wrote DO NOT DISTURB in big black letters on yellow paper and taped it to my door.

Then I fell across my bed and passed out.

25

I was savagely awoken the next morning by Hugo jumping up and down on my bed, announcing, "Tandy, you have to get dressed. Sam's mother died."

"Sam's what?"

It felt like someone was hammering nails into my skull, and Hugo's bouncing was making me sick. It took many splintered sunlit moments to get what he was telling me.

"Stop jumping!"

He threw himself down on top of me.

"We're going to the funeral, Tandy. Matty said so. He chartered a plane."

Samantha Peck had been my mom's personal assistant. She lived with us for several years and had been a great friend to us all. We didn't know until after Maud died that Sam was my mother's lover. After my parents' funeral, Sam moved out and Uncle Pig moved in, just when we needed her the most and needed him the *least*.

"What happened to Sam's mom?" I asked.

Hugo shrugged. "I think it was old age. Listen, get dressed. We have to leave."

Ninety minutes later, my three brothers and I were locked and loaded into a small single-engine Pilatus aircraft taking off from New Jersey's Teterboro Airport, heading north to Lake Placid, New York.

The plane was sturdy and elegant, and the pilot introduced himself as "Thomas Trotti. Call me Tom."

Tom was in uniform; he had longish blond hair under his hat, a dimple in each cheek, and a spray of lines at the outer corners of his eyes.

The takeoff got my blood motoring and actually lifted my crappy mood. Once we were airborne, Tom said through the mic, "Folks, it'll be an easy-breezy fifty-five-minute flight, which includes a breathtaking view over the Adirondacks. Because it's such a short hop, we'll only be flying at ten thousand feet, cruising at two hundred seventy knots. What a beautiful day to fly."

It *was* a beautiful day: crisp and clear with a lavender-blue-and-white sky. Matty sat at the window to my left, and Hugo and Harry took the two-seater on the other side of the narrow aisle.

We'd unboxed our snacks and beverages and had

been in flight for about forty minutes when something changed—and it felt terribly wrong.

I grabbed Matty's arm and said, "Did you feel that?"

"Yes. The engine cut out," he said. "Don't worry. The pilot can bring it back to life."

I didn't believe Matty. I *knew* he was wrong.

Up ahead, there was frantic action in the cockpit. Red lights flashed on the control panel, accompanied by a rhythmic beeping alarm. Tom was throwing levers and speaking into his headset.

I shouted, "*Tom*, what's happening?"

Our pilot said tersely, "Excuse me, but no talking, please."

Harry and Hugo were awake and looking petrified as the plane not only decelerated but was now sailing downward at a ten-degree angle. Without an engine, we were a giant glider—without power, and maybe without a prayer.

I broke out in a sweat over my entire body.

I thought, *Okay, okay, okay, the engine will catch in a moment*—but it did *not*.

Matty groaned. "This is my fault. Why did I have to book this plane? Oh, God, oh, God. Tandy. Forgive me."

"This is not the end," I told my brothers as we went into an even steeper descent. "We're going to make it."

That was when Hugo screamed.

26

"Mommmmmyyyy!" *Hugo screamed shrilly.* It shattered my heart to hear his fear.

I turned to see him and Harry, but I couldn't reach them, touch them, kiss them, do anything to make them less afraid.

Matty bellowed at the pilot, "Do something, dammit!"

Captain Tom shouted back, "Assume brace position, sir! And shut the hell up."

Matty gripped my hand too hard. It didn't matter. I was sure that in seconds we were going to crash and burn to death, which was the worst possible way to die.

The visceral memories of a different fire swamped me now: the darkness, the fight for air, the choking, the burning in my lungs, and the fierce scalding heat on my face as my nerves shrank back from the flames eating through my grandmother's house in Paris.

I thought, *God, I don't want to die.*

Please. Not us. Not Hugo.

While we were still in the grip of the sickening downward pressure, time stretched out to the horizon. I waited for the shattering moment of impact. How long does it take to fall ten thousand feet? Somewhere, in that time between a split second and an eternity, I lost hope.

There was no way out. No parachute or ejection seat or hand of God to pluck up the plane before it was dashed to the ground.

Shadows flashed across the windows: white, black, white, black again; a stroboscopic light show of trees and sky and snow. Tom was talking gibberish into his headset, probably Maydays and our coordinates to alert rescuers to the fireball we were about to become.

I locked eyes for a moment with Harry, my twin. He reached out his hand, and with tremendous effort against physical forces, we touched fingers. And then he bent over his knees and interlaced his hands behind his neck.

As if that would do any good against what was coming.

I pulled my hand from Matty's and braced, too.

Even though it was hopeless, I prayed. *Please, God, forgive me for whatever I've done and please don't let it hurt.*

And then I felt a noticeable change in our angle of

descent. I looked up to see Tom hauling back on the yoke. As the plane leveled out a bit, I saw our crash path through the forest in the narrow slice of windscreen. The thick woods were wall-to-wall evergreens coated with yesterday's snow. But there, between the trees, was a straight patch of snow, like a ski trail.

The pilot yelled, "*BRAAAAAACCCCE!*"

I hugged my knees and closed my eyes and felt the plane smash into the evergreens. Trunks whumped the belly of the plane; then there were more violent bumps and crunches, accompanied by a horrid scraping and ripping sound from my side of the aircraft.

We rolled violently to the left, and I was slammed against Matty and the armrest. I heard my own scream, as if it was coming out of the top of my head.

We hit something unyielding. Like stone.

Matty cried out in agony. How badly was he hurt? I opened my eyes, but then the plane twisted violently around and we were skidding, sliding to the loud, high-pitched screeching of shearing metal.

I screamed, "*Mattyyy!*" but all I heard was another ripping noise that lasted longer than the first. Out the window I could see the wing being torn from the right side of the plane.

The smell of jet fuel permeated the cabin.

Gasoline.

It was going to happen now. We were all going to burn.

This was my last living moment.

27

Jacob was sitting in a chair beside the bed when I came out of the dark.

Was this real? Or had I passed into death, with Jacob the image left in my mind?

"Uncle Jake?"

He reached for me, hugging me so gently I wasn't sure he'd actually touched me, but I was in his arms anyway.

"Tandy, Tandy, my dear heart. I want to hold you, but I don't want to hurt you."

"I'm alive?"

Our voices sounded very soft and far away.

Jacob sat back in his chair. He put his hands over his eyes and sobbed. I'd never heard Jacob cry. I wasn't sure I was hearing it now.

I made a few false starts before I was able to ask, "How is...everyone? Are they...alive?"

"Everyone survived. You were lucky, Tandy. All of you."

The hospital room was faintly lit by a crack of light under the door and the glow of the vital signs monitor just to my right.

I smelled antiseptic and had to double-check with my brain that it was not gasoline. And at the same time, I realized that I hurt *everywhere*. I was a great throbbing mass of pain, but as constant and pervasive as the pain was, it was muted.

Whatever drugs were coming through my IV, they were definitely working. I had enough doped-up presence of mind to ask Jacob, "How lucky were my brothers?"

"Matthew's left femur is broken."

I couldn't hear for a moment, and then I asked, "Will he be able to play ball?"

"It's too soon to know."

Jacob's voice was cutting in and going out. I heard, "Hugo and Harry...soft tissue bruising...no head or internal injuries...Thank God."

My monitor beeped as my heart rate picked up. Joy that my brothers were alive. Sadness for Matty, who'd already had enough sadness. And something like hope for myself.

I wiggled my toes. I wasn't paralyzed. I wasn't in bandages. I wasn't burned. *I wasn't burned.* But the plane was still tumbling. I could feel it, skidding, slamming into trees, rolling over and over.

"And Tom?"

"He's going to make it. His family is with him now."

I lost track of time.

When I came back to myself, Jake was talking about the crash, saying Tom had found a short, narrow ridge where he took a chance on a belly landing. We were low enough, going slow enough, and he was pilot enough.

"What guts. What skill," Jacob said.

I heard him say that medevac had arrived within minutes, assessed us, and brought us directly to New York Hospital.

Jacob said, "I wanted you here."

With the pain pulsing softly in the background, my mind set out on several different tracks. I remembered black cars on a beach six months ago. I remembered being kidnapped and locked up and electroshocked until my brain was wiped clean.

I remembered the scorching house fire and the armed cars that had followed me and the gunfire from men who wanted to kill me. I had gotten warnings and threats from friends and enemies. And I could still hear Katherine pleading with me to lie low because we were all in danger.

Nausea surged, violently. I leaned over the bed rail, and Jacob had a pail ready. He held my hot forehead with his cool hand and said, "I've got you, Tandy."

I heaved up nothing and then, panting, I collapsed back into the bed just as nauseated as before.

A nurse appeared. I'd never seen him before. Who was he?

"Time to go to sleep, Ms. Angel."

"Jacob?"

"I hear you, Tandy. I'll be here when you wake up."

A needle went into the tube in my arm.

I said to my commando uncle, "That plane...shouldn't have gone down. Right, Jacob...?"

If he answered, I didn't hear him. I was asleep.

28

I woke up to snow sheeting sideways outside my hospital window. It was good to see all that white, my friend. It was like fresh paint covering up the remains of the terror.

Where was Uncle Jacob?

I turned from the hypnotic snowfall and punched on the TV. I clicked on six hundred stations up and down the dial, but I found no news about a small-plane crash outside Lake Placid.

I rang the bell for the nurse, and when he appeared, I said, "I need my laptop. I need my phone. I need to speak with my family."

I listed my uncle and my brothers' names.

The nurse said, "You came in with the clothes you were wearing, dear. Nothing else."

"What's your name?" I asked him.

"Frankie. I'm on duty for another three hours."

Frankie handed me a glass of water and a paper cup of pills. I shook the little cup.

"What are these?" I asked.

"Pain pills, mostly."

"And what are the ones that aren't for pain?"

"Anti-inflammatory pills. You're running a little fever. And vitamins, of course. You need to rebuild your immune system...."

"Who makes these vitamins?" I asked.

The nurse looked at me blankly. "I get them from the pharmacy, already dispensed."

I flung the pills across the floor. I enjoyed the rattle and roll sound as they bounced off walls and chairs.

"I want to see my uncle Jacob."

Frankie scurried out of the room and I lay back, staring at the swirls of plaster in the ceiling. I thought about the plane crash, and snatches of the aftermath came to me.

I dimly heard the rhythmic whacking rotor blades of the helicopter dropping down on the hospital's helipad. Next, there were the sounds of wheels rolling under me, amplified voices through a PA system, and then hands lifting me from one bed to another.

A watery image came to me, the face of someone I'd seen through a gap in the curtain around my emergency room stall. The man had a short nose, honey-colored eyeglass frames, and hard little eyes. Uncle Pig. And I saw that he was talking to—Uncle Jacob.

Why had Peter been talking with Jacob?

More questions rose up from the bottom of my conscious mind. Why had our plane gone down? Why hadn't Jacob been with us? Had Sam's mother really died? Had there been a conspiracy? Had the whole airplane trip been cooked up so that all the Angels would die?

The single answer came to me as if I'd known it all along—and the horrible truth stunned me.

The crash had been no accident.

We were all supposed to die.

CONFESSION

Friend, I'm not afraid of death.

I'm not a religious person, and I've seen more than my share of dead bodies for a seventeen-year-old, including those of my parents. Thanks to my scientist father, I was raised with a healthy respect for the expiration date that we're all born with. We all have our moment in the sun, and it's what we do during our lives—not how or when we die—that makes up the interesting part of our obituaries.

But I refuse to go before my time.

I know I'm meant to do extraordinary things. Perhaps my personality has been shaped by the pills I've been taking my whole life, but I was never going to be a shrinking violet, drugs or not.

Here's a fairy tale for you. Once upon a time, I dreamed of a life where I went to an Ivy League college, then a Top Three business school, and eventually inherited the command of Angel Pharmaceuticals. I'd marry James, have a few kids, and live my life in fabulous luxury. It had all been perfectly mapped out.

Now I'm facing the very real possibility that I won't live to see my eighteenth birthday. Before that happens, I'm going to make sure that Angel Pharma—the company my father founded and hoped I'd helm one day—is completely destroyed.

Isn't it *crazy* how things change?

The light was pale blue in my hospital room. I found
the call button, pressed it, and held it down until the
door to my room opened and my nurse came in with
Jacob behind him.

"Tandy, I'm here," my uncle said.

"Have you learned the cause of the crash?"

"Tandy, I haven't been home. I've been here with
you and your brothers. The authorities will look into
it. Everyone *lived*."

"It was a highly suspicious accident, wouldn't you
agree?"

"You're understandably upset—"

"Have you forgotten the fire? Have you forgotten
the dead children in France, and that my brothers and
I are a threat to Peter as long as we live?"

A doctor came into the room. He said, "I'm Dr. Reese. What's wrong here, Ms. Angel? Are you in pain?"

"I have to leave *now*."

He said, "Do you remember when we discussed taking something to calm you down?"

I'd never seen Dr. Reese before, ever, but I saw the needle coming toward me, and I began screaming, *"No, no, no!"* as I thrashed from side to side.

Alarms shrilled outside the door; the room filled with orderlies and nurses, and a gurney rolled into the room. Two people held me down, and I felt the prick of the needle in my hip.

I was lifted on the count of one-two-three. Jacob walked alongside me as we rolled down the corridor and into the elevator. I thought about Jacob talking with Peter.

What the hell was that?

I flailed and tried to climb off the gurney. I couldn't move except to open my mouth and howl. I screamed and clawed and twisted, and I cursed the men and women who loaded me into the ambulance.

I was still screaming when we pulled up to the emergency bay at Waterside.

30

The knockout drugs wore off pretty soon, a testament to how mad I was. And I mean mad as in *angry*, not *crazy*.

I was taken to a room that wasn't as nice as my old one. I didn't have a view of the highway and the river, but frankly, my friend, I didn't give a flying F about the view.

A nurse came in, one I knew quite well. Luann. She helped me into a long white cotton nightgown and snapped a plastic bracelet around my wrist with my name on it in capital letters.

She said, "Be right back," and when she returned, she had one little pill for me, not a cup of them.

"It's eight hundred milligrams of ibuprofen," she said, handing me a cup of water. "Let's see you wash that right down."

I did it and got into bed.

I was in the white bed in the white room when Dr. Robosson arrived, wearing royal purple. She shrugged off her coat and sat down next to the bed, where I lay with hardly enough strength to get into a sitting position.

Without preamble she said, "I heard about the plane crash, Tandy. I think you've just overshot the amount of terror allowed by law."

"Look," I said. I pulled my nightgown up to my neck. My body was all bruises, especially vivid on my left side where I'd smashed into the armrest of my seat on the plane, but my neck, shoulders, breasts, both legs, and my left arm down to the wrist matched Dr. Robosson's coat, like they'd been colored by paint from the same pot.

"Jesus, Tandy," she said.

"Yeah. He was there, all right, or Uncle Peter would have had a very successful day's work."

"What do you mean?"

Dr. Robosson had a very, very, and I mean *very* concerned look on her face.

"I can't prove anything," I said. "But why, on a sunny day, in a new ten-million-dollar plane with a first-class pilot, did we have engine failure that should have taken out all four Angel kids at the same time?"

"What are you suggesting?"

I glared at her, like, *Come on. I have to spell this out?* Fine.

I said, "Peter did it, Dr. Robosson. It totally fits him. And he had reason to want to get us out of the way."

"Tandy, how? How could Peter know Sam's mother had died? How could he have known that Matty would book a private plane? Even if he had known all of that, how could he have gotten to a mechanic to tamper with that aircraft in such a short period of time?"

I shrugged. I had been doped up for God only knows how long. Was I imagining things? Maybe I had never left Waterside. Maybe the last three weeks had been a dream.

"Let me ask you something," Dr. Robosson said. "Is it possible that because you had just seen Peter in court, and he won the case against you, your terribly traumatized mind made him the villain in this plane crash?"

"Let me ask *you*, Dr. Robosson. Do you think Peter Angel would let me live after I exposed his criminal activities in court, whether I won the case or lost? Do you think sabotaging an engine is impossible for him to do if he was determined to do it? Do you doubt he could tap phones, put fingers in pies or flies in ointments, and throw wrenches in the works if he wanted to?

"Because if you doubt that, you haven't been listening to me, Dr. Robosson. You've simply been placating me and wasting three full months of our lives."

"Of course I've been listening to you."

"You said I'm not paranoid," I said to her with all the power I could muster.

"You're not paranoid. But you're definitely a victim of too much brutality, both circumstantial and deliberate. I want you to rest, dear. You're very safe. Leo is outside now, watching the door. And he showed me his gun."

I smiled.

"I'll see you at lunchtime," said Dr. Robosson.

"Thanks, Mom."

Every time I called her Mom, I thought how much I wish my actual mom had been anything like her, anything at all.

I closed my eyes and tried to sleep.

31

Five days after I was admitted to the Waterside Center for Those Who Can't Cope or Don't Want To, Dr. Robosson released me back into the larger pool of misfits inhabiting New York City.

I couldn't *wait* to go home, but I also couldn't quite bring myself to call Leo. I wanted to walk for a bit and gather my thoughts in the crisp air.

Bundled up in my coat, scarf, hat, and boots, I walked east from Waterside in the morning light. I caught the downtown express at Dyckman Street, transferred to the local at 125th, and eventually came up for air on 72nd Street, just a few blocks south of the San Remo.

I was walking uptown on the sidewalk between the looming apartment buildings on my left and the wide avenue of Central Park West, when a deep masculine voice called out, "Hey, Tandy!"

Who, me?

I looked up and saw that a black BMW was slowing as it approached. There were two men inside the car: the driver and a passenger, who seemed to be beckoning to me.

I was squinting into the sun, asking myself, "Do I know these men?" when a glint of sunlight hit something metallic in the passenger's hand.

I stopped moving. Every bit of me, including my brain, froze solid. That man was pointing a gun at me.

As sweat broke out over my entire body, the passenger took aim. I dropped to the sidewalk and rolled behind a parked car. I was hugging its rear tire when three sharp cracks rang out.

Yes, they were gunshots.

Jesus Christ. Someone was really trying to kill me. *Again.*

I felt cold, sick, and absolutely terrified, but I stayed balled up in a crouch as the BMW drove past. Then it was gone, but was I safe? Or was the shooter now walking up the street getting ready to take another shot at me?

I got out my backpack and dug around until I found my phone. I had to call 911.

But no. Not so fast, Tandy. My phone was dead.

What now?

I inched up from the sidewalk and looked around.

I saw no black BMW, no man with a gun advancing on me. But I did see a yellow cab slowing to pick up a woman with a walker who was waving him down.

I jumped out of my hiding place and ran between this poor woman and the taxi. I may even have shoved her aside in my rush.

She yelled out, "Hey! That's mine!"

"Sorry," I said as I got in, pulled the door closed, and locked it.

I was shaking from the adrenaline overload, but I had to get it together. I shouted at the reflection of the driver's hard eyes in the rearview mirror.

"Twentieth Precinct. Eighty-Second between Amsterdam and Columbus. Floor it," I said. *"Fly."*

32

I was thrown against the backseat as the driver peeled away from the curb. He made a hard right and sped up Amsterdam.

Was this guy on speed? In a way, I hoped he was.

It was only a ten-block ride to the police station, but I had to call Jacob *now*. I grabbed the hand strap and put my mouth up to the holes in the Plexiglas divider separating me from the cabbie.

"Please, I need to use your phone."

"If I do that, miss, I'd have to let anyone use it."

"That makes no sense. I'll pay you for the call."

His eyes flashed to the rearview mirror. He looked angry. Definitely unstable. I probably looked that way, too.

He said, "I'll bet you not only have no phone, but no money, either."

"What did you say?"

He braked hard at a light, then turned to face me through the scarred plastic divider.

He said, "Show me your money. Or get out."

Was he insane? Yes. But I needed him.

I was panting, my heart going a hundred miles an hour. I shot him the dirtiest look possible, but I went through my wallet and pulled out my American Express Black Card.

"I need to use your phone," I said. *"Now."*

He passed his phone through the small door, and I called my uncle. No answer, so I left a message and held on to the armrests. Five minutes later, the cab stopped across the street from the brick and stone precinct house. I swiped my Amex through the card reader, left the bastard a generous tip, then sprang out of the cab.

I saw Caputo and Hayes halfway down the block, getting out of their squad car. I would recognize them from ten thousand feet away—in the dark.

Sergeant Capricorn Caputo is about six feet tall, stringy and dark-haired. His pants cuffs stop four inches above his ankles, and he has a vivid tattoo of a goat—his zodiac sign—on his left wrist. He's never in his life been called nice.

Detective Ryan Hayes is his partner's total opposite. He's stocky with thin brown hair, is a family man with kids, has no visible tattoos, and doesn't hide his soft side.

These were the cops who had come to our door when my parents had died. They were sharp, which I liked. But they had rushed to a faulty judgment that one or all the Angel kids had killed their own parents. That led to all-night interrogations, borderline harassment, and three of us being charged with murder and jailed.

Of course, the charges didn't stick.

No kidding. We hadn't done it.

After I solved the case, Caputo and Hayes knew I was solid. I worked other cases with them, solving those, too, and we had even become friends. Now I made my hands into a megaphone and called down West Eighty-Second Street, "Sergeant Caputo. Detective Hayes. It's Tandy...

"I need help!"

33

The squad room was tiny, crowded with four desks, four detectives, and no windows. I fixed my eyes and the force of my personality on Caputo and Hayes and said, "A man just fired three shots at me through a car window on Central Park West. It was a drive-by, but the shooter knew me. He called my name."

"So who was it that took shots at you, Tandy?" Hayes asked me. He looked worried.

"I don't know. But I have a pretty good idea who paid him to do it."

I quickly sketched in the horrific and humiliating recent events—the imploding lawsuit, the airplane crash, my history with my uncle, whom Caputo and Hayes had met.

"I have a lot of bad stuff on him, and—no lie—it

all adds up to motive. It has to be Uncle Peter," I said. "He's tried to have me killed before."

"What happened exactly?" Hayes asked me as Caputo rooted around in his desk for a working pen. I told the detectives everything I knew about the shooter, which was pretty damned little: two seconds of staring at a car and a gun, and about ten seconds of hugging a tire.

"My take on it? He had to be a professional," I said.

Caputo said, "A pro? And he missed? You're not dead, right?"

"I ducked."

"And so he, what, figured out that you'd be on that block at that moment in time, and so he was ready to bump you off?"

"I don't know how he knew where I'd be."

"What kind of car?"

"BMW. A black sedan."

"Year?"

"I don't know."

"Plate number?"

"I wish. It happened too fast."

"The shooter. Was he white, black? Did he have facial hair?"

"White. I didn't see any facial hair."

Hayes asked, "Did anyone else see this drive-by?"

I said, "I was hiding behind a parked car."

Caputo stared at me, tapping his skeletal fingers on the desk as the other cops in the room talked loudly into their phones. How *had* that shooter known where to find me?

"Listen, Pansy, I don't know what you expect me to do. You can't identify the shooter, don't have a plate number, and there couldn't be more than fifty thousand BMWs in this city. Gimme a break."

"You *know* me. You know I don't make shit up."

Caputo sighed. "Candy, *if* the shots were fired and no one got hit and there're no witnesses, I've got nothing to go on and neither do you."

"Don't say *if*. It happened," I said, slapping Hayes's desk, hard. "So let's go to the scene and find the evidence. You can look for shell casings. Bullet holes. You can make this official. Besides, you owe me."

Hayes rubbed his chin and said, "Cap, we're not busy. We should do this for Tandy."

I beamed at Hayes.

"Thank you," I said. "Thanks very much."

34

Our sirens screamed as we sped down CPW toward the spot between Seventy-Third and Seventy-Fourth where I'd almost been shot.

The closer we got, the more anxious I became. I was starting to doubt myself. Had that shooting really happened? Had an unknown shooter really tried to kill me? How had he known how to find me? He could have tracked my phone using GPS, but my phone was dead.

I pointed out where I'd been walking when I saw the gunman. Caputo and Hayes gloved up and then unspooled yellow crime-scene tape, closing off the chunk of sidewalk I'd identified. They began to walk along the sidewalk. I saw them stop, stoop, and keep walking. Would they find pockmarks in the wall of the building, or maybe spent shells in the street, or bullet holes in a door or window?

And most importantly, would Caputo and Hayes find enough evidence to arrest my uncle Peter?

I watched Hayes talking to a doorman, and then my cop friends were stripping off their gloves, ripping down the tape, and stuffing it into a trash can.

Caputo came back to the car and, sneering, got in. Hayes confirmed what I had already guessed.

"We found no shell casings, no weapon, no evidence of any kind, Tandy. I'll file a report in case something turns up."

"You still have my number?" I asked him.

"I've got everything I need. We'll give you a lift home."

I said to Hayes, "Tell me you believe me."

"I believe you. But there's nothing to follow up. Do you understand, Tandy? We've done our best."

Why had there been no evidence of the shooting? Was this the right block? Had I gotten it wrong?

When we got to the entrance of the San Remo, I told Hayes I could take it from there. As the elevator rose to the sixteenth floor, I talked to myself.

I listed Peter Angel's crimes against me and my siblings, added up all the potentially deadly assaults that involved black cars and automatic weapons, house fires and knockout drugs, a kidnapping, having my memory wiped in a mental institution, a fatal car crash, a downed airplane, and about fifteen years of ingesting Angel Pharma drugs.

It was an outrageously long list, but I didn't feel sorry for myself. I was furious and trying to keep a lid on my emotions so that I could think logically.

I had no doubt that Peter was going to keep trying to kill me until he had done it. All evidence proved that he'd try to destroy my siblings, too. And with Katherine, he likely thought he'd succeeded.

The man kept trying and missing.

How long would it be before he got it right?

35

Jacob was waiting when I opened the front door. He was red-faced and clearly distraught, saying, "Tandy, my God. What happened? I got your message, but when I called back, I got someone who didn't know what the hell I was talking about or who you were. And he hung up on me. Did you say someone shot you? Are you hurt?"

I hugged my dear old uncle and then sang, "Lots of bad things keep happening, Uncle Jake. Lots of bad things. Lotta lotta lotta bad things. Lotta—"

"Shhh, Tandy, shhh. I've got you." He put his hands on my shoulders. "I'm here. You can count on me."

I felt the stress relax a bit and looked up at Jacob. "I'm sorry for scaring you and for not calling you back. My phone was dead. A man I don't know fired three shots at me," I said. "He missed. This time."

"Oh my God. Tell me everything," said Uncle Jake, walking me into the living room. Daylight was streaming through the windows from across the park, filling the apartment with a feeling of lightness and hope.

I didn't trust it.

I sat on the edge of the sofa, and Jacob took the chair. I told my uncle about the men in the car, my discussions with the cops, and how things had been left.

"No evidence. No case. Good-bye and good luck. Jacob, I'm a tough kid, right? I can take a lot. But no joke, I can't leave the apartment without a shitstorm raining down on me. Is this all for real or just my imagination?"

"I was at All Saints when you called," Jacob told me. "Oppenheimer asked me to come in."

"Okay," I said, asking myself, *What now?*

"He's suspending you for an indeterminate period, to be decided."

"What? Why?"

I was genuinely shocked. I had missed some time, but I could make it up. This term was just starting.

"He doesn't think you're well enough for school. He said you've missed a lot of days and that you were heard talking to yourself in class before the accident. He says you behave as if you're on drugs. That's what he said. Have you been using drugs, Tandy?"

Fury bloomed in my mind like a black flower.

"He thinks I'm on *drugs*?"

"You're not taking those pills again, are you, dear?"

"You cannot seriously be asking me that, Jacob. I sued to put Peter out of business over those pills and you ask me if I'm taking them?"

He looked at me with the question still on his face. The black flower in my mind was now full-blown. It blocked out the sun.

I snapped.

"Don't talk to me, okay? This is our apartment, not yours, so don't talk to me. Get it?"

Jacob snapped, too. "I'm your court-appointed guardian and your oldest living relative, Tandoori. When I speak, you will listen. And you will obey. Get *me*?"

I flew up to my room and slammed the door. I was hyperventilating and had that feeling you get when you know you've hurt someone but still feel you're right.

I felt trapped.

What the hell was I going to do now?

GASLIGHT

36

That night, Jacob and I exchanged tearful apologies, and over the following two weeks, my life quieted down. At least, it looked calm on the surface.

I didn't leave the apartment without the panicky feeling that someone would call my name and then gun me down. I could see this so clearly, it was as if it had already happened.

I took classes at home, Skyping with a witty college-girl tutor from NYU who had a keen knowledge of my high school subjects. I was luxuriating in my one-girl homeschooling program when C.P. started sending me spite mail. I got this one day: "James and I were just wondering, do you miss us, Tandoo?"

Seeing the name James in an e-mail from C.P. felt like an unknown assailant's bullet slamming into my rib cage and ricocheting around my chest cavity before ripping through my heart.

I wrote, "You need to stop obsessing over me, C.P. It's more than just a little pathetic." I changed my e-mail account *again*, then went outside my room and called down to Jacob.

"I need Leo to be my bodyguard tonight, okay?"

Later that day, I wriggled into a skintight black crepe dress with a low-cut asymmetrical neckline, heels high enough to make me look at least twenty, and Mom's wonderful spangled Madonna jacket. I slicked my hair back behind my ears and put on red lipstick and a pair of large black shades.

I looked like the very picture of *Vogue* Beverly Hills, eighties edition.

Hugo said, "You look hot. For you."

Hugo's broken nose was taped. He had two yellowish-black eyes, stitches in his upper lip, and a purple-green sunset of a bruise across his forehead.

I said, "You, on the other hand, look like you belong on *The Walking Dead.*"

Hugo laughed out loud, which made the rest of us laugh, too. Once we were all inside the bulletproof car, Leo drove Jacob, Hugo, and me to Carnegie Hall, one of the premier concert venues in the world.

Because Harrison Angel was playing tonight. My wonderful talented twin had the stage to himself.

Walking into the auditorium took my breath away with its grandeur. From the five-story-high tier of gold and red velvet seats that form an elongated semicircle to the glorious stage on which hundreds of eyes would be fixed all evening, the entire vast space is both a visual and an acoustic wonder.

Around us, people were talking about my brother. I heard one elegant lady saying to her husband, "This boy—he's something else, Bennett. I've been following him since his incredible debut in Paris. Prepare to have your shoes, socks, and jacket blown off. Hold on to your shirt and tie, too."

Concertgoers swirled around, finding their seats, the excitement on their faces making me so proud of my brother that my eyes welled up with tears—and he hadn't even taken the stage.

And then he did.

Wearing a tux, looking like the romantic hero in a Victorian novel with his dark curling hair and brooding eyes, my genius brother bowed at center stage. After a rolling tsunami of thunderous applause, he sat down at one of the two pianos on the stage, the Steinway grand.

I gripped Hugo's left hand and Jacob's right as the lights went down. There was an interminable silence as Harry sat on, his arms at his sides.

Whispers fluttered up to the ceiling like trapped birds, and I was suddenly afraid for Harry. Did he have stage fright? Was he having a panic attack?

For a moment, in the darkened hall, I thought I saw Katherine—and then Harry's hands jumped to the keys of the Steinway and he struck the opening notes in the concert he called "Acoustic Electric." His interpretation of "Black and White" by Reginald Trudeau resounded and filled the vast hall, and when I looked for my sister, I didn't see her at all.

But on the stage, Harry absolutely shone. After the first piece, he played three more in a series of four stunning compositions made famous by four pianists who had started out playing acoustic piano, only to move later to pickups, plugs, and amps.

The audience applauded their approval. I grinned at Jacob and shouted into his ear, "I can feel the vibrations through the soles of my shoes."

After intermission, Harry went to the electric piano and played a second piece by each of the four composers. Again the audience went crazy. Harry bowed deeply, then walked into the wings, and of course, the almost three thousand people packing Carnegie Hall demanded an encore.

I had thought the concert was over, but when Harry returned to the stage for another bow, I saw that he had a microphone in his hand.

He said into the sudden hush, "I want to close with a song I wrote for my sister Tandy. I call it 'We Will Always.' "

Sitting back down at the grand piano, Harry moved quickly into a catchy bossa nova tune. With its upbeat melody and distinctive beat, it surprised and delighted everyone.

I had wanted to be in disguise tonight. I wanted no attention at all, but I blushed as the whispers swelled and heads turned and people smiled, wiped away tears, and dipped their heads toward me as Harry played and sang his sweet and loving song about the two of us growing up together.

> *There's a place I remember,*
> *One my heart won't surrender.*
> *We could go there tomorrow.*
> *You could lead, I would follow.*
> *You've been with me for ages,*
> *Stumped the wits and the sages,*
> *Held my feet to the fire,*
> *Raised my sights a bit higher.*
> *We've known Paris in autumn.*
> *We grew up in New York.*
> *We recall the Dakota—*
> *Everything that we lost.*
> *I will never forsake you,*
> *Force or remake you.*
> *You've been one of a kind, dear.*
> *You're my twin and my sister.*
> *There's a place I remember,*
> *Somewhere east of September.*
> *We will someday return there,*
> *We will always belong there.*
> *There's a place I remember.*
> *There's a place I remember.*

37

At eleven thirty PM, just after Harry's concert, I boarded a Delta flight from New York's JFK Airport to Charles de Gaulle in Paris.

I never wanted to get on another airplane. Ever. But despite my stamping and pouting and the impressive, self-indulgent fit I threw, Jacob remained firm.

"Pack something nice to wear. Don't lose your passport. And try something new, why don't you? Trust me."

And now I was sitting in a window seat in first class with a glass of orange juice and a cup of warm nuts. I opened the note Jacob had slipped into my coat pocket curbside and read it again.

Tandy,
  Life goes on. It just does, whether we're ready
  for the next chapter or not. Embrace it.

  Love,
  Uncle Jacob

I folded the note, placed it back into my pocket, and stared at the seat backs and the curtain drawn across the front of the cabin. The other passengers were asleep, but not me.

I would never forget the sickening sensation of gravity on a falling plane, knowing that I was about to die—and that the person responsible was going to get away with it.

Now, in the body of a big jet, I gripped the armrests so hard, I broke a nail. Peter wouldn't dare bring down a commercial airliner with hundreds of passengers just to get me out of his way. Would he?

I swear, I think he *would.*

That thought occupied me for hours. I sat upright, listening to air hissing through the vents and the snoring of the man in the seat beside me. I hummed "We Will Always" under my breath, and somewhere over the enormous Atlantic Ocean, I must have fallen asleep, because I was suddenly awakened by the bright sun in my window and an announcement. "Ladies and gentlemen, we will be landing shortly...."

I had traveled light, so I cleared customs quickly and emerged on the other side of the arrivals door to see a blond-haired man in livery holding up a sign with my name.

Georges greeted me in heavily accented English, took my bag from me, and led me out to the car. I asked him where he was taking me.

"The hotel is very nice, *mademoiselle*. At six this evening, a friend of yours will come to pick you up."

A friend of mine? Would it be my sister, Katherine?

"He is Monsieur Delavergne," said my driver.

Monsieur Delavergne is my deceased grandmother's head lawyer and director of her estate. What did this mean? Why was I meeting with Monsieur Delavergne?

I checked into Hôtel le Bristol on Rue du Faubourg Saint-Honoré, hung up my clothes, and slept as though I'd never been in a bed before. And sometime around six that evening, in the middle of the day according to my sleep cycle, Monsieur Delavergne rang up to my room.

"I'll be right down," I told him.

I'd been having a dream. I could still feel James's hands on me as we lay together in a small bed with moonlight coming through the window. We'd been looking into each other's eyes. He'd told me he loved me.

That bastard.

I showered and dressed in my new peaches-and-cream silk dress, which felt like clouds wafting around my legs. I stepped into a new pair of strappy pumps and finger-combed my hair. I slicked on some pale lip gloss and gave my eyelashes a hit of mascara.

Then I casually threw on a pale cashmere coat and scarf, softer than soft.

I checked myself out in the beveled pier glass.

I looked good. Actually, I looked my best. I snapped a selfie and texted my brothers:

This is me before my surprise evening with Monsieur Delavergne. What will happen next? ☺

I pressed send. I grabbed my room key.

Ready or not, a new chapter was beginning.

Showtime.

38

Short, balding, about sixty years old, with hair sprouting on his knuckles and creeping out of his shirtsleeves, Monsieur Delavergne is not gorgeous, and in my experience, not exactly fun, either. So I was surprised to see him behind the wheel of a shiny blue Mercedes-Benz in a sport jacket, pink linen shirt, no tie, loafers, no socks. And he was smiling at me.

"Tandy, are you feeling well?" he asked me in French.

I thought of all the possible answers to that one and decided to lie.

"*Bien,*" I said. "*Je suis très bien.*"

He smiled.

He also looked very pleased with himself, and that was good. The Angel kids really needed Monsieur

Delavergne on our side. But as the car slowed to navigate the *très charmantes* winding streets of Paris's Le Marais district, I started to enjoy the lawyer's cheerful side. It felt like I was leaving the scary past behind.

When the car stopped in front of the powder-blue-and-gold building that housed the perfume company my grandmother had founded so many years ago, the attorney said, "This is a very big event. I'm pleased for you to be the flower of Parfumerie Bellaire. I hope you are ready for your close-up, yes?"

"What is it? What is happening?" I asked.

"It is your perfume," he said. "It is, how you say, rolling out today, worldwide."

My perfume?

Beautiful people in gorgeous clothes were spilling out from the store onto the adorable shop-lined street. There was a huge banner over the entrance to the shop that read INTRODUCING TANDOORI, THE SCENT OF LOVE.

I clapped my hands to my mouth. *This* was the reason I'd flown all this way. That a fragrance named for me was being introduced to the world, and this was the launch party. No wonder Monsieur Delavergne had been so lighthearted, pulling off such a stupendous treat.

But that was only the beginning.

The driver opened my door for me, and as the soles of my strappy shoes touched the street, a wonderful man who had loved my gram Hilda came out of the store, opened his arms, and embraced me. His name was Guillaume Laurier; he'd been with this company since my grandmother's time and had been the president for many years.

He had to be the one who had named a fragrance for me.

"You look beautiful," he said, kissing both my cheeks. He lifted two glasses of champagne from a tray, handed me one, and toasted me, saying, "To the original Tandoori."

I returned the toast. "I am so honored, Monsieur Laurier. I can only say, thank you so much."

"You wish to smell 'Tandoori, the scent of love'?"

"Oh, of course I do."

My silk skirts swirled around me as we parted the crowd and went into the shop. The walls were hung with huge, luminescent photos of flower fields in the French countryside: lavender and roses, and tall grasses backlit by the setting sun. There was a video playing on monitors: a gorgeous commercial for Tandoori.

Monsieur Laurier brought me to a table near the center of the store. A pinlight in the ceiling lit a rounded bottle of frosted glass with my name etched in the center.

My grandmother's old love lifted the bottle, tipped it gently, righted it, and removed the stopper. Then he touched the stopper to the inside of my wrist.

All the people standing around us, the celebrities

and the executives and the factory workers and the media, inhaled as one, their eyes filled with hope and sweet expectation.

I raised my wrist and let the scent of love come to me. It was floral and luxurious, spicy with striking notes of freesia, mandarin, bergamot, orange blossom, and orchid. It was simply delicious.

"How do you like it?" Monsieur Laurier asked me.

"*Parfait*," I said. "It is so absolutely perfect."

He took my hand and twirled me around as Monsieur Delavergne and all the other guests clapped their hands.

A man with a violin appeared and, unbelievably, played "We Will Always." My twin's song to me.

It *was* perfect.

But will it surprise you if I say that in that perfect moment, I couldn't help thinking of love lost?

I missed James.

CONFESSION

I was having a lucid dream.

I knew that I was dreaming and that I could control the whole story and even the ending—but I didn't want to change anything. I wanted the dream to spool out from my subconscious just as it was doing.

You see, I'd had this dream before.

In it, James and I were in bed together. Even though my eyes were closed, I saw him look at me in a special way. He reached out and touched my hair. Then he got out of bed and walked naked across the frayed carpet to the rickety old desk beside the armoire. There he wrote a note on a sheet of hotel stationery. I could read it as if I was standing behind him and looking over his shoulder.

Dear Tandy,
My father will seriously hurt you if he finds us together
and I can't stand for that to happen. Don't ever think
that I don't love you. I'm sorry.

James

In this dream, so much like the way it had actually happened, James dressed while standing in a fine beam of moonlight. Then he dropped the note onto the bedcovers, pulled on his leather bomber jacket, and left the room. The door closed behind him with a sharp clack.

When the door closed in my dream, I opened my eyes. I might have been able to manipulate the outcome of the dream: I could have made love to James, listened to him tell me he loved me over and over again.

But I preferred the truth…that James had firmly, decisively, closed the door.

39

I awoke in my huge bed on the top floor of the Hôtel le Bristol with its perfectly framed view of the City of Light. As I returned to the real world, I recognized the fragrance in the air as the perfume I had sprayed on my pillow last night.

Tandoori, the scent of love.

What a joke that was, linking my name to *love*.

To lift my despondent mood, I thought of Uncle Jacob. He had been emphatic: "Enjoy your time in Paris," he'd said. "Take it all in."

It was good advice. I needed a mental health break, and I was in the haute couture capital of the world and in need of smart new clothes to make my nasty schoolmates jealous.

And I *would* be going back to school.

But first, shopping.

A few hours later, I was in a cab to Rue Montorgueil, a walking street lined with sidewalk cafés and shops in the Châtelet–Les Halles district in the center of Paris.

I paid my driver and had just stepped out onto the street when a woman's voice called my name.

This time I ducked first, *then* looked for the gun.

Meanwhile, my taxi zoomed off, leaving me exposed on all sides to the traffic whizzing past—and I heard her call me again.

"Tandy. It's *me*. It's Katherine."

I looked around. Was it really my sister? Or was this a trick? Then, through a break in the traffic, I saw her waving to me from across the street.

Oh my God, oh my God, oh my *God*. It was her. Katherine was wearing a blue shawl-collar wool coat and high boots. Her dark hair flowed over her shoulders, and sunlight limned her in a halo from shining head to polished toe.

She looked angelic.

I jumped up and down and waved, and she waved back, yelled my name again, and made her way to me. She dropped her bag to the street and hugged me hard.

"I love you, love you, love you so much," she said.

I said into her shoulder, "I love you so much, too, and, Kath, in the future, will you give me a heads-up, please? So I don't go into cardiac arrest every time you just appear."

She laughed. "Okay. If possible."

I'd last seen Katherine here, in Paris, and it had been absolutely heart-stopping to see her alive when I had long believed her to be dead.

She'd explained how she had survived the fiery accident that was no accident, but a deliberate attempt on her life. She revealed that she'd been rescued by a stranger who was hiding her in a mysterious location—secret even from me. She had told me then that we might never see each other again. It was much too dangerous, because of Uncle Peter.

But here she was.

Now, at this radiant, unexpected second meeting, Katherine said, "I went to your hotel, but I'd just missed you. Oh, I love your perfume. It must be Tandoori."

I said, "Good guess," and grinned like a fool. Then I asked, "Kath, how did you know where I'm staying? How do you always know how to find me?"

"The less you know, the better, Tandy. Come. Let's walk. We shouldn't stand together in one place for too long."

40

I was strolling again with my wonderful big sister on a gorgeous avenue in this inimitable city, but instead of feeling content, I was watching everything and everybody, ready to scream, *"Gun!"*

We went to a bistro called Café du Centre at the end of the street. It's a wide-open restaurant with red awnings and lots of tables and chairs outside, with the best views of historic pastry, hardware, shoe repair, and tobacco shops.

"I saw Beyoncé here once." Kath laughed. "Really."

We took seats inside for privacy, and over cafés au lait and Niçoise salads, Kath showed me pictures of her little boy. He was adorable and looked so much like Kath, but I couldn't get her to tell me about the baby's father, if she was married, or even what *continent* she called home.

She was saying, "When I heard about the launch of your perfume, I knew you would be there. I booked a flight, but it was delayed, dammit. Sorry I missed the party. Look at what I was going to wear," she said. She opened her bag wide and showed me a blond wig and big wraparound shades.

"You were going to go in disguise?"

"Nothing has changed, Tandoo. Be careful. Watch everything around you and maybe, one day..."

Just then, I saw a gray car, a Peugeot, speeding past the café. It cut off a blue Renault, and I watched the T-bone collision accompanied by the blare of car horns.

The cars were still rocking from the impact when Katherine's phone pinged. She glanced at it, then said to me, "Sorry. I have to take this."

She texted a message, read another, and typed a second text, then apologized again and called for the check.

"I have to go right now," she said. "I love you, T."

I said, "Kath, are you serious? What's wrong? I can't believe you're leaving already."

Katherine said nothing.

She kissed me on both cheeks, then held my head with her cheek pressed to mine as if she was saying good-bye forever. When she released me, she put money down on the table, then fled. Baffled, I watched her run directly toward the dusty gray Peugeot that had caused the accident. By now it had backed away from the other car and was readying to take off in the opposite direction. I couldn't make out who was driving.

I was out of my chair, knocking into the waiter as I ran after my sister. I called to her from the doorway.

"Katherine, *wait*! I'll come with you!"

She waved and blew me a kiss before getting into the passenger seat of the Peugeot and closing the door. And then my beautiful, mysterious sister was gone. Again.

41

That night, I sat by myself in the first-class lounge with my new, oversized Gerard Darel handbag, *Marie Claire* Paris, and a glass of Perrier, waiting for my flight to be called.

I wasn't actually reading the magazine. I was replaying my meeting with Katherine. Having felt for a short while that we were closer than ever before, I now began to question all of it.

How *had* Katherine found me after I had left the hotel? I hadn't told anyone where I was going. Who was driving the gray Peugeot? Why had he caused that crash? Had that driver and my sister been following me? They must have been—but why?

These thoughts circled in an endless loop as I sat alone in the timeless vacuum of the flight lounge. Then my thoughts were derailed by an incoming phone call from Monsieur Delavergne.

I picked up.

"Tandy, I am sorry I didn't say good-bye in person."

"No worries, Monsieur Delavergne. Thanks for sending a car."

"You're welcome, *mademoiselle*. Also, I wanted to confide something to you."

He had every bit of my attention. The only sound in the world was Monsieur Delavergne's voice in my ear.

"What is it, Monsieur Delavergne? What's wrong?"

"It's about Jacob," he said.

"What about him?" I gripped the phone so tightly that I snapped a photo of my knees and almost disconnected the call. "Monsieur Delavergne? Can you hear me?"

"I am still here, Tandy," he said in French.

And just then my flight was announced right over my head. I asked Monsieur Delavergne to wait for the announcement to end, and when I finally had reestablished a cone of silence, I asked him again, "What *about* Jacob?"

"It is not going so well for him," Monsieur Delavergne said. "Just watch him. And if you need to call me, I am always here for you."

"Be more specific," I said. "*Please.* What should I look for? What's wrong with him?"

But Monsieur Delavergne was saying, "Have a safe flight. It was good seeing you again, Tandoori. Be kind."

Be *kind*?

"Au revoir, ma chérie."

"Au revoir," I responded, to a dead phone line.

I went to the gate and boarded my flight to New York. Then I went into my head for the next eight hours, wondering what the hell Monsieur Delavergne had been hinting at.

Add to that my plane-crash paranoia, which had me jumping at every hum, rattle, hiss, and captain's announcement. In between hyperlistening, I prayed that the plane would stay aloft until it landed smoothly on the runway in New York.

I couldn't eat or read or sleep. Instead, I watched a movie without the sound while I pondered the imponderable.

How had Katherine found me? Why had she left in such a rush?

Why was everything about Katherine so mysterious?

42

The next morning, Jacob was making hot cocoa when I trundled wearily into the kitchen.

"Welcome home," he said. "Come in and pull up a chair, Tandy. I want to hear all about your trip in actual words, not bloody texts."

"Pictures, too, right?"

"You bet."

The kitchen in our new home was airy and modern. Jacob poured hot cocoa into mugs and placed a platter of just-baked cookies on the long metal table. I thanked him. Actually, I totally needed the warmth and the sugar.

"Start talking," Jacob said when we were both sitting down. "Don't leave anything out."

I'd been wide-awake since leaving Paris, wondering

about Monsieur Delavergne's oddly veiled warning, but I kept that part to myself and gave Jacob some highly animated highlights of the Tandoori launch party.

"Monsieur Delavergne is nicer than I thought," I told Jacob, showing him a selfie of me with the lawyer in the pink linen shirt, photo-bombed by a cute woman spraying perfume over our heads.

Jacob grinned. "That's a keeper."

"And I saw Katherine," I said, scrutinizing Jacob's face, looking for any cracks in his affect that should worry me. I saw nothing.

I swiped my phone and showed him pics of the two of us in the bistro. "We were just having the greatest time, and then there was a deliberate car crash on the street. A second later, Katherine got a text, said, 'I've gotta go,' and then ran outside, got into one of those cars—and *poof*! She was gone."

"Tandy, was she scared? Or what did you make of that?"

I shrugged. "It seemed like her ride called her and she had to go. Another mystery," I said. "And how have you been, Uncle Jake?"

"Me? Same as always. Harry stayed home from school for a couple of days, recuperating, catching up on his mail, and so on. Hugo has been steady. I haven't heard from Matthew."

"How are *you*?" I insisted.

"What are you getting at, Tandy? I take care of things. That's my job. Are you done with your cocoa?"

He took away the mug and I told him I'd be in my room. I unpacked the bags I hadn't wanted to deal with earlier and charged up my electronics and then sat at my desk and watched the sky darken above the park. I thought about Jacob. I couldn't even guess at what he might be hiding, but he was definitely holding something back.

Why would he hide anything from me? I considered this question through my new, highly focused lens of paranoia.

Jacob had been in France the day my brothers and I took Peter to court. If he had been with us, he would have lent credibility to our case. Jacob knew that Angel Pharma pills had killed people.

Another thing—Jacob hadn't been with us when our plane crashed on the way to Lake Placid. But *after* the crash, while I was in the emergency room, I'd seen Jacob speaking with Peter.

And that led me to a long-standing mystery that had never been answered to my satisfaction. Why had Peter turned over the guardianship of the Angel kids to Jacob, an uncle we had never even known existed before our parents' deaths?

Was Jacob even our uncle at all?

I was nearly overwhelmed with confusion—and I didn't like that one bit. I flashed on the hundreds of pills I had emptied out onto the conference table at Peter's lawyer's office. I had more pills stashed in the apartment.

If only I could sedate myself with a handful of Num.

Who could blame me for wanting the clarity of a crisp, emotionless state? How else could I know up from down in my Alice-in-Horrorland existence? Was what I believed to be my life history in any way real? Or was it all a dream?

If so, whose dream was it?

And who was I? That was the question.

Did anyone know the answer?

43

I awoke out of a dreamless black hole of sleep to find myself staring at a star field of sleet coming straight at me, stinging my cheeks. A wet wind was blowing hard at the skirt of my nightgown; my arms were stretched out like wings in flight.

It took a second to understand, to really *get* that this was no dream.

I was standing outside on the ledge of the living room terrace with the railing *behind* me, my toes curled over the wet, slippery edge, *sixteen stories above the street.*

I screamed and beat at the air as I started to teeter. This could *not* be happening—but it *was.*

I made a backward grab for the railing behind me and caught it, tightening my cold hands around the wrought iron, holding on tight even as my legs shook and wobbled.

What had happened? How had I gotten out here?

Have I gone crazy?

I had no memory of unlocking the French doors, crossing the terrace, and climbing over the railing, let alone making my way downstairs. I couldn't conceive of deliberately going out to the gritty edge of the building like it was a diving board.

But this was not a hallucination or a dream...no trick of an overactive mind. Two hundred feet below me, cars sped through the slush on the avenue.

If I fell, I would make a snow angel like no other.

Screw *that*.

I had to get off this ledge, and there was no room for error. If I sneezed or panicked or lost my awkward backhanded grip, I wouldn't get a second chance. I was going numb, quaking with terror, when a sober, instructive voice inside my head said, "Turn around, Tandy. Take your time."

With precise attention to where I placed my frozen toes and how I reversed the grip of my rigid fingers, I turned little by little, finger over finger, until I was facing away from the street, holding the railing tightly with both hands.

I wasn't safe yet. I still had to climb over the railing and onto the terrace. From there, I could get to a door or a window.

Just then, as I carefully began to haul my numb and

shaking limbs over the rail, things went from horrific to hellish. As if I'd been punched in the gut, I was hit with stomach cramps. I fought back the pain and nausea and pulled myself up and over the railing. As soon as my weight was over the terrace, I let go of the railing and collapsed in a heap, retching helplessly in the snow.

I lay there, sick and panting from fear and exhaustion. *What was happening to me?*

Was I overdosing? But I hadn't taken any drugs. Had I?

I heard glass shattering several yards away; then Hugo's face poked out through a broken window. "Tandy, what's wrong?" he cried.

I gathered myself and rolled up onto my hands and knees. Hugo was there beside me, trying to help me stand, but my legs wouldn't hold me.

I saw blood streaking my nightgown. Panicking, I realized it was streaming from his wrist.

I screamed, "Hugo, you're hurt! Go get Jacob...*now!*"

44

I pulled myself to my feet using a deck chair as a crutch. I was still trying to get my balance when Harry came flying through the terrace doors and ran over to me.

Jesus, he was scared. I could hardly look at him because I didn't know what the hell to say.

He grabbed my arm and shook it until I looked at him. "Are you hurt? What happened to you?"

"I'm freezing," I said.

"Okay, okay, I've got you."

He put my arm over his shoulder and walked me carefully through the mushy snow on the terrace, through the French doors, and into the living room.

My lips were frozen and my voice shook as I said, "Harry, Hugo is bleeding."

And then Jacob was there in front of us, absolute shock and horror on his face. He looked at me, at the blood on my nightgown, and I knew he thought I'd attempted suicide.

That wasn't true. Was it?

I said, "Jacob. Hugo cut himself badly on the window glass. Please see to him."

At any other time, Jacob would have said, "It's going to be okay. I'm here."

But he said, "Tandy. Take a hot shower. Then call Dr. Robosson's service. Say it's an emergency and make an appointment for first thing tomorrow morning. If you don't do it, I will take you there myself."

I nodded numbly and headed for the stairs.

Jacob was right to think I had lost my mind. If I didn't get help, I didn't know how I was going to get it back. As I climbed the spiral staircase, I watched Jacob wash Hugo's arm in the kitchen sink. Blood ran down the drain, and Hugo screamed when the peroxide followed the soapy water.

"Does he need stitches?" Harry asked.

"I don't think so," said Jacob. "The cut is shallow. More like a scratch, right, young man?"

This was my fault.

What the hell was wrong with me?

45

It was Saturday, the day after I had almost flown off the sixteenth-floor balcony. I had just come home from my emergency session with Dr. Robosson, who had explained that my nocturnal and unconscious trip to the ledge was sleepwalking, possibly caused by so much stress.

If she was right, it was the first time I had ever walked in my sleep. But I had no better explanation.

Before I had been discharged from Waterside, Dr. Robosson had given me a prescription for sleep meds and a few samples, which I had in my backpack. I hadn't taken one of those samples, had I? Dr. Robosson and everyone else knew I was against pills. *All* pills.

But I had a plan... what to do for everyone's safety

and peace of mind. It was a sickening plan, but it was necessary.

I called Uncle Peter from the sanctuary of my pretty blue bedroom. "We need to talk."

"Go ahead," he answered.

"I want to talk to you in person."

"Do you wish to meet under the clock in Grand Central? I'll wear a carnation in my lapel. Pink."

"That won't be necessary," I said. "I'll come to you."

I still saw it as my life's mission to put Angel Pharma out of business, but I wanted to buy a little time to live without fearing the sound of my name. I needed to think, to plan, rather than react. To gather myself. And I was willing to humble myself and promise anything to get Peter to give me and my brothers some space.

I made sure my phone was charged and that I had Jacob, Leo, Harry, and the Twentieth Precinct all on my speed dial. I dressed modestly in dark trousers and a turtleneck for my meeting with my would-be assassin. Then I called Leo and asked him to bring the car around.

I had only been to Peter's apartment once.

I had been in the fourth grade, and he had invited all of us to dinner. Katherine was still with us then, and as usual, all of Peter's attention was on her. He seated her in the chair next to his at the table. He gave her a gilded book on Catherine the Great and asked her opinion on all manner of things. He was really, really nice to her.

At fifteen, Katherine was already a mathematical prodigy and a superb athlete, and she was becoming a real beauty. Peter asked her if she would like to go to Europe with him that summer, and my parents seemed to think it was a wonderful opportunity.

Why hadn't they seen Peter for the monster he was?

I now knew that this was the summer when Katherine had gone to France. I knew from Jacob that Peter had used my sister as a lure, a recruitment tool to persuade parents to sign up their children as guinea pigs for Angel Pharma.

Jacob had introduced me to one of those sets of parents when I was in Paris last fall. I had seen pictures of their triplet sons who had taken the pills and had died before they reached their twentieth birthdays.

Was what happened to those children happening to me and my brothers and sister now?

Leo pulled up to the Smithfield, an apartment building at Eighty-First and Columbus, close enough to our home on the West Side of Manhattan. The doorman rang up to Peter's apartment, and I heard my uncle's voice over the intercom.

"Send her up."

I was afraid of what was about to happen. Would Peter hear me out? Would I lose my nerve? I pushed the elevator button, then clasped my shaking hands.

The elevator took me to the tenth floor, and the

doors opened. I looked in both directions and saw that an apartment door had been left ajar at the far end of the hallway. It gave the appearance of a trap.

I shook out my hands and thought of Leo circling the block in the car. If I didn't call him in a reasonable amount of time, he would come upstairs looking for me.

I walked down the long carpeted hallway to the half-open door. It swung open on soundless, well-oiled hinges. I peered into the foyer and called out, "Uncle Peter?"

His voice came to me from the depths of his apartment.

"Come on in, Tandoori. I'm here."

Said the spider to the fly.

46

I found Peter sitting in front of a drafting table at one end of the room. He was working at a sleek computer but looked up when I came in and said, "Be with you in a minute. Have a seat."

He pointed to the other side of the room, which was furnished with two red upholstered office chairs, a square metal table between them. There were no paintings on the walls, no clue to the nature or interests or personality of the man who lived here, no signs that Peter Angel was the devil incarnate. Which he was.

As directed, I took a seat.

While my uncle finished what he was typing, I took in the closed doors and wondered what they led to. I smelled a faint fragrance that I almost recognized.

And I noticed two cups and saucers on a tray on the kitchen counter.

Finally, Peter pushed back his chair, then came over and sat down next to me. He stared at me through his thick glasses with the butterscotch-colored frames, which matched his messy ginger hair.

He said, "What do you want, Tandoori?"

I stammered as I tried to get out my rehearsed request, finally managing it.

"I want to call a truce, Uncle Peter."

"Spell it out," he said.

"Okay. I will stop invoking your name as an enemy. I will not look for legal redress for any crimes you may have committed against me and my brothers, nor will I testify against you if I'm ever asked to. I will put that in writing. All I want in exchange is for you to leave us alone. I especially want Hugo to grow up in complete safety."

Peter sat back in his chair and shook his head.

Was he turning me down? Was he actually saying no to my proposal?

I think I saw smoke coming out of his mouth when at last he said, "I am a ruthless businessman. I'm proud of that. Would I destroy you if you got in my way? Of course. But I'm not a murderer. I would never try to kill you, and I never have. Any other questions?"

"So we have a deal?" I said in a squeaking voice.

"We don't *need* a deal," he said. "Now get out."

Now get out was more than a slap across the face.

It was like a crowbar to the side of my head. Emotionally, I reeled. I realized that I had actually expected him to shake my hand, to lay down arms, to agree to agree.

Jamming my trembling hands into my pockets, I left my uncle's apartment knowing that nothing had changed. Whatever he planned to do to me—to *us*—there was nothing I could do to stop him.

I had stood up to Peter with all my drive, ingenuity, and determination, and I'd even come begging. Nothing had worked.

I had never felt so completely powerless in my life.

Leo was waiting for me outside the Smithfield. He opened the car door, and I got in. As we pulled out into traffic, he looked back at me through the mirror. He must have read the total defeat in my face.

"Is there anything I can do for you, Tandy?"

Leo's hat was lying on the seat beside him, so I was looking at the lifeless eyes tattooed on the back of his scalp.

For the first time, I asked myself if Leo was who he seemed to be.

He worked for us, but Jacob had hired him and Jacob paid his salary. Supposedly. Or did Leo work for Peter, the mastermind of the plan to wipe out our family?

Was pistol-packing Leo one of Peter's plants?

Now, *that* was crazy. Right?

"Thank you, Leo. There's nothing you can do."

There was nothing anyone could do.

47

That evening, we had takeout from Curry in a Hurry. Everyone seemed preoccupied and moody, but at least we were together. After tidying up, I went to my room, shut off the lights, and covered myself with blankets to my chin. I needed sleep, badly.

But I hardly got any.

I was ripped out of sleep by a shocking, agonizing pain in my abdomen. My eyelids flashed open, and I instantly got my bearings. I was in my bed, for sure.

But I was very over-the-top sick to my stomach.

I balled up my pillows, held them tight against my belly, and curled around them, but that didn't help. It was just past midnight. Jacob would still be awake.

Groaning, almost doubled over, I hobbled along the hall to Jacob's door and fell against it. I knocked weakly and called him. He appeared almost instantly in his doorway, wearing shorts and a T-shirt and a fearful, almost angry look on his face.

I'm sure he was thinking, *What the hell is it now?* Honestly, I don't know how he can stand me.

"What's wrong, Tandy?"

"I'm very sick, Jacob. The pain is—oh my God— *excruciating*. I think I've been poisoned."

My knees buckled, and I collapsed at his feet, rolled into a fetal curl. He stooped down and put his hand on my forehead. Right after that, I heard him calling for help, waking up my brothers. I felt like a jerk, but I couldn't do anything to help myself. I couldn't even sit up.

Jacob and Harry wrestled me into a pullover and a pair of corduroy pants right over my pajamas. Hugo worked on getting socks and boots on my feet.

And that was when I lost it. I heaved, and a wastebasket somehow appeared under my chin. I used it, but instead of feeling relief, I felt worse, and now a rubber hammer had begun banging inside my head.

I must have blacked out, because the next thing I remember is a pair of EMTs lifting me onto a stretcher. There was a long trip through the lobby, radios crackling in my ears and my twin's reassuring voice saying, "We're with you, Tandy. We're right here."

The temperature outside was twenty degrees, but I was sweating like it was high noon in the Amazon rain forest. Jacob sat with me in the ambulance while I writhed and twisted and moaned.

He said, "We're almost there, Tandy. Hang on."

I grunted and managed to say, "I saw Peter today."

"Really?" Jacob said. He didn't believe me, but I needed to confess.

"I waved the white flag, Jacob. Total surrender. *Owwwwww!*" I yelped, grabbing my belly. "My God, this really hurts."

I fought through the pain and kept talking.

"I told Peter I wouldn't bother him anymore. Just to leave us alone. He didn't go for it. I'm sorry, Jacob."

"Don't be sorry. You'll feel better as soon as the doctors see you."

"I've doubted you, too."

"What do you mean?"

"I've questioned you because too many bad things have happened since you came to live with us. I've been thinking you—*Oh, this hurts so much.*"

Jacob took my hand.

"Rest, Tandy, please just rest," he said.

"No, I have to say this. Please forgive me, Jacob. I thought you could be working with Peter. His inside man."

"That's the pain talking," Jacob said. "You're really sick, Tandy. I don't know for how long, but you've been suffering from one thing or another since I met you."

"Do you think I'm crazy?" I asked him.

Tears leaked out of the corners of my eyes.

"Define *crazy*," he said.

I laughed one short *ha*. For a second or two, I felt good. Jacob wasn't mad at me, but the memory of all my suspicions about him came back with the pain.

The emergency room was packed with the sick and sicker. When someone got to me, my stomach was pumped, my blood was pulled, and I was sponge-bathed by a nurse with a very rough hand.

After checking my chart, the emergency doctor said, "Looks like you had food poisoning. Did you eat something in the last few hours that the other members of your family didn't eat?"

I thought about dinner. I pictured the table and the dishes we had ordered. And I remembered.

"We had Indian takeout. I had the tandoori prawns," I said. "Everyone else had curry. Lamb. Beef."

"Yep, seafood will do it. You feel a little better now?"

"When can I go home?"

"I want you to spend the night here. Let's see how you're feeling in the morning," said the doctor. "The nurse will give you something to help you rest."

I took the pills without protest and collapsed into a deep, troubled sleep.

48

Dr. Robosson *was highly concerned.* *"Tell* me what's hurting you," she said.

"Physically?"

"Emotionally."

"I don't know where to start. And please don't tell me to start at the beginning. I don't think I know what the beginning is."

"Tandy, start wherever you want to."

"I think I could die soon, Dr. Robosson."

"Are you suicidal?"

"Not in the least," I said. "I'm fighting off every attack. You know that."

"Then you're not going to die."

"I thought you wanted me to talk."

"I do. I'm sorry. Go ahead," said my shrink, leaning back in her brown velvet recliner.

I took some long breaths in and out. I spoke to myself inside my head about how I really liked Dr. Robosson but thought there was a good chance she wasn't enough shrink for me. I was too odd a case. Too smart, too damaged—physically, mentally, and psychologically. And I was a target. I had to tell her all of this.

Confession time.

"Don't take this the wrong way," I said. "I'm sick on too many fronts for one doctor to handle, even you. The damage was done long before I met you. And when I say I could die, I'm not being dramatic. Many attempts have been made on my life."

"Go on," she said.

"My uncle Peter wants me dead. He is crafty and rich and doesn't want to get actual blood on his hands. But I believe he has paid some people I count as friends to watch me and to report back to him. I believe that he has hit men at his disposal."

"Your uncle wants to kill you."

"Yes."

"So, please indulge me, sweetheart. Do you think he caused that airplane to go down?"

"There's a very strong possibility. It would have saved him a lot of trouble if my brothers and I had all died at the same time."

"And the drive-by shooting?"

"I would say a definite yes to hired gun."

"And the sleepwalking?"

"I looked up sleepwalking. It's caused by 'uninhibited REM' or 'sleep behavior disorder.' Stress contributes to that."

"Correct," said Dr. Robosson.

"Now, did Peter stress me out? Absolutely. Did he give me food poisoning? I don't know. Let's say he didn't do that. But there are too many other things that I can point to, Dr. Robosson—kidnapping and gunmen and fires—that just cannot be accidents."

She didn't protest. I saw love and concern in her face.

I said, "I need someone I can trust to know that if I die, it's murder, so that my uncle won't get away with it."

"Do you trust *me*, Tandy?"

I had to think about it. "Yes."

"Then here's what I need you to do."

49

I went directly from Dr. Robosson's cream-colored office to the high-tech lab on the floor above it. My blood was drawn for the second time in two days—six big vials of it this time—and I also had a CT scan of my brain.

After all that, I was taken to a pleasant white room with a big electric clock on the wall and a clean pine desk upon which were a stack of paper and a lot of pens. I started working on a battery of psychological and neurological tests, similar to ones I had taken before.

Usually, a person takes these tests over four nonsequential days.

I did them all in six hours.

After setting down my pen, I was escorted back to Dr. Robosson's office, and I took my seat opposite her in her big brown recliner. I could see through the window behind her. Wet snow fell and stuck to the leafless branches.

"Tandy. How are you feeling right now?"

"Do you have the test results?" I asked her.

"I do."

"I'm ready."

She had a couple of papers on a clipboard on her lap, but she didn't look at them.

She said, "Your cortisol is through the roof. That's a result of stress. Otherwise, your blood work is normal. Your CT scan is the same as when you came here for the first time. You have no tumors, no aneurysms, no brain damage.

"Intellectually, you are off the charts," she said. "High genius, as you know. Very high. Psychologically, you have severe trust issues and fears of many things. Given your history, I don't find these fears psychotic."

"So I tested normal, right?"

"Well, normal for someone who has seen active duty in a war zone."

"Okay."

"I'm prescribing antianxiety medication and something for your uninhibited REM sleep disorder. We have to monitor your reactions to these meds and perhaps make adjustments."

"You know how I feel about 'medication,'" I said, making air quotes around the last word.

"I understand," said Dr. Robosson. "The meds are not permanent, but you need help now in order to go back to school and function in daily life. They can give you some relief from stress until your life normalizes, and it will. And you definitely need to sleep."

"Thanks, Mom. Please don't forget what I've told you."

"I won't," she said.

Dr. Robosson wrote out the scrips, set up another appointment for us later in the week, and gave me a big hug.

The snowstorm had turned the sky dark, and everything else was pretty much a whiteout.

Leo drove slowly and carefully to a twenty-four-hour pharmacy, where I picked up my thirty-day supply of pills, and then he took me home.

We had a late dinner of comfort foods: mac and cheese, creamed spinach, chocolate pudding with whipped cream. Nothing hard, crunchy, chewy, or spicy. It was a pretty tame family dinner—for us.

The first chance I got, my friend, I flushed the drugs down the toilet.

CONFESSION

Can't sleep. My mind is racing.

I'm thinking of the Angel pills, and how I would've solved this case by now if I was still taking them. Just one little Lazr, and my focus would be unmatched. Uncle Peter would be behind bars by now.

Would it be worth it, just to see that happen?

Just this one time?

50

The next morning, Leo parked our car outside Matty's apartment in Tribeca. He started to get out, but I stopped him, saying, "Wait here, Leo. I'll go."

"The snow is deep and slippery," Leo said.

"Not a problem. Really."

I opened my door and stepped knee-deep into the slush at the curb. Icy water spilled in over the tops of my boots, but I didn't flinch.

I crossed to Matty's building, rang his bell, and entered at the buzz. There was an arrhythmic thump and drag of his footsteps inside his apartment, and then my brother flung open the door.

"I want to talk to you privately," I said.

"Good morning to you, too, Tandoo."

He cracked a big smile.

He was wearing jeans, one leg of them cut off at the thigh to accommodate his broken leg; he also had on a beautiful white shirt, a silk tie, and a nice blue jacket. He looked *great*.

"Don't say anything personal in front of Leo," I said. "I just don't trust him, okay? Where's your coat?"

I helped Matty on with his overcoat and filled him in briefly on the drive-by shooting as well as my sleepwalking and food poisoning incidents.

"Christ, Tandy. You need an exorcism," he said.

"Ha. Exorcism for an Angel. Perfect."

Leo helped Matty into the backseat of the car, then drove us uptown to an office building on Third Avenue where Gram Hilda's estate lawyers had rented a conference room for the sole purpose of meeting with Matty.

I think we both knew what was coming: a strong admonition, a heartfelt apology from Matty, and then a check.

I entered the room with my arm around Matty's waist. Monsieur Delavergne greeted me with a smile, but he was once again in his professional role. He reintroduced us to the four lawyers accompanying him, but clearly, as before in Paris, it was Monsieur Delavergne's meeting.

When we were seated, Monsieur Delavergne addressed Matthew.

"Mr. Angel," he said in his accented English, "I

understand the gravity and the impact of our decision on you, and that is why we have made this trip."

Matty nodded his big head and said, "Thanks for giving me a chance to speak for myself."

"Eh, actually, that won't be necessary," said the head lawyer. "The committee has met to discuss the terms of your inheritance and unanimously agreed that you violated the one condition of your trust fund. I am referring to the drunk-driving incident involving property damage and underage female passengers. This disgraceful occurrence reflects badly on the family name. But you know this.

"I'm very sorry, but you left us no choice but to terminate your inheritance."

"What do you mean *unanimously*?" Matty asked. I felt his body tense up. "You met with my uncle Jacob. I'm sure he voted *against* this decision."

"As I said, the decision was unanimous," said Monsieur Delavergne. "We are sorry, but we have to follow the dictates of the trust. We all wish you well."

"Like hell you do," Matty roared. "I have bills. I can't play football. People are suing me."

"I'm sorry," Monsieur Delavergne said again.

"Not sorry enough," my brother bellowed, rising to his full six-foot-two-inch height. Even with one of his legs encased in plaster, Matthew Angel had strength and balance to spare.

I watched in shock as Matty picked up his chair, raised it over his head, and threw it toward the windows. After the chair bounced off the reinforced glass, it knocked over a gigantic coffee urn, and china cups flew off the credenza.

Before the crashing subsided, Matty pushed me aside with one arm, then flipped the conference table. The lawyers scrambled to their feet and just barely got out of the way as the table upended.

Matthew was out of control, and it was worse than scary. What would he do next? What did the *pills* make him capable of doing?

Matthew looked at each of the lawyers in turn with his laserlike blue-eyed stare. I'd seen him steamroll professional football players many times. He'd broken ribs and shattered femurs. What else could he do?

Was he capable now of murder?

I was yelling his name, telling him to calm down.

He said, "I *am* calm, Tandy."

Then he blew out of the conference room like a hurricane on a crutch. The meeting about Matty's inheritance was officially over.

Matthew was *done*.

51

I left a devastated Matty in Charlie's Tap Room on Mott Street and arrived home at three that afternoon. I was in a black and violent mood, and for that I blamed Uncle Jake.

My poor brother.

How could Jacob have gone against Matty, siding with Gram Hilda's callous board when Matty was so down and so out?

I dropped my bag in the foyer and went looking for my uncle. I found him at his desk in his bedroom, talking on the phone.

I said, and not too nicely, "We have to talk."

He held up his index finger, the universal signal for *I'll be with you in a minute.*

"We need to talk right *now*," I said.

"Hold on, Peter," he said into the phone. "Tandy, please leave and close my door as you make your dramatic exit."

This was my Israeli former commando uncle speaking: a killer with lethal, registered hands. When he gave an order, you had to obey.

But you didn't have to like it.

I shot him one of my filthiest looks and left his room, slamming the door, then put my ear to the wood. I heard Jacob throw the lock, then continue conversing with Peter, pausing for Peter to speak and then speaking again himself.

I could only make out one word. *Tandy*.

Then I heard Jacob say, "Okay. Later."

I stood at the door like a freaking sentry outside Buckingham Palace. I waited. I heard drawers open and close. And finally, when I was about to kick the door down, it opened.

Jacob jumped back.

"For God's sake, Tandy."

"What you did to Matthew was really dirty, Jacob."

"You obviously don't know what you're talking about."

"No? While we were in court facing off with Peter, while we were flying in a sabotaged airplane, you were supposedly in Paris fighting for Matty to retain his inheritance."

"I *was* in Paris," Jacob said. "I went to the meeting.

My input was requested and then, after listening to the others, I voted with the board."

"You were supposed to *fight*."

"I'm on the board, Tandy. It's a responsibility. Matty violated the terms of the trust. I didn't call for punitive action, but I don't disagree with the decision to withhold his inheritance.

"If I start blindly throwing my vote to you kids, then I'll have no credibility and maybe no seat at the table, either. And I can almost guarantee that in the next forty years, you will *want* me at the table," Jacob said.

"Matty's *broke*."

"Matty was making ten million dollars a year. What happened to it all? Tandy, listen, he brought this trouble on himself, and now he needs to get his life back. By himself. All of you need to work on getting a life. You can't rely on Peter forever."

What had Jacob just said?

I think time actually stopped. It felt as if a gigantic sinkhole opened between Jacob and me and swallowed up all my belief in him, and my understanding of the world as I knew it.

When time resumed, all I could manage to say was, "What does Peter have to do with this?"

52

I was stunned, thunderstruck, and all my attention was on Jacob. It looked like he wanted to take back what he had said, but it was too late.

I asked him again. "Rely on Peter? What do you mean?"

He said, "For one of the brightest people I've ever met, you can be unbelievably clueless, Tandy."

He walked past me, heading downstairs, and I followed him down the spiral staircase. We passed Mercurio, hooked a right at Robert, and headed for the Pork Chair, which was in the open area behind the lipstick-red sofa and Harry's Pegasus piano.

When Jacob sat down hard in the chair, it grunted and squealed like it was being slaughtered. Any other day, I would have fallen apart, laughing at the surprised look on Jacob's face. But not today.

Uncle Jake recovered his angry face pretty fast and continued his totally unexpected rant.

"Did you ever ask yourself who pays the very pricy monthly charges for this apartment, Tandy? Have you wondered who pays me and Leo, and three private school tuitions, not to mention those thousand-dollar-a-night spa days at Waterside?"

I stared into Jacob's eyes. They were like small twin mirrors reflecting me back to myself, making me say to myself, *How could you be so stupid?*

This breaking news was far worse than I had imagined, but I wanted to make sure I understood. "When we got our inheritance, Phil bought the apartment. Jacob, you said you were rich."

"Right, Tandy. Phil bought the apartment with a onetime multimillion-dollar lump sum from the estate. But there are bills, plenty of them: taxes, common charges, insurance, food, utilities, salaries, and much more.

"Your grandmother didn't know there would be an apartment to buy or tuition or mental health care. She didn't even know that any of you would exist. The money left in her trust for you and your siblings was a 'just in case' plan and, when divided up among you, amounted to about a million dollars each, to be doled out to you in monthly payments until you're fifty-eight years old. That's about two thousand dollars a month.

"It's spend-and-save money. It's hard-times money. But if you get a scholarship to college, if you invest your stipend wisely, it will be a good safety net when you start out in life on your own."

I was hearing this for the first time.

It was a shocking jolt of reality, but it made sense—except for the part about Peter.

My mind raced forward and back and round and round as I examined our relationship with Peter over all the years I had known him. Disdain hardly begins to describe his show of feelings for us.

Jacob was saying, "Peter is carrying you because of his love for your father. He didn't want you to know because he didn't want your thanks. I accepted this guardianship out of loyalty to the family, but I love all of you, Tandy. Even Matthew. I think you know this."

I nodded dumbly as Jacob rested his arms on his knees. I saw the shiny scars on his forearms from the burns he'd suffered while rescuing me from the "accidental" fire, the latest of the three times Jacob had saved my life at risk of his own. No questions about whether he was with *us* or with *Peter* could stand up to those facts.

I got to my feet and he got to his, and I hugged my good uncle, who had sacrificed so much to take care of very difficult kids who totally needed him.

But my mind was blown regarding Uncle Peter.

If I'd been wrong about Peter, then who had been trying to kill us?

53

It was what some might call a lull in the storm.

My tutor, Jackie Rogers, a dean's list student from NYU, wrote to Dr. Oppenheimer saying, "Ms. Angel has gotten perfect test scores, and honestly, she doesn't need me. I recommend she be readmitted to All Saints."

Oppenheimer relented, so I was back at school. Defiantly so.

I wore my old wardrobe with aplomb. I sprayed Tandoori on my underwear, and my expression said *Don't mess with me.* And no one did.

By now, thanks to C.P., my former bestie, everyone knew that I'd spent three of the last four months in a nuthouse. Kids who knew me avoided me. The ones I didn't know stared at me from afar.

I liked that. I wanted to be left alone.

One day during lunch, I left school and walked a couple of blocks along Columbus. I bought a bag of chestnuts from a vendor and was heading back to school when a woman with long brown hair wearing a blue coat grabbed my attention.

She was half a block away, facing away from me, hailing a yellow cab that was coming to a stop.

Was that my sister?

I called out, "Katherine. Katherine, *wait!*"

I had that feeling of déjà vu as I ran toward the woman in the blue coat. But I had no chance to catch her as the cab took off, sending a wave of slush onto the sidewalk.

Had I really seen Kath?

Why would she be in New York and not let me know?

Or was this a sign that my brain had gone off the rails and that I couldn't even trust myself anymore?

I got back to All Saints, still shaken by the possible sighting of my sister, and took a front-row seat in my history class.

When the room was full, Mr. Conroy Brown, my twenty-five-year-old instructor, began his lecture. He was saying that New York, as part of the British imperial trading system, had acquired its mercantile character from Great Britain.

And that was just dead wrong.

As Mr. Brown pontificated, I muttered to myself,

still jacked up by seeing a Katherine look-alike on the street.

I was jolted into the moment when Mr. Brown called me out.

"Speak up, Ms. Angel. We all want to hear what you have to say."

That snarky expression must be given out to every graduate in education along with their diplomas, but I was glad of the opportunity to speak up. And I did.

I got to my feet and straightened my shoulders.

"If you were factually accurate," I said, "I would have kept quiet, but since you clearly need my help, I might as well set the record straight."

No one laughed, sneezed, or even exhaled.

Even Mr. Brown seemed paralyzed.

I went on, "So, Mr. Brown, to be fair to the class, the Dutch came to Manhattan well before the British. And they came for one reason—to make a profit. The Dutch named this city New Amsterdam and endowed it with its mercantile character. It's part of our *Dutch* legacy, not British.

"Any questions?"

54

It turns out Mr. Brown did *have* a question.

His face was a weird, stiff mask of high dudgeon as he asked me, "Do you want to get expelled from school, Ms. Angel?"

"Why would that happen?"

He said, "It would happen because you're rude, insubordinate, and extremely disruptive."

The room had been as quiet as a hole until then, but now there was snickering and raucous laughter. And I'm pretty sure my classmates weren't laughing at me.

"*Not another word*," said the instructor, addressing me and everyone else in the room.

I didn't crack a smile. I locked in on Mr. Brown with my deadly serious gaze—and he blinked first.

"Go to the headmaster's office, *now*," said Mr.

Brown, "and wait there. I'll join you when class is over."

I sat down and said, "I'm not going anywhere, Mr. Brown. If the headmaster wants to talk to me, he can come here."

There were claps and even a few whistles, and Mr. Brown slammed a ruler down on his desk and demanded silence. He took his phone and went outside the classroom, where you didn't have to be brilliant to guess that he phoned Oppenheimer and relayed to him what a scourge I was.

When Mr. Brown returned, he gave a shaky lecture on the history of trade in Manhattan. He included the Dutch influence on trade without citing me, and finally, the bell rang.

Students thundered out from behind their desks, and as the classroom emptied, Dr. Oppenheimer waded in.

He was a prim and fussy man with a pinched face who looked to me like his parents had chained him to the radiator as a child until he ate his peas. And that angry little kid had vowed that once he grew up, he would get back at everyone in the world.

I watched his muted back-and-forth conversation with Mr. Brown, and then the two of them advanced upon my front-row desk. Their anger made me feel pretty powerful. I wasn't used to feeling powerful anymore, but I liked it.

"Ms. Angel, you seem bent on destroying your opportunity to attend this school," Oppenheimer said.

"You're a smart girl, but not smart enough to make yourself small and avoid scrutiny. Why is that, do you suppose? Looking for drama is my guess. Looking for attention. Which is not a survival trait at All Saints, is it? Think about that, young lady. All Saints is your ticket to your future. This is your very last chance—"

"I don't want a last chance," I cut in, realizing that I'd made a huge snap decision in the last three seconds. "And I don't need your ticket. I'm a person, Dr. Oppenheimer. I have feelings and intelligence, and being small has never been one of my goals.

"In the short time I've known you, Dr. Oppenheimer, you've offended me every time I've seen you. So I'm leaving All Saints, effective this minute. You're *fired*. No second chances for you."

I picked up my bag, and before Oppenheimer could say, "You can't fire *me*," I stalked out of the room and into a small mob of classmates, who put their hands together for Tandy Angel, who was not small at all.

Hugo was there, my irrepressible booster. He hugged me and said, "Way to go, T."

He walked me out to the street, where Harry was leaning against the wrought-iron fence in front of the school, surrounded by fans.

Harry's long hair was thick and shiny, and his shirt was open under his unzipped jacket. His slouchy posture and general lack of starch had taken on a sexy appeal now that he was signing autographs for jumping, squealing girls.

He grinned and waved to me, and I waved back. It was surprising and a little bit hilarious. My twin brother was giving Harry Styles some competition.

I ordered Hugo back to class.

He said, "If *you* don't have to go, *I* don't have to go."

"Hugo. Go to class. You have to get into MIT one day."

I left my brothers at school and walked the few blocks toward home with my mind circling my major preoccupation.

I had an enemy. A dangerous one.

And I had no idea who that enemy was.

55

The San Remo's criminally outdated laundry room is in the vast, cavernous basement, one of many large and small rooms connected by long, dimly lit passageways leading to the stairs and service elevators.

It was late on a weeknight. I was wearing leggings, ballet flats, and one of Matty's winter-weight Giants sweatshirts. I was alone in the laundry room, but the smell of dryer sheets and the hum of the machinery were soothing and homey.

I put a load of whites into a washer and was thinking of dinner as I headed toward the elevators, about forty feet away down a darkened corridor.

I never saw the foot that shot out, tripping and sending me to the floor, or the hand that grabbed me by the back of my sweatshirt and pulled me back to my feet.

"Get off me!" I screamed, and tried to twist away, but the crook of a heavy arm clenched around my neck.

A male voice hissed, "Die, bitch."

I saw a flash of metal near my throat, the blade of a knife. I kicked behind me—a judo self-defense move—and my foot slammed into a knee. There was a yowl of pain, and I pushed away and ran like a bomb had gone off behind me.

My slippery shoes flew off my feet as I ran along the brightest of the dim hallways, past the closed elevator doors. I couldn't stop to push the call button. I just ran, taking corners when they appeared, afraid that my attacker would catch up with me any second, screaming for help as I ran.

I heard footsteps behind me. I think.

There were gigantic industrial fans in the basement ceiling, there to move the heat and static underground air. Between my screams and the *whack-whack* of the fans, the echoes of the pumps and furnace, and the rasp of my own panting, I couldn't be certain I still heard footsteps. But I did see that blood was dripping from the fingers of my right hand.

I grabbed my right shoulder as I ran and found a slash in the sweatshirt a few inches down on the outside of my right arm. *That bastard cut me.* I kept running, even though I was lost and confused and losing blood.

My bare feet slapped the cement floor as I forced

myself onward, yelling "Help!" all the while. I slipped and fell against a stack of empty cartons, then scrambled up and looked around. I didn't see him, and now I realized that I had boxed myself into a dead end—the corner between the bike room and the exit door to the street.

The exit door!

I yanked on the handle and threw my full weight against the door, but it didn't budge. And then I did hear footsteps, echoing against the cement walls and getting closer.

There was nowhere left to go that wouldn't take me directly past my attacker, so I gathered all my fear and rage and braced myself to face him. I would have to fight hard. I would have to kick at his junk, slam an elbow into his throat, use my clasped hands as a club at the back of his neck—and that was when I saw a kitchen knife lying on the ground.

Was it really a knife? *It was.*

I grabbed it up and clutched it. It was long, thin, sharp. It had to be the knife my attacker had used on me, but how had it gotten here? Had he snuck by without me seeing him?

I was trying to catch my breath and get my bearings when I keyed into the footsteps again. The figure of a man materialized from around a bend in the hallway.

I held the knife in front of me with both hands and screamed, *"Get away from me or I'll kill you!"*

The man shouted back, "Who's there?"

And then I recognized Benny, our night doorman.

"Ms. Angel? Was that you screaming?" he asked. "What's wrong? Did someone hurt you?"

Was Benny my attacker? Was he trying to kill me?

He came toward me saying, "Ms. Angel, what happened? Are you hurt?"

Benny was only feet away, his face full of concern. He was sixty and way out of shape. He couldn't have been chasing me.

I held out the knife and said, "Benny, look. Someone used this on me." I pulled at the neckline of my sweatshirt so that he could see the gash below my shoulder.

"You've got blood all over your face."

I touched my chin and cheek, felt where the skin had gotten scraped when I fell—and then I started blubbering. Dammit. I just hate that.

"Benny, thank God you chased him away."

He looked at me strangely. Like, *I did what?*

I said, semihysterically, "Did you see who was after me?"

"I didn't see anybody, Ms. Angel. Maybe you got spooked. Maybe you fell and cut yourself on something?"

"No, Benny. He said, 'Die, bitch.' He cut me with this." Hands shaking, I showed him the knife again, and he shrank away.

"That's sick. Can you walk okay? Here. Lean on

me. Let's get you upstairs so your uncle can take you to a doctor."

Benny walked me to the elevator bank, all the while throwing nervous glances at my face and at the knife.

As he repeatedly jabbed the elevator call button, I could tell what he was thinking. He couldn't get this crazy girl off his hands soon enough.

56

It had been a half hour since the murderous thug had slashed me in the basement.

My pulse had slowed to about eighty, but I was still pumping adrenaline. I was panting, sweating, and pressing a washcloth to the slash on the side of my arm, which now hurt like crazy.

Caputo and Hayes sat across the kitchen table from me and Uncle Jacob. The knife between us was spotlighted by the overhead fixture. It was six inches long, with a black handle and a narrow blade that had been sharpened to a razor edge. If I hadn't been wearing Matty's thick sweatshirt, that blade might have sliced my arm to the bone.

Caputo leaned across the table and said, "Let's take it from the top one more time, okay, Brandy?"

"Stop. Doing. That," I said. "I know you're pretending you don't know my name to throw me off. But you're forgetting one thing, Sergeant. I'm not a suspect. I'm the freaking *victim*."

Caputo leaned back, not quite suppressing a smirk. Both he and Hayes were treating me as if I was in the psych ward at Bellevue. Why didn't they write up the incident report and do some detecting? Why didn't they believe me?

Caputo said, "Once again, Tandy. Start at the beginning."

"As I said before, I didn't see him. He came from behind. He tripped me. Then he grabbed at the back of my sweatshirt and pulled me up. He put his arm around my neck. I saw the knife, so I kicked back at his knees. That's when I ran."

"He said something, right?"

"Right. Before I kicked him, he said, 'Die, bitch.' "

"Does that sound familiar to you? Has anyone ever said that before?"

"No."

"Did he call you by name?" Caputo asked.

"No."

"Unlike the guy who took a shot at you on the street?"

That wasn't really a question, so I didn't answer it.

Hayes said, "And this knife? Your, uh, attacker just dropped it?"

"I found it, that's all I know. And I was glad to have it. I thought I would have to use it."

"Too bad you held on to it with your sweaty hands," Caputo mused. "I suppose, if you don't mind waiting about a month, the lab can test it for DNA."

"You should do that," I snapped, "and put a rush on it. I resent your implication that I would cut myself."

Caputo said, "It's a valid hypothesis, Tootsie. Is that what happened? You're desperate to get us to believe you, so you pushed the envelope a little bit—"

I jumped up, losing it, and at the same time not.

"How about getting the security footage from inside the basement and outside the exits? How about interviewing the doormen? Why not see if any other tenants used the laundry room tonight or went down to the garbage room and if they saw anyone they didn't know or who looked suspicious?"

Caputo said to Jacob, "Letting you know. We can't be responding to these kinds of calls anymore."

Jacob said, "Tandy is not a liar."

I shouted at Caputo. "*Someone is trying to kill me!* What are you going to say when you find me dead?"

Chairs scraped. Cops got to their feet. Caputo said, "If I learn anything, I'll get in touch. Meanwhile, Sandy, maybe you ought to become a writer. Fiction, of course."

"Screw you!" I shouted at Caputo's back.

Jacob gripped my arm to stop me from following the cops to the front door. I felt as crazy as everyone thought I was. Had I fabricated this assault?

My cheek and my chin were scraped from my

fall. My arm was cut. I'd heard what I'd heard: "Die, bitch." Footsteps.

Hell, no, I didn't make this up. I don't lie and I'm not crazy. I'm also the leading authority on my own state of mind, thank you.

You can trust me on that.

57

I *was still shaky when Jacob* and I returned from the emergency room late that night. Hugo was still awake, and he demanded to see the fifteen neat little stitches closing the gash on my arm.

I took a hot shower, then pulled on Harry's pajamas and Hugo's socks for some added comfort. Jacob brought a few of Dr. Robosson's prescribed and newly refilled antianxiety pills up to my bedroom with a cup of herbal tea and a plate of cookies.

I said, "Thanks. And you don't have to watch me swallow the pills. I *want* to take them."

"Good. Do you need anything else right now? I'm going down to the laundry room."

"My whites need to be dried."

"No problem."

"If you see an unknown or imaginary attacker looking for his knife, kindly beat the hell out of him and hold him for questioning."

"Will do. That's a promise."

I swallowed the pills and gathered my two brothers in residence for a meeting on my bed.

I said, "Guys, once again, my sanity is in question. If you think someone threatened and slashed me, please raise your hand."

"We were on the plane together, remember?" Hugo said. "I know a death threat when I see the ground coming up at me."

Harry said, "Seriously? You need a show of hands?"

"Yes. I do."

Hands went up.

"Excellent. Okay. I'm back in detective beast mode. You know my motto: *Mystery solved. Case closed.*"

I repeated to my brothers what Jacob had told me about Peter: that he was supporting our fantastic lifestyle. They were as shocked as I had been, and they had the same questions I had hurled at Jacob.

Why was Peter supporting us when he clearly hated us? And why hadn't we been told?

Harry said, "If he's paying the bills, he could plant spies."

Hugo added, "And spies would tell his hired thugs when to sneak up on you. Like whoever knifed you tonight."

"Agreed," I said. "People we don't even know could be watching. Mailmen. That old couple who are always hanging out in the lobby. By the way, everyone's a suspect until I clear you. Where were you when I was attacked?"

Harry said, "We were both in my room when you went down to do your laundry, goofball. We can alibi each other."

"Okay. You're both not guilty."

I bumped fists first with Harry, then with Hugo.

Hugo said, "*Booooommmm!*" and shot his fingers out in an "explosion," then rolled off the bed and kept rolling until he hit the wall, where he played dead.

Sometimes I forget he's only eleven. "Get up, Hugo."

"You blew me up," he said. "I saw you."

We all cracked up, and it took a while to call my meeting back to order.

When we'd collected ourselves, I said, "So let's say Peter is guilty of being a pig, but not of trying to kill me. Who else would want me crazy or dead?"

I handed out pads and pens, saying, "Put your number one suspect first, your number two after that, and so on, for a total of five."

After our lists were done, we compared notes and had a heated discussion about the suspects, each of us defending names on the list and providing reasons for other suspects to go to the top.

We firmed up our lists. Then I adjourned the meeting and took a sleeping pill.

Sorry, Dr. Robosson. I have no idea if I dreamed. But when I woke up the next morning, I was breathless, as if I'd been running hard.

Was I fleeing or chasing?

I wish I knew.

CONFESSION

Friend, the names on my list were frightening, even to me. They were people I *knew*, some I've been close to most of my life. And some I hardly knew at all.

Not being able to trust anyone is enough to drive someone crazy. Was that what was happening to me? Had the *pills* finally kicked in with their poison to debilitate me mentally, if not physically? Was I going crazy?

I felt hot tears well up in my eyes. I let them flood and spill over. When I was younger, obediently taking my course of "vitamins" every morning, I never cried. It felt good to have emotions again, even if they were painful and harrowing. But maybe my chaotic thoughts and emotions were hard to manage because I was so out of practice.

My parents had done this to me. And my uncle.

Could I trust anyone ever again?

58

I was in a state of high anxiety the next morning. The pain in my arm reminded me how much I wanted to get ahead of the psycho who had attacked me last night and was still at large.

Hugo, our in-house tech wiz, hacked into the Violent Criminal Apprehension Program and ran a search on our driver, Leonard Peavey. Leo was on Peter's payroll, carried a gun, and knew where I was at all times. He was my number one suspect.

But Leonard Peavey had no criminal history. *Au contraire.* He had been a cop for twenty years in Schenectady, retired with distinction, and became security chief for Target in Albany before coming to work for us at the age of fifty-five.

He was clean.

We ran a similar search on Philippe Montaigne, our attorney, who had also once worked for Uncle Peter. I ran global searches on Sergeant Capricorn Caputo and Detective Ryan Hayes, and we screened our night doorman, Benito Rodriguez, and the rest of the San Remo staff.

There were no red flags on any of our top suspects, but we continued to throw spaghetti against criminal databases all morning. None of our suspects stuck.

At noon, I decided to call Samantha Peck for help.

Sam, my mother's former personal assistant and—as we'd recently found out—lover, knew the Angel family extremely well, maybe better than I did. She also knew about the plane crash that came *this close* to killing us all and was the reason my brothers and I had missed her mother's funeral.

After we'd exchanged fond hellos, I brought Sam up to the minute on my recent near-death experiences.

"Trust your gut, Sam," I urged her. "Who would want me crazy or dead?"

There was a silence, and then Sam started crying so hard, she couldn't speak. I waited while she blew her nose and went for a glass of water, and when she came back to the phone, she said, "My mother was a mean old bitch, Tandy, but even with her rough edges and hoarding and inappropriate comments and judgments and rudeness, I still miss her. And I miss Maud, too, so much. I even miss Malcolm. I still believe your mom and dad were murdered."

"Sam. You know that's not true."

"I don't know much anymore, sweetie. I'm sorry. I think I've crossed over the line into crazy."

Everything Sam said pulled at my head and my heart in ways I hadn't predicted. I commiserated with our family friend, brought her up to date on my brothers, and finally got her laughing before we said good-bye.

But *I* wasn't laughing.

I sat for a while in my blue room, staring at the sky, remembering my parents' wretched deaths. The end of their lives meant the end of the pills and an epic turning point in the lives of everyone who loved them.

Sirens blaring on Central Park West brought me back to the present. They sounded like a call to action.

I texted Leo and asked him to drive me downtown.

59

I found Matty sitting on the steps outside his apartment building, drinking a forty-ounce bottle of Bud. He hadn't shaved in a while. His dreadlocks were so disreputable that they had shot past cool and rolled right up to homeless. He was cheerful, however, and somewhat lucid.

I sat down next to him, facing glinting snowbanks, and I told him everything. He heard me out, including my suspicions.

"Me?" he asked. "Why would I want to kill you?"

"Well, maybe it's not personal. You're prone to violence, Matty. You have an anger problem, and let's face it, you're a professional thug. And now that you're broke, you could have a financial motive. If the rest of us are out of the way, you might get money from the estate. Or maybe you've got a split personality. I've heard that craziness runs in the family."

Matty laughed and said, "You don't really think I tried to kill you. Come here."

He put his arm around my good shoulder and pulled me close. He hugged me really hard and I liked it. Correction. I *loved* it.

"I never have and never will hurt you, Tandoo. You've been my strongest, most loyal supporter always, and I've loved you since you were born. But I *am* worried about you."

"And I'm kind of worried about *you*, big brother."

I crossed Matty off the list and asked Leo to drive me uptown to Sarabeth's, a trendy tea shop on the Upper East Side.

I was on time. I took a sunny table at a zebra-striped banquette and asked the waiter for lemon cake and peppermint tea. But before I put cup to lip, the door opened with a jangle and James walked in.

He looked like the girl-crush he was, perfectly dressed to show off his great body and his huge pots of money. He slipped into the seat across from me and said, "Hey, Tandy, you're looking like, uh, someone hit you. Or something."

My heart, traitor that it is, took off at a gallop and sent blood rushing into my cheeks—and down below. But I did my best to seem unaffected by the sight and smell of a boy I still loved.

I said, "I'm okay, James. I'm not going to take up much of your time. I'm not recording this meeting"— his eyebrows shot up at this—"so I want you to be honest with me."

"Not recording? What do you mean?"

"That this conversation is strictly confidential and will never come back to bite you. Oh. Here she is."

The door jangled and C.P. came in. She was in private school slut mode—miniskirt up to her smile, tights, knee-high boots, and an open fur coat over all of that. Skunk, I think. Or hyena.

She sat down next to James and put her hand in his lap, smirking.

I wanted to slap her. But I *had* invited her. Know thy enemy. Keep her close.

Once they'd both ordered tea, I asked, straight-out, "Does either of you have any idea who may have been responsible for the attempts on my life?"

"Huh?" C.P. said. "What attempts? Oh, I forgot. You're out of your mind."

I ignored her and turned to James.

"James, your father was Uncle Peter's partner for a while. That's a fact. So have you stepped into your father's shoes? Do you have a partnership with my uncle?"

"Me? And your uncle Peter? You can't be serious." Peter was there when I was ripped from James's arms that long-ago night on the beach. At the time, we both had reason to hate him. But that James—the one who cared—was not the boy sitting across from me now.

Screwing the lid tightly closed on those memories, I cut to the chase. "Do you have any idea who might want to kill me?" I asked crisply.

"No, but I think you might be a little grandiose," said James.

"Or delusional," C.P. added. "Megalo-something."

"Megalomaniacal," said James.

C.P. said, "Yeah, that's it." And they both laughed.

I couldn't hide my disgust, so I just went with it.

"Thanks. You've reminded me that neither of you has the brains or the wherewithal to come after me. You're off the list. The tea is on me."

I dropped a fifty on the table and walked out.

"Where to, Ms. Tandy?"

"One Hundred Fifty-Fifth Street and Broadway, please. Thanks, Leo."

I was just about out of suspects.

This would be my last stop.

60

Trinity Church Cemetery is on a sloping twenty-three acres, tucked between banks of nondescript apartment buildings in Washington Heights. It runs downhill between Amsterdam Avenue and Riverside Drive, and from the top of the hill, it owns a commanding view of the Hudson.

I left Leo at the gate and walked uphill under a gray, snow-laden sky to the mausoleum where my parents were interred. It was easy to pick out their final resting place because of the angel statues on each side of the doors and the name Angel carved above the lintel.

I sat on a stone bench fronting the mausoleum, with its view in one direction of the Church of the Intercession and, in the other, of the river. I took in cold breaths and let out frosted ones as snowflakes began to float down.

I was still thinking about my conversation with Sam and felt the ache of irreplaceable loss, maybe more than ever before.

Sam had said, *"My mom was a bitch, but I miss her so much."*

Maud was worse than a bitch. But now I wasn't thinking of her aloofness or her tough lessons "for my own good." I was remembering lying on the couch with her on Sunday mornings when she did the crossword puzzle in her yellow silk pj's. She asked for my help with the puzzle and shared her tea and toast, and those mornings were so precious, I could almost smell the ink from the *New York Times* and the fragrance of her shampoo.

I was having similar thoughts about my distant and preoccupied father. I saw myself as a little girl, playing in his lab and working with him in the kitchen. He taught me to cook and told me that the best cooks were scientists, whether they knew it or not. Just thinking about him saying that I had a scientific mind made me feel good about myself, then and now.

Sitting there, I decided to relinquish my anger over the stiff punishments and the tight leash and the wretched pills. I even forgave them for my time at Fern Haven, which was Waterside on steroids, where there were electroshock treatments, heavy medications, and controversial therapy, all in the interest of getting me away from James.

Looking back, I had to give it to them. They'd been right about James.

Sweet images came to me of party hats, and ball games where we watched my big brother take punts and kickoffs to the house. I thought about growing up with Katherine and swimming with gentle sharks the size of whales and about preparing for a future where all of us would become... something more than just nature and nurture combined.

I walked up to the gates of the mausoleum and touched each of the carved stone angels and said, "I know you loved us in your way and that you did your best. I get that now, and I'm very grateful. I wish I could talk to you, or even just see you. I love and miss you both."

And then I let them go.

I found the car on Amsterdam. Leo jumped out and opened the back door for me. I brushed snow from my coat and stamped my boots. Then, when I had strapped in, Leo turned and fixed me with his pale gray eyes.

"Ms. Tandy, I'm asking you again. This isn't bull. Is there something I can do for you?"

I knew now that Leo used to be a cop. I searched his face for the truth of him and saw nothing to be afraid of.

"Do you mean it?" I said.

"Absolutely," he said. "I'm here for you. Whatever you need. Just ask."

"I need you to tail someone."

"No problem," said Leo. "Who?"

CONFESSION

The nightmare was back again.

The one in which someone—Peter? James? *Malcolm?*—is slowly and firmly pushing my head underwater. I don't know if I'm in a bathtub or a pool or a lake. My guttural screams are abruptly cut off by the water flooding my throat. I fight and flail, but the iron hand steadily, inexorably pushes me down.

I gasp and choke as fluid fills my lungs.

I look up—

61

After a night of tumultuous, haunting dreams, I finally gave up on sleep. I was brushing my teeth, wondering what my parents would advise now that I'd quit school, when Jacob called up to me from downstairs.

"In a minute," I shouted.

"Now," he shouted back.

I was in pajamas—but fine. I went down the stairs, and when I cleared the spiral, I saw a lot of people filling the living room. At eight in the morning?

Harry and Hugo were dressed for school, but their faces were frozen in an expression I could read only as shock. What the hell was going on?

Jacob looked agitated, and that was when I saw that Dr. Robosson, warm and fuzzy in gray cashmere, was sitting in the Pork Chair and two young women were standing behind her.

I knew the women, Luann and Stella, a nurse and an orderly from Waterside. From the corner of my eye, I saw another figure standing between me and the door. I turned my head for a better look.

He was male, white, about twenty-eight, wearing blue scrubs with the name LOUIS stitched over the breast pocket. He had a blond brush cut and fire tattoos spiraling around his huge arms. I had never seen him before.

Dr. Robosson said, "Tandy, don't be afraid. This is a good thing. I want you to come with us to Waterside."

"But why? I'm fine. I'm taking my medicine."

"You had an incident the other night that required stitches. It's been suggested that you may have cut yourself. Honey, just look at what you've done to your face."

I shot a furious look at Jacob and said, "Are you serious? Is this what's happening now? I'm being committed?"

Jacob looked at me helplessly. "I had to call your doctor," he said. "As your guardian, I had to."

Hugo was off the couch like a shot. He had his arms around me and he was saying, "For your own good, Tandy. For your own good."

I unlocked Hugo's arms and started backing away. I knew there was nowhere to go, but I wasn't going down easily. I made a feint toward the kitchen, then an end run around the muscle-bound goon who was still blocking my path to the doorway.

He moved fast—a football player of some type, I could tell. He caught me and twisted my good arm behind my back and lowered me facedown to the floor.

"Honey, please," said Dr. Robosson. She came over to where I was lying and spoke really close to my face. I smelled wintergreen and hair spray. "You *like* Waterside, remember? We're going to take good care of you."

I screamed *"No!"* loud enough to make my shrink pull back and to make my twin brother put his hands over his ears and turn away from me. I lost track of Hugo and Jacob as the orderlies lifted me up and— even as I fought them—strapped me to a gurney.

I yelled, "You can't do this to me! I'm a citizen of the United States!"

I screamed inside the elevator. I shocked the porters, and the doormen and the residents in the lobby. The gurney rattled as it went over the cracks in the sidewalk. Snow swirled around us like ghosts. I called to the people walking past our building, "They're trying to kill me!"

Cell phones came out. Videos were shot.

"I'm being held against my will," I pleaded. "I'm being kidnapped."

A private ambulance with the wavy blue logo of Waterside Center was waiting at the curb. Parked behind the ambulance was our bulletproof car.

Leo got out. He stood beside the open door and tracked me with startled eyes but didn't make a move to help.

"They're doing it, Leo!" I screamed. "Help me, please! They're going to make me *disappear*!"

62

I came out of a deep, thick sleep to find myself in a hospital bed with side rails in a darkened room. I was facing a single casement window. The moon was up, and I recognized the view of the river.

I knew where I was.

This was Waterside, but my room was at an unaccustomed height. I was on a high floor, the psycho ward where the certifiably insane were housed.

It was coming back to me, what had happened that morning. I tried to sit up, but I had so little strength that even using the side bars for leverage didn't help.

I thought at first that I was strapped down, but no.

I'd been drugged.

The heaviness was pinning me to the bed and tamping down whatever emotions that, without the drugs, I would certainly be having. Like justifiable three-alarm fury and overwhelming heartbreak, to name just two.

I was here. Again.

I turned my head to the left and saw amber pill bottles on the nightstand. Some had been tipped over, and pills were scattered everywhere.

What had happened?

Had I fought to stop them from gagging me with pills?

I turned my head to the right, and there, sitting in a chair beside the door, was Leo.

I drew in my breath, a long, sucking gasp.

He put his finger to his mouth, like—*Shhh. Don't scream.* He leaned toward me and said quietly, "It worked, Tandy. You were right."

It was coming back now. All of it.

"I was right? Really?"

Leo nodded, and as muzzy as I was, my head almost exploded. It was as if too much was flooding in—the good and the great; the bad and the horrible. It was cosmic.

"Is it done?" I asked.

"Not yet."

The door to my room opened slowly, and Jacob slipped in as Leo melted into the background. Jacob walked over to my bed and asked softly, "How do you feel, sweetheart?"

"Like I weigh four hundred pounds."

"Can you sit up?"

He put his arm behind me and adjusted the bed.

He said, "I'll help you get dressed. We have to leave now. You've been out of it for the whole day."

Just then, a noise came from the bathroom. Like someone was trying to speak. Leo opened the bathroom door and turned on the light.

"This is Louis," he said to me.

It was the body builder who had been in the apartment this morning, all muscle with flame tattoos wrapping his biceps. Now he was sitting on the floor, subdued, not struggling. I looked at Leo. He showed me a stun gun in his waistband.

Oh.

Jacob brought my clothes from the closet, and I dressed in slow motion while Leo helped Louis to his feet.

"Are we good to go, Lou?"

The man nodded vacantly.

The four of us left the room in pairs.

Groggily, I leaned on Jacob, and we went quietly down six flights of fire stairs. When we reached the ground floor, we ducked through the side door to the garbage room. From there, the outer door opened easily, and we were standing in crisp night air on the tree-lined street lit by the full moon.

As we got into the bulletproof car, I noticed the gray sedan parked behind us. It was a police car.

"Cops?" I asked Jacob.

"Yep. Friends of yours."

I saw Leo transferring Louis to a sergeant I happen to know by heart from ten thousand feet away and in the dark. He was lanky with wild dark hair, his pant cuffs hanging above his ankles and his zodiac goat tattooed on his wrist.

Sergeant Caputo gave me a little wave.

Bemused, I waved back.

Doors slammed. Headlights flashed on. Leo got behind the wheel of the bulletproof car, and both vehicles moved away from the curb.

Jacob said, "Tandy, this could get rough. Emotionally and physically. Are you sure you're ready for this?"

I nodded.

As we drove down the halogen-lit West Side Highway, my uncle Jacob told me all that he knew.

My nerve endings were tingling. My brain was humming with good vibrations. This was going to be an evening to remember always.

I was about to solve my greatest mystery.

63

I was still woozy and nauseous from the load of drugs in my system when our car pulled up to the curb on Eighty-First near Columbus and parked in front of an apartment building that I recognized all too well.

Caputo and Hayes parked their unmarked gray Chevy sedan behind us. Caputo transferred Louis, the handcuffed orderly, to another unmarked car across the street while Hayes opened my door and helped me out to the sidewalk. I hung on to his arm to steady myself.

He said, "Tandy, we'll be with you the whole time, okay? Mr. Peavey, if you don't mind, stay here and keep your phone line open."

Jacob, Caputo, Hayes, and I entered the foyer of the posh apartment building, where Caputo badged the doorman and said, "Police. Call up to Mr. Angel and tell him that his brother, Jacob, is here to see him. Nothing else."

I flashed on the last time I'd seen my loathsome uncle as the elevator ascended and we four approached the door at the end of the hall.

Caputo indicated to Jacob to come right to the door, while the rest of us flattened ourselves against the wall.

Is this really happening?

Are the police really at Peter's door?

Jacob rang the doorbell. Locks clacked, and the door opened wide enough to accommodate Peter's face. He was wild-haired and wild-eyed as he looked at Jacob and snapped, "What's this about, Jake? I have company. It's midnight, for Christ's sake."

Caputo stepped forward, showed Peter his badge, and said, "I'm Sergeant Caputo. This is my partner, Detective Hayes. Mind inviting us in for a minute or two?"

That was when Peter saw me. His eyes widened, but then he scoffed, flung open the door, and said, "Jacob, you're a damned fool. What wild story has my niece been telling you now? I suppose she's been accusing me of trying to murder her. And now the police are involved? Bad move, brother."

I held back snarky retorts in the interest of letting the police run this show. We followed Peter into the apartment, through the foyer, and into the barely furnished living room.

Hayes said, "Mind if I take a look around?" He went directly to the closed doors beyond Peter's desk.

"Of course I mind. You didn't answer my question," said Peter. "What's this about?"

Caputo pulled a folded paper from his inside pocket. "This is an arrest warrant, Mr. Angel. As a matter of fact, I have two of them."

Hayes knocked on the bedroom door. A woman's voice said, "Peter?"

"It's the police, ma'am. Please step outside."

Peter's face was flushed as he said, "What is this trumped-up whatever? I'm under arrest for *what*, exactly?"

"As you said," Caputo said, "you're under arrest for the attempted murder of your niece. Put your hands behind your back, Mr. Angel."

The bedroom door opened, and I clawed my hands down my face. I was glad to be right, but at the same time, this was the worst betrayal, *ever*. I'd asked Leo to follow the one person who knew my movements to the minute, who understood the workings of my mind, maybe better than I knew them myself.

"Peter, what's going on?" asked Dr. Mary Robosson. She was wearing a Waterside Center robe and her hair was bunched in a messy ponytail, making her look completely alien to me. She seemed strangely composed.

Hayes said, "You're under arrest as well, Dr. Robosson."

"Do *not* touch me," she said.

I wanted to feel something—rage, jubilance, ecstasy—but I was still numb and nauseated from the damned drugs.

This was emotional robbery.

Peter's fury, however, was obvious. He said to me, "You wretched girl. I'll sleep in my own bed tonight, but I'm officially done with you and your idiot brothers, Tandoori. My checkbook is closed. You have nothing on me but your hysterical, girlish imagination—no evidence, no proof, no *nothing*."

I cleared my throat a couple of times.

Then I said, "Actually, we have something—your girlfriend and coconspirator. We also have her hired thug. If she's offered a deal, I think she's going to take it, Uncle Peter. She has no conscience. I think she'll tell us everything."

64

We were at the Twentieth Precinct, sitting around the scarred metal table in the break room.

Peter and Dr. Robosson had been charged with conspiracy to commit murder. While they were chilling out in separate interrogation rooms, Leo, Jacob, and I sipped cold coffee with Caputo and Hayes and tried to fit the pieces together. It was a high: three cops, a former Mossad intelligence officer, and me, a seventeen-year-old former high school student who had, as Caputo said, "earned a seat at the table."

I was thinking, *Thanks, Cappy. That's not quite an apology*—but I didn't say it. He had finally collared my monstrous uncle, as well as my wretched shrink.

As an added bonus, Robosson's killer for hire, Louis Caltrane, was in a cell because Leo had caught him "holding the bag"—an IV bag of sedatives, that is. An overdose that was meant to kill me.

Leo was running the story again, how after my cemetery visit, he'd followed Dr. Robosson to a coffee shop, where she had met Uncle Peter. Leo had taken a booth behind them and listened as they discussed "a permanent solution to the Tandy problem."

Their plan was too easy.

They decided that after my next therapy session, she would check me into Waterside for observation. And then my dear uncle Peter, my father's brother, my own blood relative, had suggested to his lover, "I think Tandy will commit suicide, don't you?"

The coffee was coming on and the drugs were wearing off. I knew this because listening to how Dr. Robosson and my uncle had plotted to murder me sent a jolt of pure white fury right through me. I could have flipped the table. I could have flipped a *car*.

But I forced myself to be quiet while Jacob explained that the so-called intervention in our living room had been my idea. It had given Dr. Robosson and Uncle Peter the chance they were looking for to lock me up at Waterside, while giving us an opportunity to take control of their plan.

Leo continued his story by saying that he had followed the ambulance to Waterside, where Caputo and Hayes talked to the management, who gave Leo scrubs, a name tag, and cover. He'd gone to the seventh floor, where he'd introduced himself to Louis as a new hire, and then he'd watched my room.

Leo said to me, "Robosson gave you a sedative right away, but your vital signs were all good. So while you slept, I helped Louis mop floors, and when he prepared your overdose, I busied myself cleaning the bathroom. Christ, I had to wait until he had emptied all the drug bottles on the bedside table and had the IV needle in his hand."

He shook his head, remembering.

"That's when I took him down," Leo said. "I roughed him up a little until he spilled."

"A pretty good move," said Caputo. "Hats off, buddy."

"Outstanding," I said. "Then what happened?"

Leo said, "Louis told me that Dr. Robosson paid him 'a bomb' to kill you, Tandy, and to make it look like a suicide. He said that Dr. R. was working with her 'boyfriend'; he didn't know the guy's name."

Leo went on. "I secured Louis in the bathroom. Then I gloved up, bagged the IV bag in a clean trash bag, and left the empty bottles on the table, so as to preserve the evidence."

Caputo picked up where Leo left off. He said, "Louis's statement will indict Dr. Robosson, but all we have on Peter is an overheard conversation. It's hearsay. If we want to hold Peter, the doctor is going to have to implicate him by name and on the record."

Hayes said, "Cappy's going to interrogate Peter. And while he's doing that, Tandy, if you're willing, you could have a private chat with Dr. Robosson. I'll be right behind the glass."

65

The interrogation room was the size of a walk-in closet, furnished with a metal table, four chairs, a two-way mirror, a light fixture, and a camera in a corner of the ceiling.

Dr. Robosson was sitting at the table, wearing the clothes she'd worn yesterday: a tan gabardine suit, a silk blouse with a stain on it, and diamond studs.

She looked up when I opened the door.

"Oh, Tandy. I thought you were those horrible cops. Where are they?"

"Interrogating Peter and Louis, I think. I shouldn't be here, but we have to talk. Don't you agree, you heinous bitch?"

I pulled out a chair and sat down.

"Of course. Tell me what you're feeling," she said.

Like this was a therapy session and she was still my doctor.

"I feel glad to be alive," I said. "But how do *you* feel about yourself, Doctor? I trusted you more than anyone in the world, and you betrayed that trust completely."

"It's not what you think," she said.

"No? You aren't sleeping with my uncle? You didn't conspire with him to kill me?"

"Tandy, yes, I've been seeing Peter since you first came to Waterside. You were convinced that he was out to kill you, and I had to see for myself."

"And one thing led to another?" I said.

"It's a cliché, but that's right. We did connect over concern for you. We fell in love."

I guess I thought she'd be furious, or apologetic or ashamed—*something*. But her affect was flat. Like this was happening to someone else.

"Is that ethical?" I asked. "Are you allowed to sleep with a patient's close family member without telling them?"

"Strictly speaking, there's nothing unethical about it. Peter is not your parent or boyfriend or child. But I can see how you might find it uncomfortable."

Uncomfortable? She was delusional—or worse. How had I missed this?

"You've got your uncle all wrong, you know," she said. "He's a good man, Tandy. A big thinker. A humanitarian."

"Peter is a humanitarian? Is that right?"

"You think the pills damaged you, when everyone

knows that you and your siblings are extraordinary. Don't you see that if those pills were readily available, they would benefit other children, and that that would be a tremendous asset to all of mankind? You were trying to stop that."

"The pills kill your emotions," I said. "Is it a benefit for mankind to have no feelings, no conscience? You're a psychiatrist, for God's sake."

"I've had a real breakthrough since I met Peter. I see now that emotions impede success in life. They cause broken homes and destroy marriages and damage children. I should know. I've been a practicing therapist for twenty years. Has talk therapy helped you, Tandy?"

I couldn't answer her. Surely talk therapy with her had been a total sham.

"I started taking the pills, Tandy. Yes, *me*—and they've given me wonderful clarity."

"I'm not following you," I said, dropping a hunk of bait into the trap.

"It's simple, Tandy. Look. If you'd gotten your way, Angel Pharmaceuticals might have closed. The groundbreaking work your father and Peter have done would be lost along with the promise of pure analytical thinking for millions who need clear minds to survive in this challenged world."

Dr. Robosson was glowing. She was high on a mission that overrode common sense. Talk about drinking the Kool-Aid...did this clueless freaking maniac know what she was saying?

"I tried to help you, Tandy, but you wouldn't leave it alone. So you had to be sacrificed. One person for the greater good of humanity. You see that now, don't you?"

Not really. She was mentally disintegrating in front of my eyes. Had the shame of getting caught caused Dr. Robosson to have a psychotic break? Had the pills done this to her? Had Peter brainwashed her? Or had she been freaking crazy all along?

"Okay, let me see if I've got this right. You're saying that when Peter's attempts to kill me failed, you decided to get me out of the way. For the common good."

She smiled agreeably. "You would have just drifted off to sleep."

That was an admission of wrongdoing.

The trap slammed shut.

It took everything I had not to look up at the camera. I got out of my chair and stood over her.

"I've had a breakthrough, Dr. Robosson. I just realized you're a psychopath. Like my uncle Peter. Thanks for the session."

I stalked out of the interrogation room and ran right into Hayes. He grabbed my shoulders, then shook my hand.

"You did it," he said. "Nailed her like a pro."

"What about Peter?"

"He's asked for his lawyer."

Crap. No doubt Peter would hire the best lawyer in New York, who could get him off.

5

THE BEST DAY OF MY LIFE

66

Months had passed since the conspiracy to kill me at Waterside Center had been thwarted. Now it was a warm summer evening in Manhattan, a long holiday weekend in July.

Leo was at the wheel, Uncle Jake was riding shotgun, and the rest of us were in the backseats of the long black car: me and Harry, Hugo, Matthew, and Kath, along with her baby son, George.

Yes, *Katherine*. My brave, sweet, wonderful big sister, who no longer had to hide her very existence from our uncle Peter.

It's been said that the wheels of justice grind slowly, but Matthew's lawsuit against the owner of our crashed aircraft had been quickly settled in our favor, and we were paying our own bills now.

Dr. Robosson agreed to testify against Peter in exchange for a lighter sentence and was now residing at Bedford Hills Correctional Facility, working off her next ten years, one slow day at a time.

Peter's trial date was still in the indeterminate future, but until then, he was being held without bail at Rikers Island. Most importantly, he no longer owned Angel Pharmaceuticals.

Philippe Montaigne, our family lawyer, good friend, and protector, produced the founding documents that my parents and Peter had prepared and signed twenty-five years ago. Despite the change of management due to the company's short-lived bankruptcy, once Peter resumed ownership, the original regulations were reinstated. Namely, that in the event none of the founders were available to run the company, control would pass to a committee of their offspring. By unanimous decision, my siblings elected me CEO of Angel Pharmaceuticals with fifty-one percent of the voting shares.

I had voted—and my siblings had gone along with me.

That was why we were all together now, heading downtown toward a gray concrete-slab factory in Hell's Kitchen as dusk settled over the city.

Our excitement was palpable as Leo slowed the car and pulled into an empty parking lot two blocks east of the Angel Pharmaceuticals plant. From this spot, we had a clear view of the factory, which was dark and empty on a Sunday evening.

Jacob and Leo opened the car doors and we all got out, breathless with anticipation. Speaking for myself, I was also a little bit fearful.

Harry put it into words.

"This might be the craziest thing you've done yet, Tandy. There are so many options that make more sense."

"I know," I said. "But this puts an end to this dirty business forever. I'm not going to regret it."

"No regrets here, either, Tandoo," said Katherine. "Nothing but blood money came from that horrible place."

She put her arm around my waist, and we lined up in a row facing Angel Pharmaceuticals.

Jacob looked at his watch.

"Ten seconds and counting," he said.

I grinned at him and he grinned back. We bumped fists, and of course, Hugo said, *"Booooommmm!"*

It was as if Hugo had pressed the detonator himself. Small controlled explosions erupted on several floors of the building like the beginning of a fireworks display.

All of us said *"Boom,"* even Leo and Uncle Jake.

And then, with sharp crackling sounds and huge clouds of dust, the whole freaking building crumpled, folding in on itself, and Angel Pharma, along with too many family nightmares to count, once and for all came tumbling down.

In the eerie aftermath of the explosions, as the dust clouds blended with the darkening sky, there was a surprising moment of silence. As Dr. Robosson had said, my father's dreams and Peter's had materialized in this place, and now all that was left of their terrible experiments were our wounded hearts and terrible memories.

I saw that Harry had tears on his cheeks. I hoped this was the end of his deeply felt grief at being the least-loved child.

And then the breeze coming off the Hudson River blew off the momentary sadness. I was filled with exhilaration. I felt liberated, as though Independence Day was inside *me*.

I was actually free.

My siblings and I whooped and embraced one another, and Matty cracked open a bottle of champagne and poured it over my head. More corks popped, and we all laughed and danced like fools in the delicious sparkling rain. I loved everyone here.

The wide-open views of the West Side of New York were wider and more open now that Angel Pharmaceuticals was rubble.

My God.

This was truly the best day of my life—so far. And I'm not done yet, not even *close*. But I know this right now. No other kids will take Angel Pharmaceuticals' heinous, unpredictable, brain-changing "vitamin pills" ever again.

And that's all I ever really wanted.
Game *over*. Case closed.
Wishing you the best of everything.
Your friend,
Tandoori Angel

ACKNOWLEDGMENTS

Our thanks to John A. Duffy for his touching lyrics, pilot Pete Colomello for his super aerodynamics, attorney Philip R. Hoffman for weighing in on the law, and Ingrid Taylar for her thorough research.

JAMES PATTERSON received the Literarian Award for Outstanding Service to the American Literary Community at the 2015 National Book Awards. He holds the Guinness World Record for the most #1 *New York Times* bestsellers, including *Confessions of a Murder Suspect* and the Maximum Ride series, and his books have sold more than 325 million copies worldwide. A tireless champion of the power of books and reading, Patterson has created a new children's book imprint, JIMMY Patterson, whose mission is simple: "We want every kid who finishes a JIMMY Book to say, 'PLEASE GIVE ME ANOTHER BOOK.'" He has donated more than one million books to students and soldiers and funds over four hundred Teacher Education Scholarships at twenty-four colleges and universities. He has also donated millions to independent bookstores and school libraries. Patterson invests proceeds from the sales of JIMMY Patterson Books in pro-reading initiatives.

MAXINE PAETRO has collaborated with James Patterson on the bestselling Women's Murder Club and Private series. She lives with her husband in New York State.

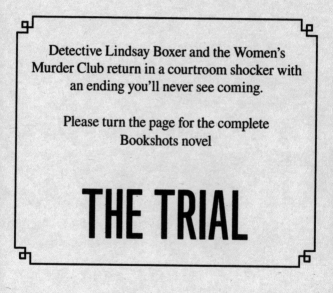

Detective Lindsay Boxer and the Women's
Murder Club return in a courtroom shocker with
an ending you'll never see coming.

Please turn the page for the complete
Bookshots novel

THE TRIAL

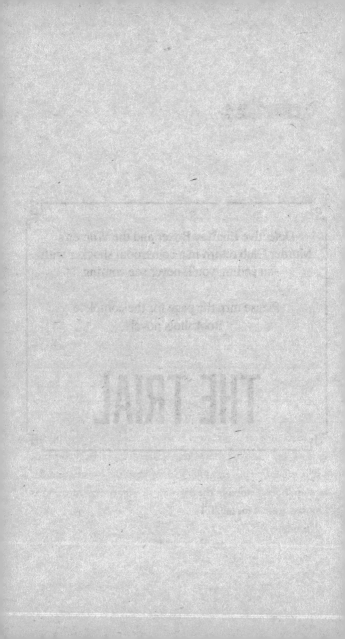

CHAPTER 1

IT WAS THAT CRAZY period between Thanksgiving and Christmas when work overflowed, time raced, and there wasn't enough light between dawn and dusk to get everything done.

Still, our gang of four, what we call the Women's Murder Club, always had a spouse-free holiday get-together dinner of drinks and bar food.

Yuki Castellano had picked the place.

It was called Uncle Maxie's Top Hat and was a bar and grill that had been a fixture in the Financial District for 150 years. It was decked out with art deco prints and mirrors on the walls, and a large, neon-lit clock behind the bar dominated the room. Maxie's catered to men in smart suits and women in tight skirts and spike heels who wore good jewelry.

I liked the place and felt at home there in a Mickey Spillane kind of way. Case in point: I was wearing straight-legged pants, a blue gabardine blazer, a Glock in my shoulder holster, and flat lace-up shoes. I stood in the bar area, slowly turning my head as I looked around for my BFFs.

"Lindsay. Yo."

Cindy Thomas waved her hand from the table tucked under the spiral staircase. I waved back, moved toward the nook inside the cranny. Claire Washburn was wearing a trench coat over her scrubs, with a button on the lapel that read SUPPORT OUR TROOPS. She peeled off her coat and gave me a hug and a half.

Cindy was also in her work clothes: cords and a bulky sweater, with a peacoat slung over the back of her chair. If I'd ducked under the table, I'm sure I would have seen steel-toed boots. Cindy was a crime reporter of note, and she was wearing her on-the-job hound dog clothes.

She blew me a couple of kisses, and Yuki stood up to give me her seat and a jasmine-scented smack on the cheek. She had clearly come from court, where she worked as a pro bono defense attorney for the poor and hopeless. Still, she was dressed impeccably, in pinstripes and pearls.

I took the chair across from Claire. She sat between Cindy and Yuki with her back to the room, and we all scooched up to the smallish glass-and-chrome table.

If it hasn't been said, we four are a mutual heart, soul, and work society in which we share our cases and views of the legal system, as well as our personal lives. Right now the girls were worried about me.

Three of us were married—me, Claire, and Yuki—and Cindy had a standing offer of a ring and vows to be exchanged in Grace Cathedral. Until very recently you couldn't have found four more happily hooked-up women. Then the bottom fell out of my marriage to Joe Molinari, the father of my child and a man I shared everything with, including my secrets.

We had had it so good, we kissed and made up before our fights were over. It was the typical: "You are right." "No, you are!"

Then Joe went missing during possibly the worst weeks of my life.

I'm a homicide cop, and I know when someone is telling me the truth and when things do not add up.

Joe missing in action had not added up. Because of that I had worried almost to panic. Where was he? Why hadn't he checked in? Why were my calls bouncing off his full mailbox? Was he still alive?

As the crisscrossed threads of espionage, destruction, and mass murder were untangled, Joe finally made his curtain call with stories of his past and present lives that I'd never heard before. I found plenty of reason not to trust him anymore.

Even he would agree. I think anyone would.

It's not news that once trust is broken, it's damned hard to superglue it back together. And for me it might take more time and belief in Joe's confession than I actually had.

I still loved him. We'd shared a meal when he came to see our baby, Julie. We didn't make any moves toward getting divorced that night, but we didn't make love, either. Our relationship was now like the Cold War in the eighties between Russia and the USA, a strained but practical peace called détente.

Now, as I sat with my friends, I tried to put Joe out of my

mind, secure in the knowledge that my nanny was looking after Julie and that the home front was safe. I ordered a favorite holiday drink, a hot buttered rum, and a rare steak sandwich with Uncle Maxie's hot chili sauce.

My girlfriends were deep in criminal cross talk about Claire's holiday overload of corpses, Cindy's new cold case she'd exhumed from the *San Francisco Chronicle*'s dead letter files, and Yuki's hoped-for favorable verdict for her client, an underage drug dealer. I was almost caught up when Yuki said, "Linds, I gotta ask. Any Christmas plans with Joe?"

And that's when I was saved by the bell. My phone rang.

My friends said in unison, "NO PHONES."

It was the rule, but I'd forgotten—again.

I reached into my bag for my phone, saying, "Look, I'm turning it off."

But I saw that the call was from Rich Conklin, my partner and Cindy's fiancé. She recognized his ring tone on my phone.

"There goes our party," she said, tossing her napkin into the air.

"Linds?" said Conklin.

"Rich, can this wait? I'm in the middle—"

"It's Kingfisher. He's in a shoot-out with cops at the Vault. There've been casualties."

"But—Kingfisher is *dead*."

"Apparently, he's been resurrected."

CHAPTER 2

MY PARTNER WAS DOUBLE-PARKED and waiting for me outside Uncle Maxie's, with the engine running and the flashers on. I got into the passenger seat of the unmarked car, and Richie handed me my vest. He's that way, like a younger version of a big brother. He thinks of me, watches out for me, and I try to do the same for him.

He watched me buckle up, then he hit the siren and stepped on the gas.

We were about five minutes from the Vault, a class A nightclub on the second floor of a former Bank of America building.

"Fill me in," I said to my partner.

"Call came in to 911 about ten minutes ago," Conklin said as we tore up California Street. "A kitchen worker said he recognized Kingfisher out in the bar. He was still trying to convince 911 that it was an emergency when shots were fired inside the club."

"Watch out on our right."

Richie yanked the wheel hard left to avoid an indecisive panel truck, then jerked it hard right and took a turn onto Sansome.

"You okay?" he asked.

I had been known to get carsick in jerky high-speed chases when I wasn't behind the wheel.

"I'm fine. Keep talking."

My partner told me that a second witness reported to first officers that three men were talking to two women at the bar. One of the men yelled, "No one screws with the King." Shots were fired. The women were killed.

"Caller didn't leave his name."

I was gripping both the dash and the door, and had both feet on imaginary brakes, but my mind was occupied with Kingfisher. He was a Mexican drug cartel boss, a psycho with a history of brutality and revenge, and a penchant for settling his scores personally.

Richie was saying, "Patrol units arrived as the shooters were attempting to flee through the front entrance. Someone saw the tattoo on the back of the hand of one of the shooters. I talked to Brady," Conklin said, referring to our lieutenant. "If that shooter is Kingfisher and survives, he's ours."

CHAPTER 3

I WANTED THE KING on death row for the normal reasons. He was to the drug and murder trade as al-Baghdadi was to terrorism. But I also had personal reasons.

Earlier that year a cadre of dirty San Francisco cops from our division had taken down a number of drug houses for their own financial gain. One drug house in particular yielded a payoff of five to seven million in cash and drugs. Whether those cops knew it beforehand or not, the stolen loot belonged to Kingfisher—and he wanted it back.

The King took his revenge but was still short a big pile of dope and dollars.

So he turned his sights on me.

I was the primary homicide inspector on the dirty-cop case.

Using his own twisted logic, the King demanded that I personally recover and return his property. Or else.

It was a threat and a promise, and of course I couldn't deliver.

From that moment on I had protection all day and night, every day and night, but protection isn't enough when your tormentor is like a ghost. We had grainy photos and shoddy footage from cheap surveillance cameras on file. We had a blurry picture of a tattoo on the back of his left hand.

That was all.

After his threat I couldn't cross the street from my apartment to my car without fear that Kingfisher would drop me dead in the street.

A week after the first of many threatening phone calls, the calls stopped. A report came in from the Mexican federal police saying that they had turned up the King's body in a shallow grave in Baja. That's what they said.

I had wondered then if the King was really dead. If the freaking nightmare was truly over.

I had just about convinced myself that my family and I were safe. Now the breaking news confirmed that my gut reaction had been right. Either the Mexican police had lied, or the King had tricked them with a dead doppelganger buried in the sand.

A few minutes ago the King had been identified by a kitchen worker at the Vault. If true, why had he surfaced again in San Francisco? Why had he chosen to show his face in a nightclub filled with people? Why shoot two women inside that club? And my number one question: Could we bring him in alive and take him to trial?

Please, God. Please.

CHAPTER 4

OUR CAR RADIO WAS barking, crackling, and squealing at a high pitch as cars were directed to the Vault, in the middle of the block on Walnut Street. Cruisers and ambulances screamed past us as Conklin and I closed in on the scene. I badged the cop at the perimeter, and immediately after, Rich backed our car into a gap in the pack of law enforcement vehicles, parking it across the street from the Vault.

The Vault was built of stone block. It had two centered large glass doors, now shattered, with a half-circular window across the doorframe. Flanking the doors were two tall windows, capped with demilune windows, glass also shot out.

Shooters inside the Vault were using the granite doorframe as a barricade as they leaned out and fired on the uniformed officers positioned behind their car doors.

Conklin and I got out of our car with our guns drawn and crouched beside our wheel wells. Adrenaline whipped my heart into a gallop. I watched everything with clear eyes, and yet my mind flooded with memories of past shoot-outs. I had been shot and almost died. All three of my partners had been shot, one of them fatally.

And now I had a baby at home.

A cop at the car to my left shouted, *"Christ!"*

Her gun spun out of her hand and she grabbed her shoulder as she dropped to the asphalt. Her partner ran to her, dragged her toward the rear of the car, and called in, "Officer down." Just then SWAT arrived in force with a small caravan of SUVs and a ballistic armored transport vehicle as big as a bus. The SWAT commander used his megaphone, calling to the shooters, who had slipped back behind the fortresslike walls of the Vault.

"All exits are blocked. There's nowhere to run, nowhere to hide. Toss out the guns, now."

The answer to the SWAT commander was a fusillade of gunfire that pinged against steel chassis. SWAT hit back with automatic weapons, and two men fell out of the doorway onto the pavement.

The shooting stopped, leaving an echoing silence.

The commander used his megaphone and called out, "You. Put your gun down and we won't shoot. Fair warning. We're coming in."

"WAIT. I give up," said an accented voice. "Hands up, see?"

"Come all the way out. Come to me," said the SWAT commander.

I could see him from where I stood.

The last of the shooters was a short man with a café au

lait complexion, a prominent nose, dark hair that was brushed back. He was wearing a well-cut suit with a blood-splattered white shirt as he came out through the doorway with his hands up.

Two guys in tactical gear grabbed him and slammed him over the hood of an SUV, then cuffed and arrested him.

The SWAT commander dismounted from the armored vehicle. I recognized him as Reg Covington. We'd worked together before. Conklin and I walked over to where Reg was standing beside the last of the shooters.

Covington said, "Boxer. Conklin. You know this guy?"

He stood the shooter up so I could get a good look at his face. I'd never met Kingfisher. I compared the real-life suspect with my memory of the fuzzy videos I'd seen of Jorge Sierra, a.k.a. the King.

"Let me see his hands," I said.

It was a miracle that my voice sounded steady, even to my own ears. I was sweating and my breathing was shallow. My gut told me that this was the man.

Covington twisted the prisoner's hands so that I could see the backs of them. On the suspect's left hand was the tattoo of a kingfisher, the same as the one in the photo in Kingfisher's slim file.

I said to our prisoner, "Mr. Sierra. I'm Sergeant Boxer. Do you need medical attention?"

"Mouth-to-mouth resuscitation, maybe."

Covington jerked him to his feet and said, "We'll take good care of him. Don't worry."

He marched the King to the waiting police wagon, and I watched as he was shackled and chained to the bar before the door was closed.

Covington slapped the side of the van, and it took off as CSI and the medical examiner's van moved in and SWAT thundered into the Vault to clear the scene.

CHAPTER 5

CONKLIN AND I JOINED the patrol cops who were talking to the Vault's freaked-out customers, now milling nervously in the taped-off section of the street.

We wanted an eyewitness description of the shooter or shooters in the *act* of killing two women in the bar.

That's not what we got.

One by one and in pairs, they answered our questions about what they had seen. It all came down to statements like *I was under the table. I was in the bathroom. I wasn't wearing my glasses. I couldn't see the bar. I didn't look up until I heard screaming, and then I ran to the back.*

We noted the sparse statements, took names and contact info, and asked each person to call if something occurred to him or her later. I was handing out my card when a patrolman came over, saying, "Sergeant, this is Ryan Kelly. He tends bar here. Mr. Kelly says he watched a conversation escalate into the shooting."

Thank God.

Ryan Kelly was about twenty-five, with dark, spiky hair. His skin was pale with shock.

Conklin said, "Mr. Kelly, what can you tell us?"

Kelly didn't hesitate.

"Two women were at the bar, both knockouts, and they were into each other. Touching knees, hands, the like. The blonde was in her twenties, tight black dress, drinking wine coolers. The other was brunette, in her thirties but in great shape, drinking a Scotch on the rocks, in a white dress, or maybe it was beige.

"Three guys, looked Mexican, came over. They were dressed right, between forty and fifty, I'd say. The brunette saw their reflections in the backbar mirror and she jumped. Like, *Oh, my God*. Then she introduced the blonde as 'my friend Cameron.'"

The bartender was on a roll and needed no encouragement to keep talking. He said there had been some back-and-forth among the five people, that the brunette had been nervous but the short man with the combed-back hair had been super calm and played with her.

"Like he was glad to meet her friend," said Kelly. "He asked me to mix him a drink called a Pastinaca. Has five ingredients that have to be poured in layers, and I had no open elderflower. There was a new bottle under the bar. So I ducked down to find it among a shitload of other bottles.

"Then I heard someone say in a really strong voice, 'No one screws with the King.' Something like that. There's a shot, and another right after it. Loud *pop, pop*. And then a bunch more. I had, like, a heart attack and flattened out on the floor behind the bar. There was screaming like crazy. I stayed down until our manager found me and said, 'Come on. Get outta here.'"

I asked, "You didn't see who did the shooting?"

Kelly said, "No. Okay for me to go now? I've told this to about three of you. My wife is going nuts waiting for me at home."

We took Kelly's contact information, and when Covington signaled us that the Vault was clear, Conklin and I gloved up, stepped around the dead men, their spilled blood, guns, and spent shells in the doorway, and went inside.

CHAPTER 6

I KNEW THE VAULT'S layout: the ground floor of the former bank had been converted into a high-end haberdashery. Access to the nightclub upstairs was by the elevators at the rear of the store.

Conklin and I took in the scene. Bloody shoe prints tracked across the marble floors. Toppled clothing racks and mannequins lay across the aisles, but nothing moved.

We crossed the floor with care and took an elevator to the second-floor club, the scene of the shooting and a forensics investigation disaster.

Tables and chairs had been overturned in the customers' rush toward the fire exit. There were no surveillance cameras, and the floor was tacky with spilled booze and blood.

We picked our way around abandoned personal property and over to the long, polished bar, where two women in expensive clothing lay dead. One, blond, had collapsed across the bar top, and the other, dark-haired, had fallen dead at her feet.

The lighting was soft and unfocused, but still, I could see that the blond woman had been shot between the eyes and had taken slugs in her chest and arms. The woman on the floor had a bullet hole through the draped white silk across her chest, and there was another in her neck.

"Both shot at close range," Richie said.

He plucked a beaded bag off the floor and opened it, and I did the same with the second bag, a metallic leather clutch.

According to their driver's licenses, the brunette was Lucille Alison Stone and the blonde was Cameron Whittaker. I took pictures, and then Conklin and I carefully cat-walked out of the bar the way we had come.

As we were leaving, we passed Charlie Clapper, our CSI director, coming in with his crew.

Clapper was a former homicide cop and always looked like he'd stepped out of a Grecian Formula commercial. Neat. Composed. With comb marks in his hair. Always thorough, never a grandstander, he was one of the SFPD's MVPs.

"What's your take?" he asked us.

"It was overkill," I said. "Two women were shot to death at point-blank range and then shot some more. Three men were reportedly seen talking to them before the shooting. Two of them are in your capable hands until Claire takes them. We have one alive, being booked now."

"The news is out. You think he's Kingfisher."

"Could be. I hope so. I really hope this is our lucky day."

CHAPTER 7

BEFORE THE MEDICAL EXAMINER had retrieved the women's bodies, while CSI was beginning the staggering work involved in processing a bar full of fingerprints and spent brass and the guns, Conklin and I went back to the Hall of Justice and met with our lieutenant, Jackson Brady.

Brady was platinum blond, hard bodied, and chill, a former narcotics detective from Miami. He had proven his smarts and his astonishing bravery with the SFPD over the last couple of years and had been promoted quickly to run our homicide squad.

His corner office had once been mine, but being head of paperwork and manpower deployment didn't suit my temperament. I liked working crime on the street. I hadn't wanted to like Brady when he took the lieutenant job, but I couldn't help myself. He was tough but fair, and now he was married to my dear friend Yuki Castellano. Today I was very glad that Brady had a history in narcotics, homicide, and organized crime.

Conklin and I sat with him in his glass-walled office and told him what we knew. It would be days before autopsies were done and guns and bullets were matched up with dead bodies. But I was pretty sure that the guns would not be registered, there would be no prints on file, and law enforcement might never know who owned the weapons that killed those women.

I said, "Their car was found on Washington—stolen, of course. The two dead men had both Los Toros and Mala Sangre tats. We're waiting for ID from Mexican authorities. One of the dead women knew Kingfisher. Lucille Alison Stone. She lived on Balboa, the thirty-two hundred block. Has a record. Shoplifting twice and possession of marijuana, under twenty grams. She comes up as a known associate of Jorge Sierra. That's it for her."

"And the other woman? Whittaker?"

"According to the bartender, who read their body language, Whittaker might be the girlfriend's girlfriend. She's a schoolteacher. Has no record."

Brady said, "Barry Schein, ADA. You know him?"

"Yes," Conklin and I said in unison.

"He's on his way up here. We've got thirty-six hours to put together a case for the grand jury while they're still convened. If we don't indict our suspect pronto, the FBI is going to grab him away from us. Ready to take a crack at the man who would be King?"

"Be right back," I said.

The ladies' room was outside the squad room and down the hall. I went in, washed my face, rinsed out my mouth, reset my ponytail. Then I walked back out into the hallway where I could get a signal and called Mrs. Rose.

"Not a problem, Lindsay," said the sweet granny who lived across the hall and babysat Julie Anne. "We're watching the Travel Channel. The Hebrides. Scotland. There are ponies."

"Thanks a million," I told her.

I rejoined my colleagues.

"Ready," I said to Brady, Conklin, and Barry Schein, the new rising star of the DA's office. "No better time than now."

CHAPTER 8

WHEN KINGFISHER BEGAN HIS campaign against me, I read everything I could find on him.

From the sparse reports and sightings I knew that the five-foot-six Mexican man who was now sitting in Interrogation 1 with his hands cuffed and chained to a hook on the table had been running drugs since before he was ten and had picked up the nickname Martin Pescador. That was Spanish for *kingfisher,* a small, bright-colored fishing bird with a prominent beak.

By the time Sierra was twenty, he was an officer in the Los Toros cartel, a savage paramilitary operation that specialized in drug sales up and down the West Coast and points east. Ten years later Kingfisher led a group of his followers in a coup, resulting in a bloody rout that left headless bodies from both sides decomposing in the desert.

Los Toros was the bigger loser, and the new cartel, led by Kingfisher, was called Mala Sangre, a.k.a. Bad Blood.

Along with routine beheadings and assassinations, Mala Sangre regularly stopped busloads of people traveling along a stretch of highway. The elderly and children were killed immediately. Young women were raped before execution, and the men were forced to fight each other to the death, gladiator style.

Kingfisher's publicity campaign worked. He owned the drug trade from the foot of Mexico to the head of Northern California. He became immensely rich and topped all of law enforcement's "Most Wanted" lists, but he rarely showed himself. He changed homes frequently and ran his business from a laptop and by burner phones, and the Mexican police were notoriously bought and paid for by his cartel.

It was said that he had conjugal visits with his wife, Elena, but she had eluded attempts to tail her to her husband's location.

I was thinking about that as I stood with Brady, Conklin, and Schein behind the mirrored glass of the interrogation room. We were quickly joined by chief of police Warren Jacobi and a half dozen interested narcotics and robbery inspectors who had reasonably given up hope of ever seeing Kingfisher in custody.

Now we had him but didn't own him.

Could we put together an indictable case in a day and a half? Or would the Feds walk all over us?

Normally, my partner was the good cop and I was the hardass. I liked when Richie took the lead and set a trusting tone, but Kingfisher and I had history. He'd threatened my life.

Rich opened the door to the interrogation room, and we took the chairs across from the probable mass killer.

No one was more primed to do this interrogation than me.

CHAPTER 9

THE KING LOOKED AS common as dirt in his orange jumpsuit and chrome-plated bracelets. But he wasn't ordinary at all. I thought through my opening approach. I could play up to him, try to get on his side and beguile him with sympathy, a well-tested and successful interview technique. Or I could go badass.

In the end I pitched right down the center.

I looked him in the eyes and said, "Hello again, Mr. Sierra. The ID in your wallet says that you're Geraldo Rivera."

He smirked.

"That's cute. What's your real name?"

He smirked again.

"Okay if I call you Jorge Sierra? Facial recognition software says that's who you are."

"It's your party, Officer."

"That's Sergeant. Since it's my party, Mr. Sierra it is. How about we do this the easiest and best way. You answer some questions for me so we can all call it a night. You're tired. I'm tired. But the internet is crackling. FBI wants you, and so do the Mexican authorities, who are already working on extradition papers. They are salivating."

"Everyone loves me."

I put the driver's licenses of Lucille Stone and Cameron Whittaker on the table.

"What were your relationships to these two women?"

"They both look good to me, but I never saw either one of them before."

"Before tonight, you mean? We have a witness who saw you kill these women."

"Don't know them, never saw them."

I opened a folder and took out the 8½ x 11 photo of Lucille Stone lying across the bar. "She took four slugs to the chest, three more to the face."

"How do you say? Tragic."

"She was your lady friend, right?"

"I have a wife. I don't have lady friends."

"Elena Sierra. I hear she lives here in San Francisco with your two children."

No answer.

"And this woman," I said, taking out the print of the photo I'd taken of the blond-haired woman lying on the bar floor.

"Cameron Whittaker. I counted three or four bullet holes in her, but could be more."

His face was expressionless. "A complete stranger to me."

"Uh-huh. Our witness tells us that these two, your girlfriend and Ms. Whittaker, were very into each other. Kissing and the like."

Kingfisher scoffed. He truly looked amused. "I'm sorry I didn't see them. I might have enjoyed to watch. Anyway, they have nothing to do with me."

I pulled out CSI's photos of the two dead shooters. "These men. Could you identify them for us? They both have two sets of gang tats but have fake IDs on them. We'd like to notify their families."

No answer, but if Kingfisher gave a flip about them, you couldn't tell. I doubted a lie detector could tell.

As for me, my heart was still racing. I was aware of the men behind the glass, and I knew that if I screwed up this interrogation, I would let us all down.

I looked at Richie. He moved his chair a couple of inches back from the table, signaling me that he didn't want to insert himself into the conversation.

I tried a Richie-like tack.

"See it through my eyes, Mr. Sierra. You have blood spatter on your shirt. Spray, actually. The kind a person would *expel* onto you if she took a shot to the lung and you were standing right next to her. Your hands tested positive for gunpowder. There were a hundred witnesses. We've got three guns and a large number of slugs at our forensics lab, and they're all going to tell the same story. Any ADA drawn at random could get an indictment in less time than it takes for the judge to say 'No bail.'"

The little bird with the long beak smiled. I smiled back, then I said, "If you help us, Mr. Sierra, we'll tell the DA you've been cooperative. Maybe we can work it so you spend your time in the supermax prison of your choice. Currently, although it could change in the near future, capital punishment is illegal in California. You can't be extradited to Mexico until you've served your sentence here. Good chance that will never happen, you understand? But you will get to *live*."

"I need to use the phone," Kingfisher said.

I saw the brick wall directly up ahead. I ignored the request for a phone and kept talking.

"Or we don't fight the extradition warrant. You take the prison shuttle down to Mexico City and let the *federales* talk to you about many mass murders. Though, frankly, I don't see you surviving long enough in Mexico to even get to trial."

"You didn't hear me?" our prisoner asked. "I want to call my lawyer."

Richie and I stood up and opened the door for the two jail guards, who came in and took him back to his cell.

Back in the viewing room Conklin said, "You did everything possible, Linds."

The other men uttered versions of "Too bad" and left me alone with Conklin, Jacobi, Brady, and young Mr. Schein.

I said, "He's not going to confess. We've got nothing. To state the obvious, people are afraid of him, so we have no witnesses. We don't know if he's the killer, or even if he is the King."

"Find out," said Brady. He had a slight southern drawl, so it came out "Fahnd out."

We all got the message.

Meeting over.

CHAPTER 10

IT WAS JUST AFTER 8:00 p.m. when I walked into the apartment where Julie and I live. It's on Lake Street, not too far from the park.

Mrs. Rose, Julie's nanny, was snoozing on the big leather sofa, and our HDTV was on mute. Martha, my border collie and dear old friend, jumped to her feet and charged at me, woofing and leaping, overcome with joy.

Mrs. Rose swung her feet to the floor, and Julie let out a wail from her little room.

There was no place like home.

I spent a good hour cuddling with my little girl, chowing down on Gloria Rose's famous three-protein meat loaf, downing a couple of glasses of Pinot Noir, and giving Martha a back rub.

Once the place was tidy, the baby was asleep, and Mrs. Rose had left for the night, I opened my computer and e-mail.

First up, Charlie Clapper's ballistics report.

"Three guns recovered, all snubbies," he wrote, meaning short-barreled .38 Saturday night specials. "Bullets used were soft lead. Squashed to putty, every one of them, no striations. Fingerprints on the guns and shells match the two dead men and the man you booked, identity uncertain. Tats on the dead men are the usual prison-ink variety, with death heads and so forth, and they have both the Los Toros bull insignia and lettering saying *Mala Sangre*. Photos on file."

Charlie's report went on.

"Blood on the clothing of the dead men and your suspect is a match to the blood of the victims positively identified as Cameron Whittaker, white, twenty-five, grade-school substitute teacher, and Lucille Stone, white, twenty-eight. ID says she was VP of marketing at Solar Juice, a software firm in the city of Sunnyvale.

"That's all I've got, Lindsay. Sorry I don't have better news. Chas."

I phoned Richie, and Cindy picked up.

My reporter friend was a cross between an adorable, girly journalist and a pit bull, so she said, "I want to work on this Kingfisher story, Linds. Tell Rich it's okay for him to share with me."

I snorted a laugh, then said, "May I speak with him?"

"Will you? Share?"

"Not yet. We'll see."

"Fine," Cindy huffed. "Thanks."

Richie got on the phone.

He said, "I've got something that could lead to motive."

"Tell me."

"I spoke with the girlfriend's mother. She says Lucy was seeing

Sierra but broke it off with him about a month ago. Right after that Lucy believed that Sierra was dead. I mean, we all did, right?"

"Correct."

"According to Lucy Stone's mother, Sierra went to Lucy's apartment yesterday and Lucy wouldn't let him in. Mrs. Stone said her daughter called her and told her that Sierra was angry and threatening. Apparently, Lucy was afraid."

"He could have staked her out. Followed her to the Vault."

"Probably, yeah. I asked Mrs. Stone if she could ID Sierra. And she said—"

"Let me guess. 'No.'"

"Bingo. However…"

"Don't tease me, Richie."

He laughed. "Here ya go. Mrs. Stone said that the King's wife, Elena Sierra, has been living under the name Maura Steele. I got her number and address on Nob Hill."

A lead. An actual lead.

I told Richie he was the greatest. He laughed again. Must be nice to have such a sunny disposition.

After hanging up, I checked the locks on the door and windows, double-checked the alarm, looked in on my darling Julie, and put my gun on my night table.

I whistled for Martha.

She bounded into the bedroom and onto the bed.

"Night-night, sweet Martha."

I turned off the light and tried to sleep.

CHAPTER 11

WE MET IN THE squad's break room the next morning: Conklin, Brady, ADA Schein, and me.

Schein was thirty-six, married, and a father of two. He reported directly to DA Len "Red Dog" Parisi, and he'd been pitching no-hitters since he took the job, sending the accused to jail every time he took the mound. Putting Kingfisher away would be Schein's ticket to a five-star law firm if he wanted it. He was suited up for the next big thing even now, close shaved and natty in this shabby setting, and he was all business. I liked it. I liked him.

Schein said, "Summarizing what we have: A 911 tape of a male with a Spanish accent reporting that he's seen Kingfisher at the Vault, and we presume that that's the man we arrested. The tipster said he was a kitchen worker but could have been anyone. He called from a burner phone, and this witness hasn't stepped forward."

Conklin and I nodded. Schein went on.

"We have a witness who saw the run-up to the shooting but didn't see the actual event."

I said, "We've got blood on the suspect's shirt."

"Good. But a juror is going to ask if he could have gotten that blood spray if he was near the victim but he didn't fire the weapon."

Schein shrugged. "What can I say. Yeah. Bottom line, twenty-four hours from now we get a 'proceed to prosecution' from the grand jury, or our suspect goes out of our hands and into the lap of a higher or different jurisdiction."

"Spell out exactly what you need," said Brady. He was making a list with a red grease pencil on a lined yellow pad.

"We need legally sufficient evidence and probable cause," said Schein. "And I can be persuasive up to a point."

"We have to positively ID our man as Jorge Sierra?"

"That's the price of admission. Without that, no hearing."

"Additionally," said Brady, "we get a witness to the shooting or to Sierra's intent to kill."

"That would nail it."

When the coffee containers and doughnut box were in the trash and we were alone at last, Rich said, "Cindy should run it in the *Chron* online."

"Like, 'SFPD needs info from anyone who was at the Vault on Wednesday night and saw the shooting'?"

"Yep," said Rich. "It's worked before."

CHAPTER 12

RICH WENT BACK TO the crime scene for another look, and I called the former Mrs. Jorge Sierra, now Ms. Maura Steele. She didn't answer the phone, so I signed out a squad car and drove to her address in Nob Hill.

I badged the doorman and asked him to ring up to Ms. Sierra-a.k.a.-Steele's apartment.

He said, "You just missed her."

"This is important police business," I said. "Where can I find her?"

"She went to the gym. She usually gets back at around ten o'clock."

It was quarter to. I took a seat in a wingback chair with a view of the street through two-story-tall plate-glass windows and saw the black limo stop at the curb. A liveried driver got out, went around to the sidewalk side of the car, and opened the rear door.

A very attractive woman in her late twenties or early thirties got out and headed toward the lobby doors while she went for the keys in her bag.

Ms. Steele was slim and fine boned, with short, dark, curly

hair. She wore a smart shearling coat over her red tracksuit. I shot a look at the doorman and he nodded. When she came through the door, I introduced myself and showed her my badge.

"Police? What's this about?"

"Jorge Sierra," I said.

She drew back. Fear flickered in her eyes, and her face tightened.

She said, "I don't know anyone by that name."

"Please, Ms. Steele. Don't make me take you to the station for questioning. I just need you to ID a photograph."

The doorman was fiddling with papers at the front desk, trying to look as though he wasn't paying attention. He looked like Matt Damon but didn't have Damon's talent.

"Come upstairs with me," Ms. Steele said to me.

I followed her into the elevator, which opened directly into her sumptuous apartment. It was almost blindingly luxurious, with its Persian carpets, expensive furnishings, and what looked to me like good art against a backdrop of the Golden Gate Bridge and San Francisco Bay.

I'd looked her up before getting into the car. Ms. Steele didn't have a job now and had no listing under Sierra or Steele on LinkedIn, Facebook, or Who's Who in Business. Odds were, she was living on the spoils of her marriage to one of the richest men west of the Rockies.

Steele didn't ask me to sit down.

"I want to be absolutely clear," she said. "If you quote me or depose me or in any way try to put me on the record, I will deny everything. I'm still married. I can't testify."

I took the mug shot out of my pocket and held it up for her to see. "Is this Jorge Sierra?" I asked. "Known as Kingfisher?"

She began nodding like a bobblehead on crack. I can't say I didn't understand her terror. I'd felt something like it myself.

I said, "Thank you."

I asked follow-up questions as she walked with me back toward the elevator door. Had her husband been in touch with her? When was the last time she'd spoken with him? Any idea why he would have killed two women in a nightclub?

She stopped moving and answered only the last question.

"Because he is *crazy*. Because he is *mental* when it comes to women. I tried to leave him and make a run for the US border, but when he caught me, he did this."

She lifted her top so that her torso was exposed. There was a large scar on her body, about fifteen inches wide by ten inches long, shirring her skin from under her breasts to her navel. It looked like a burn made by a white-hot iron in the shape of a particular bird with a prominent beak. A kingfisher.

"He wanted any man I ever met to know that I belonged to him. Don't forget your promise. And don't let him go. If he gets out, call me. Okay?"

"Deal," I said. "That's a deal."

CHAPTER 13

EARLY FRIDAY MORNING CONKLIN and I met with ADA Barry Schein in his office on the second floor of the Hall. He paced and flexed his hands. He was gunning his engines, which was to be expected. This was a hugely important grand jury hearing, and the weight of it was all on Barry.

"I'm going to try something a little risky," he said.

Barry spent a few minutes reviewing what we already knew about the grand jury—that it was a tool for the DA, a way to try out the case with a large jury in an informal setting to see if there was enough probable cause to indict. If the jury indicted Mr. Sierra, Schein could skip arraignment and take Sierra directly to trial.

"That's what we want," said Barry. "Speed."

Rich and I nodded that we got that.

Schein said, "There's no judge, no attorney for the defense, as you know. Just me and the jury," Schein said. "Right now we don't have sufficient evidence to indict Sierra on a murder of any degree. We can place him at the scene of the crime, but no one saw him fire his gun, and the forensics are inconclusive."

I said, "I'm ready to hear about your 'risky' move."

Schein straightened his tie, patted down his thinning hair, and said, "I've subpoenaed Sierra. This is rarely done, because the putative defendant is unlikely to testify against himself.

"That said, Sierra *has* to take the stand. Like most people in this spot, he'll plead the Fifth. So I'm going to try to use that to help us."

"How so?" I asked.

Schein cracked his first smile of the day.

"I'll lay out my case to the jury by asking Sierra: 'You had a plan in mind when you went to the Vault on the fourteenth, isn't that right? Lucille Stone was your girlfriend, correct, sir? But she rejected you, didn't she? You followed her and learned that she was involved with a woman, isn't that right, Mr. Sierra? Is that why you murdered her and Cameron Whittaker?'"

I didn't have to ask Schein to go on. He was still circling his office, talking from the game plan in his head.

"The more he refuses to answer," Schein said, "the more probable cause is raised in the jurors' minds. Could it backfire? Yeah. If the jury doesn't hold his refusal to testify against him, they'll hand me my hat. But we won't be any worse off than we are now."

An hour later Rich and I were in the San Francisco Superior Court on McAllister Street, benched in the hallway. Sierra had been brought into the courtroom through a back door, and as I'd seen when the front doors opened a crack, he was wearing street clothes, had shackles around his ankles, and was sitting between two hard-boiled marshals with guns on their hips.

Sierra's attorney, J. C. Fuentes, sat alone on a bench ten yards from where I sat with my partner. He was a huge, brutish-looking man of about fifty wearing an old brown suit. I knew him to be a winning criminal defense attorney. He wasn't an orator, but he was a remarkable strategist and tactician.

Today, like the rest of us, he was permitted only to wait outside the courtroom and to be available if his client needed to consult with him.

Rich plugged into his iPad and leaned back against the wall. I jiggled my feet, people-watched, and waited for news. I was unprepared when the courtroom doors violently burst open.

I jumped to my feet.

Jorge Sierra, still in chains, was being pulled and dragged out of the courtroom and into the hallway, where Mr. Fuentes, Conklin, and I stood, openmouthed and in shock.

Sierra shouted over his shoulder through the open doors.

"I have all your names, stupid people. I know where you live. Street addresses. Apartment layouts. You and your pathetic families can expect a visit very soon."

The doors swung closed and Fuentes rushed to Sierra's side as he was hauled past us, laughing his face off.

It was twenty past twelve. Rich said to me, "How long do you think before the jury comes back?"

I had no answer, not even a guess.

Fourteen minutes later Schein came out of the courtroom looking like he'd been through a wood chipper.

He said, "Sierra took the Fifth, and the jurors didn't like him. Before he got off the stand, he threatened them, and he didn't quit until the doors closed on his ass. Did you hear him? Threatening the jurors is another crime."

Rich said, "When do they decide, Barry?"

Schein said, "It's done. Unanimous decision. Sierra is indicted on two counts of murder one."

We pumped Schein's hand. The indictment gave us the time we needed to gather more evidence before Sierra went to trial. Conklin and I went back to the Hall to brief Brady.

"There is a God," Brady said, rising to his feet.

We high-fived over his desk, and Conklin said, "Break out the Bud."

It was a great moment. The Feds and the Mexican government had to step back. Jorge Sierra had been indicted for murder in California.

The King was in our jail and he was ours to convict.

CHAPTER 14

JOE AND I WERE dancing together close and slow. He had his hand at the small of my back, and the hem of my low-cut slinky red gown swished around my ankles. I couldn't even feel my feet because I was dancing on cotton candy clouds. I felt so good in Joe's arms—loved, protected, and excited, too. I didn't want this dance to ever end.

"I miss you so much," he said into my ear.

I pulled back so I could look into his handsome face, his blue eyes. "I miss you—"

I never got out the last word.

My phone was singing with Brady's ring tone, a bugle call.

I grabbed for the phone, but it slipped out of my hand. Still half under the covers, I reached for it again, and by that time Martha was snuffling my face.

God!

"Boxer," I croaked.

Brady's voice was taut.

"A juror was found dead in the street. Gunned down."

I said, "No."

He said, "'Fraid so."

He told me to get on it, and I called Richie.

It was Saturday. Mrs. Rose was off, but I called her anyway. She sounded both half asleep and resigned but said, "I'll be right there."

She crossed the hall in her robe and slippers and asked if I wouldn't mind taking Martha out before I took off.

After a three-minute successful dog walk I guzzled coffee, put down a PowerBar, and drove to Chestnut Street, the main drag through the Marina District. This area was densely lined with restaurants and boutiques, normally swarming with young professionals, parents with strollers, and twentysomethings in yoga pants.

All that free-spirited weekend-morning traffic had come to a dead halt. A crowd of onlookers had formed a deep circle at the barrier tape enclosing a section of street and the victim's body.

I held up my badge and elbowed my way through to where Conklin was talking to the first officer, Sam Rocco.

Rocco said, "Sergeant, I was telling Conklin, a 911 caller reported that one of the grand jurors in the Sierra jury had been 'put down like a dog.'"

"The operator said the caller sounded threatening. She got the street and cross street before the caller hung up," Rocco continued. "Feldman and I were here inside of five minutes. I opened the victim's wallet and got her particulars. Sarah Brenner. Lives two blocks over on Greenwich Street. From the coffee container in the gutter, looks like she was just coming back from Peet's on Chestnut."

"Anyone see the shooting?" I asked.

"None that will admit to it," said Officer Rocco.

"Cash and cards in the wallet?"

"Yep, and she's wearing a gold necklace and a watch."

Not a robbery. I thanked Rocco and edged around the dead body of a young woman who was lying facedown between two parked cars. She wore jeans and a green down jacket with down puffing out of its bullet holes, and nearby lay the slip-on mules that had been blown off her socked feet by the impact or the fall. Shell casings were scattered on the asphalt around the body, and some glinted from underneath the parked cars.

I lifted a strand of Sarah Brenner's long brown hair away from her face so that I could see her features. She looked sweet. And too young. I touched her neck to be sure she was really gone. *Goddamnit.*

Putting Sarah Brenner "down like a dog" was a crude term for a professional hit meant to scare everyone connected with Sierra's trial. Inciting fear. Payback. Revenge.

It was just Kingfisher's style.

I thought he might get away with killing this young woman as he had done so many times before. He would hit and run again.

CHAPTER 15

MONDAY MORNING RICH AND I reported to Brady what we had learned that weekend.

Rich said, "Sarah was twenty-five, took violin lessons at night, did paperwork for a dentist during the day. She had no boyfriend, no recent ex, and lived with two other young women and an African gray parrot. She had a thousand and twenty dollars in the bank and a fifty-dollar credit card balance for a green down jacket. No enemies, only friends, none known to have a motive for her killing."

"Your thoughts?" Brady asked me.

"Maybe the King would like to brag."

Brady gave me a rare grin. "Knock yourself out," he said.

I took the stairs from our floor, four, to maximum security on seven. I checked in at the desk and was escorted to Sierra's brightly lit, windowless cell.

I stood a good five feet from the bars of the King's cage.

He looked like someone had roughed him up, and the orange jumpsuit did nothing for his coloring. He didn't look like the king of anything.

He stood up when he saw me, saying, "Well, hello, Officer Lindsay. You're not wearing lipstick. You didn't want to look nice for me?"

I ignored the taunt.

"How's it going?" I asked him.

I was hoping he had some complaints, that he wanted a window or a blanket—anything that I could use to barter for answers to questions that could lead to evidence against him.

He said, "Pretty good. Thank you for getting me a single room. I will be reasonably comfortable here. Not so much everyone else. That includes you, your baby girl, even your runaround husband, Joseph. Do you know who Joseph is sleeping with now? I do. Do you want to see the pictures? I can have them e-mailed to you."

It was a direct shot to the heart and caught me off guard. I struggled to keep my composure.

"How are you going to do that?" I asked.

Sierra had an unpleasant, high-pitched laugh.

I'd misjudged him. He had taken control of this meeting and I would learn nothing from him about Sarah Brenner—or about anyone else. The flush rising from under my collar let both of us know that he'd won the round.

I left Jorge Sierra, that disgusting load of rat dung, and jogged down the stairs to the squad room, muttering, promising myself that the next point would be mine.

Conklin and I sat near the front of the room. We'd pushed

our desks together so that we faced each other, and I saw that Cindy was sitting in my chair and Conklin was in his own. There were open Chinese food cartons between them.

I said hello to Cindy. Conklin dragged up a chair for her and I dropped into mine.

"Nice of you to bring lunch," I said, looking at the containers. I had no appetite whatsoever. Definitely not for shrimp with lobster sauce. Not even for tea.

"I've brought you something even nicer," she said, holding up a little black SIM card, like from a mobile phone.

"What's that?"

"This is a ray of golden sunshine breaking through the bleak skies overhead."

"Make me a believer," I said.

"A witness dropped this off at the *Chron* for me this morning," Cindy said. "It's a video of the shooting at the Vault's bar. You can see the gun in the King's hand. You can see the muzzle aimed at Lucy Stone's chest. You can see the flare after he pulled the trigger."

"This is evidence of Sierra shooting Stone on film?"

She gave me a Cheshire cat smile.

"The person who shot this video has a name?"

"Name, number, and is willing to testify."

"I love you, Cindy."

"I know."

"I mean I *really* love you."

Cindy and Rich burst out laughing, and after a stunned beat I laughed, too. We looked at the video together. It was good. We had direct evidence and a witness. Jorge Sierra was cooked.

FOUR MONTHS LATER

CHAPTER 16

NO MATTER WHAT KIND of crappy day life dealt out, it was almost impossible to sustain a bad mood at Susie's Café.

I parked my car on Jackson Street, buttoned my coat, and lowered my head against the cold April wind as I trudged toward the brightly lit Caribbean-style eatery frequented by the Women's Murder Club.

My feet knew the way, which was good, because my mind was elsewhere. Kingfisher's trial was starting tomorrow.

The media's interest in him had been revived, and news outlets of all kinds had gone on high alert. Traffic on Bryant and all around the Hall had been jammed all week with satellite vans. None of my phones had stopped ringing: office, home, or mobile.

I felt brittle and edgy as I went through the front door of Susie's. I was first to arrive and claimed "our" booth in the back room. I signaled to Lorraine and she brought me a tall, icy brewski, and pretty soon that golden anesthetic had smoothed down my edges.

Just about then I heard Yuki and Cindy bantering together

and saw the two of them heading toward our table. There were kiss-kisses all around, then two of my blood sisters slid onto the banquette across from me.

Cindy ordered a beer and Yuki ordered a Grasshopper, a frothy green drink that would send her to the moon, and she always enjoyed the flight. So did the rest of us.

Cindy told me that Claire had phoned to say she would be late, and once Cindy had downed some of my beer, she said, "I've got news."

Cindy, like every other reporter in the world, was covering the Sierra trial. But she was a crime pro and the story was happening on her beat. Other papers were running her stories under her byline. That was good for Cindy, and I could see from the bloom in her cheeks that she was on an adrenaline high.

She leaned in and spoke only loud enough to be heard over the steel drums in the front room and the laughter at the tables around ours.

She said, "I got an anonymous e-mail saying that 'something dramatic' is going to happen if the charges against Sierra aren't dismissed."

"Dramatic how?" I asked.

"Don't know," Cindy said. "But I could find out. Apparently, the King wants me to interview him."

Cindy's book about a pair of serial killers had swept to the top of the bestseller lists last year. Sierra could have heard about her. He might be a fan.

I reached across the table and clasped Cindy's hands.

"Cindy, do not even think about it. You don't want this man to know anything about you. I oughta know."

"For the first time since I met you," Cindy said, "I'm going to say you are right. I'm not asking to see him. I'm going to just walk away."

I said, "Thank you, God."

Lorraine brought Cindy her beer, and Yuki took the floor.

She said almost wistfully, "I know Barry Schein pretty well. Worked with him for a couple of years. If anyone can handle the King's drama, it's Barry. I admire him. He could get Red Dog's job one day."

None of us would ever forget this very typical night at Susie's. Before we left the table, it would be permanently engraved in our collective memories. We were chowing down on Susie's Sunday-night special, fish fritters and rice, when my phone tootled. I had left it on only in case Claire called saying she wasn't going to make it. But it was Brady's ring tone that came through.

I took the call.

Brady gave me very bad news. I told him I was on my way and clicked off. I repeated the shocking bulletin to Cindy and Yuki. We hugged wordlessly.

Then I bolted for my car.

CHAPTER 17

FROM THE LOOK OF it, the Scheins lived in a classic American dream home, a lovely Cape Cod on Pacheco Street in Golden Gate Heights with a princely view, two late-model cars, a grassy yard, and a tree with a swing.

Today, Pacheco Street was taped off. Cruisers with cherry flashers marked the perimeter, and halogen lights illuminated an evidence tent and three thousand square feet of pavement.

The first officer, Donnie Lewis, lifted the tape and let me onto the scene.

Normally cool, the flustered CSI director, Clapper, came toward me, saying, "Jesus, Boxer, brace yourself. This is brutal."

My skin prickled and my stomach heaved as Clapper walked me to the Scheins' driveway, which sloped down from the street to the attached garage. Barry's body was lying faceup, eyes open, keys in his hand, the door to his silver-blue Honda Civic wide open.

I lost my place in time. The pavement shifted underfoot and the whole world went cold. I covered my face with my hands, felt Clapper's arm around my shoulders. "I'm here, Lindsay. I'm here."

I took my hands down and said to Clapper, "I just spoke with him yesterday. He was ready to go to trial. He was ready, Charlie."

"I know. I know. It never makes sense."

I stared down at Barry's body. There were too many holes punched in his jacket for me to count. Blood had outlined his body and was running in rivulets down toward the garage.

I dropped enough f-bombs to be seen on the moon.

And then I asked Clapper to fill me in.

"The little boy was running down the steps right there to greet his father. Daddy was calling to the kid, then he turned back toward the street. Must have heard the shooter's car pull up, or maybe his name was called. He turned to see—and was gunned down."

"How old is the child?"

"Four. His name is Stevie."

"Could he describe what he saw?" I asked Clapper.

"He told Officer Lewis that he saw a car stop about here on the road at the top of the driveway. He heard the shots, saw his father drop. He turned and ran back up the steps and inside. Then, according to Lewis, Barry's wife, Melanie, she came out. She tried to resuscitate her husband. Their daughter, Carol, age six, ran away to the house next door. Her best friend lives there.

"Melanie and Stevie are in the house until we can get all of them out of here."

"What's your take?" I asked Clapper.

"Either the driver tailed the victim, or he parked nearby, saw

Schein's car drive past, and followed him. When Barry got out of the car, the passenger emptied his load. Barry never had a chance."

We stepped away from the body, and CSIs deployed in full. Cameras clicked, video rolled, and a sketch artist laid out the details of the crime scene from a bird's-eye point of view. Techs searched for and located shell casings, put markers down, took more pictures, brought shell casings to the tent.

Conklin said, "Oh, my God."

I hadn't heard him arrive but I was so glad to see him. We hugged, hung on for a minute. Then we stood together in the sharp white light, looking down at Barry's body lying at our feet. We couldn't look away.

Rich said, "Barry told me that when this was over, he was taking the kids to Myrtle Beach. There's family there."

I said, "He told me he'd waited his whole career for a case like this. He told me he was going to wear his lucky tiepin. Belonged to his grandfather."

My partner said, "Kingfisher put out the hit. Had to be. I wish I could ask Barry if he saw the shooter."

I answered with a nod.

Together we mounted the brick front steps to the white clapboard house with black shutters, the remains of the Schein family's life as they had known it.

Now a couple of cops were going to talk to this family in the worst hour of their lives.

CHAPTER 18

WE RANG THE FRONT doorbell. We knocked. We rang the bell again before Melanie Schein, a distraught woman in her midthirties, opened the front door.

She looked past us and spoke in a frantic, disbelieving voice. "My God, my God, this can't be true. We're having chicken and potatoes. Barry likes the dark meat. I got ice cream pie. We picked out a movie."

Richie introduced us, said how sorry we were, that we knew Barry, that this was our case.

"We're devastated," Richie said.

But I don't think Barry's wife heard us.

She turned away from the door, and we followed her into the aromatic kitchen and, from there, into the living room. She looked around at her things and bent to line up the toes of a pair of men's slippers in front of a reclining chair.

I asked her the questions I knew by heart.

"Do you have a security camera?"

She shook her head.

"Has either of you received any threats?"

"I want to go to him. I need to be with him."

"Has anyone threatened you or Barry, Mrs. Schein?"

She shook her head. Tears flew off her cheeks.

I wanted to give her something, but all I had were rules and platitudes and a promise to find Barry's killer. It was a promise I wasn't sure we could keep.

I promised anyway. And then I said, "Witness Protection will be here in a few minutes to take you and the children to a safe place. But first, could we talk with Stevie for just a minute?"

Mrs. Schein led us down a hallway lined with framed family photos on the walls. Wedding pictures. Baby pictures. The little girl on a pony. Stevie with an oversized catcher's mitt.

It was almost impossible to reconcile this hominess with the truth of Barry's still-warm body lying outside in the cold. Mrs. Schein asked us to wait, and when she opened the bedroom door, I was struck by the red lights flashing through the curtains. A little boy sat on the floor, pushing a toy truck back and forth mindlessly. What did he understand about what had happened to his father? I couldn't shake the thought that an hour ago Barry had been alive.

With Mrs. Schein's permission Richie went into the room and stooped beside the child. He spoke softly, but we could all hear his questions: "Stevie, did you see a car, a truck, or an SUV?...Car? What color car?...Have you seen it before?...Did you recognize the man who fired the gun?...Can you describe him at all?…Is there anything you want to tell me? I'm the police, Stevie. I'm here to help."

Stevie said again, "Was a gray car."

Conklin asked, "How many doors, Stevie? Try to picture it." But Stevie was done. Conklin opened his arms and Stevie collapsed against him and sobbed.

I told Mrs. Schein to call either of us anytime. Please.

After giving her our cards, my partner and I took the steps down to the halogen-lit hell in front of the lovely house.

In the last ten minutes the street had thickened with frightened neighbors, frustrated motorists, and cops doing traffic control. The medical examiner's van was parked inside the cordoned-off area of the street.

Dr. Claire Washburn, chief medical examiner and my dearest friend, was supervising the removal of Barry Schein's bagged body into the back of her van.

I went to her and she grabbed my hands.

"God-awful shame. That talented young man. The doer made damned sure he was dead," said Claire. "What a waste. You okay, Lindsay?"

"Not really."

Claire and I agreed to speak later. The rear doors to the coroner's van slammed shut and the vehicle took off. I was looking for Conklin when an enormous, pear-shaped man I knew very well ducked under the tape and cast his shadow over the scene.

Leonard Parisi was San Francisco's district attorney. He wasn't just physically imposing, he was a career prosecutor with a long record of wins.

"This is...abominable," said Parisi.

"Fucking tragedy," Conklin said, his voice cracking.

I said, "I'm so sorry, Len. We're about to canvass. Maybe someone saw something. Maybe a camera caught a license plate."

Parisi nodded. "I'm getting a continuance on the trial," he said. "I'm taking over for Barry. I'm going to make Kingfisher wish he were dead."

CHAPTER 19

A WEEK HAD PASSED since Barry Schein was killed fifteen hours before Sierra's trial had been scheduled to begin. We had no leads and no suspects for his murder, but we had convincing direct evidence against Sierra for the murders of Lucille Stone and Cameron Whittaker.

Our case was solid. What could possibly go wrong?

The Hall of Justice was home to the offices of the DA and the ME, as well as to the county jail and the superior court of the Criminal Division. For his security and ours, Sierra was being housed and tried right here.

Rich, Cindy, Yuki, and I sat together in the back row of a blond-wood-paneled courtroom that was packed with reporters, the friends and families of Sierra's victims, and a smattering of law students who were able to get in to see the trial of the decade.

At 9:00 a.m. Sierra was brought in through the rear door of Courtroom 2C. A collective gasp nearly sucked up all the air in the room.

The King had cleaned up since I'd last seen him. He'd had

a nice close shave and a haircut. The orange jumpsuit had been swapped out for a gray sports jacket, a freshly pressed pair of slacks, a blue shirt, and a paisley tie. He looked like a fine citizen, except for the ten pounds of shackles around his ankles and wrists that were linked to the belt cinched around his waist.

He clanked over to the defense table. Two marshals removed the handcuffs and took their seats in the first row behind the rail, directly behind Sierra and his attorney, J. C. Fuentes.

Sierra spoke into his lawyer's ear, and Fuentes shook his head furiously, looking very much like a wild animal.

At the prosecution counsel table across the aisle, Red Dog Parisi and two of his ADAs represented the side of good against evil. Parisi was too big to be a snappy dresser, but his navy-blue suit and striped tie gave him a buttoned-up look and set off his coarse auburn hair.

He looked formidable. He looked loaded for bear.

I was sure of it. Kingfisher had met his match. And my money was on Red Dog.

CHAPTER 20

THE BUTTERFLIES IN MY stomach rose up and took a few laps as the Honorable Baron Crispin entered the courtroom and the bailiff asked us all to rise.

Judge Crispin came from Harvard Law, and it was said that he was a viable candidate for the US Supreme Court. I knew him to be a no-nonsense judge, strictly by the book. When he was seated, he took a look at his laptop, exchanged a few words with the court reporter, and then called the court to order.

The judge said a few words about proper decorum and instructed the spectators in what was unacceptable in his court. "This is not reality TV. There will be no outcries or applause. Cell phones must be turned off. If a phone rings, the owner of that phone will be removed from the courtroom. And please, wait for recesses before leaving for any reason. If someone sneezes, let's just *imagine* that others are saying 'God bless you.'"

While the judge was speaking, I was looking at the back of Kingfisher's head. Without warning, the King shot to his feet.

His attorney put a hand on his arm and made a futile attempt to force him back down.

But Kingfisher would not be stopped.

He turned his head toward DA Parisi and shouted, "You are going to die a terrible death if this trial proceeds, Mr. Dog. You, too, Judge Crispy. That's a threat and a promise. A death sentence, too."

Judge Crispin yelled to the marshals, "Get him out of here."

Parisi's voice boomed over the screams and general pandemonium. "Your Honor. Please sequester the jury."

By then the marshals had charged through the gate, kicked chairs out of their way, and cuffed Sierra's wrists, after which they shoved and pushed the defendant across the well and out the rear door.

I was also on my feet, following the marshals and their prisoner out that back door that connected to the private corridor and elevators for court officers and staff.

Attorney J. C. Fuentes was at my heels.

The door closed behind us and Sierra saw me. He said, "You, too, will die, Sergeant Boxer. You are still on my list. I haven't forgotten you."

I shouted at Sierra's guards, "Don't let him talk to anyone. *Anyone.* Do you understand?"

I was panting from fear and stress, but I stayed right on them as they marched Sierra along the section of hallway to the elevators, keeping distance between Sierra and his lawyer. When

Sierra and his guards had gotten inside the elevator, the doors had closed, and the needle on the dial was moving up, I turned on Fuentes.

"Remove yourself from this case."

"You must be kidding."

"I'm dead serious. Tell Crispin that Sierra threatened your life and he will believe you. Or how does this sound? I'll arrest you on suspicion of conspiring to murder Barry Schein. I may do it anyway."

"You don't have to threaten me. I'll be glad to get away from him. Far away."

"You're welcome," I said. "Let's go talk to the judge."

CHAPTER 21

CHIEF OF POLICE WARREN Jacobi's corner office was on the fifth floor of the Hall, overlooking Bryant.

Jacobi and I had once been partners, and over the ten years we had worked together, we had bonded for life. The gunshot injuries he'd gotten on the job had aged him, and he looked ten years older than his fifty-five years.

At present his office was packed to standing room only.

Brady and Parisi, Conklin and I, and every inspector in Homicide, Narcotics, and Robbery were standing shoulder to shoulder as the Kingfisher situation was discussed and assignments were handed out.

There was a firm knock on the door and Mayor Robert Caputo walked in. He nodded at us in a general greeting and asked the chief for a briefing.

Jacobi said, "The jury is sequestered inside the jail. We're organizing additional security details now."

"Inside the actual jail?" said Caputo.

"We have an empty pod of cells on six," Jacobi said of the

vacancy left when a section of the women's jail was relocated to the new jail on 7th Street. He described the plan to bring in mattresses and personal items, all of this calculated to keep the jury free of exposure to media or accidental information leaks.

"We've set up a command center in the lobby, and anything that comes into or out of the sixth floor will go through metal detectors and be visually inspected."

Jacobi explained that the judge had refused to be locked down but that he had 24/7 security at his home. Caputo thanked Jacobi and left the room. When the meeting ended, Brady took me aside.

"Boxer, I'm putting two cars on your house. We need to know where you are at all times. Don't go rogue, okay?"

"Right, Brady. But—"

"Don't tell me you can take care of yourself. Be smart."

Conklin and I took the first shift on the sixth floor, and I made phone calls.

When I got home that evening, I told my protection detail to wait for me.

I took my warm and sleepy Julie out of her bed and filled Mrs. Rose in on my plan as we gathered toys and a traveling bag. When my bodyguards gave me the all clear, I went back downstairs with my still-sleepy baby in my arms. Mrs. Rose and I strapped her into her car seat in the back. Martha jumped after us.

Deputy sheriffs took over for our beat cops and escorted me

on the long drive to Half Moon Bay. I waited for their okay, and then I parked in my sister's driveway.

I let Martha out and gently extricated my little girl from the car seat. I hugged her awake. She put her hands in my hair and smiled.

"Mommy?"

"Yes, my sweets. Did you have a good nap?"

Catherine came out to meet me. She put her arm around me and walked me and Julie inside her lovely, beachy house near the bay. She had already set up her girls' old crib, and we tried to put a good spin on this dislocation for Julie, but Julie wasn't buying it. She could and did go from smiles to stratospheric protests when she was unhappy.

I didn't want to leave her, either.

I turned to Cat and said, "I've texted Joe. He's on call for whenever you need him. He'll sleep on the couch."

"Sounds good," she said. "I like having a man around the house. Especially one with a gun."

"Don't worry," Cat and I said in unison.

We laughed, hugged, kissed, and then I shushed Julie and told Martha that she was in charge.

I had my hand on my gun when I left Cat's house and got into my car. I stayed in radio contact with my escorts, and with one car in the lead and the other behind me, we started back up the coast to my apartment on Lake Street.

I gripped the wheel so hard my hands hurt, which was preferable to feeling them shake. I stared out at the taillights in front of me. They looked like the malevolent red eyes of those monsters you see in horror movies. Kingfisher was worse than all of them put together.

I hated being afraid of him.

I hated that son of a bitch entirely.

CHAPTER 22

AN HOUR AFTER I got home to my dark and empty apartment, Joe's name lit up the caller ID.

I thumbed the On button, nearly shouting, "What's wrong?"

"Linds, I've got information for you," he said.

"Where are you?"

"On 280 South. Cat called me. Julie is inconsolable. I know I agreed that it was safe to take her there, but honestly, don't you think it would have made more sense for me to come over and stay with the two of you on Lake Street?"

I was filled with complex and contradictory rage.

It was true that it would have been easier, more expeditious, for Joe to have checked into our apartment, slept on our sofa instead of Cat's. True that along with my security detail, we would have been safe right here.

But I wasn't ready for Joe to move back in for a few nights— or whatever. Because along with my justifiable rage, I still loved a man I no longer completely trusted.

"I had to make a quick decision, Joe," I snapped. "What's the information?"

"Reliable sources say that there's Mexican gang activity on the move in San Francisco."

"Could you be more specific?"

"Hey. Blondie. Could you please take it easy?"

"Okay. Sorry," I said. The line was silent. I said, "Joe. Are you still there?"

"I'm sorry, too. I don't like anything about this guy. I've heard that Mala Sangre 'killer elites' have come to town to deliver on Kingfisher's threats. Los Toros activity has also been noted."

"Gang war?"

"I've told you all I know."

"Thanks, Joe. Drive safe. Call me if Julie doesn't settle down."

"Copy that," said Joe. "Be careful."

And the line went dead.

I stood with the phone pressed against my chest for a good long while. Then I called Jacobi.

CHAPTER 23

I WATCHED FROM THE top of the steps up to the Hall the next morning as hundreds of people came to work, lined up to go through the metal detectors, and walked across the garnet-marbled lobby to the elevator banks.

They all looked worried.

That was both unusual and understandable. Kingfisher's presence on the seventh floor felt like a kryptonite meteor had dropped through the roof and was lodged in the jail. He was draining the energy from everyone who worked here.

I went inside, passed through metal detection, and then took the stairs to the squad room.

Brady had called a special early-morning meeting because of the intel from Joe. He stood at the head of the open-space bull pen, his back to the door, the muted TV hanging above his head.

Cops from all departments—the night shift, the swing shift, and our shift—were perched on the edges of desks, leaned against walls. There were even some I didn't recognize from the northern station crammed into the room. I saw deputy sheriffs, motorcycle cops, and men and women in plain clothes and blue.

Brady said, "I've called y'all together because we could be looking at a citywide emergency situation."

He spoke about the possibility of drug gang warfare and he answered questions about Mala Sangre, about Kingfisher, about cops who had been killed at the King's order. They asked about the upcoming rescheduled trial and about practical issues. The duty rosters. The chain of command.

Brady was honest and direct to a fault. I didn't get a sense that the answers he gave were satisfying. But honestly, he had no idea what to expect.

When the meeting was over, when the dozen of us on the day shift were alone with our lieutenant, he said, "The jurors are having fits. They don't know what's going on, but they can see out the windows. They see a lot of cops.

"The mayor's coming over to talk to them."

The mayor was a great people handler.

I was in the sixth-floor dayroom when Mayor Caputo visited the jurors and explained that they were carrying out their civic duty. "It's not just that this is important," he said. "This could be the most important work of your entire lives."

That afternoon one of the jurors had a heart attack and was evacuated. A second juror, a primary caregiver for a dependent parent, was excused. Alternates, who were also in our emergency jury lockup, moved up to full jurors.

When I was getting ready to leave after my twelve-hour day, Brady told me that an ambitious defender, Jake Penney, had spent the last four days with Jorge Sierra and had said that he was good to go.

The countdown to Sierra's trial had begun again.

CHAPTER 24

I WAS SLEEPING WHEN Joe called.

The time on my phone was midnight, eight hours before the trial was to begin.

"What's wrong?" I asked.

"Julie's fine. The SFPD website is down. The power is out at the Hall."

I turned on the TV news and saw mayhem on Bryant Street. Barricades had been set up. Reporters and cameramen shouted questions at uniformed officers. The Hall of Justice was so dark it looked like an immense mausoleum.

I nuked instant coffee and sat cross-legged in Joe's chair, watching the tube. At 1:00 a.m. fire could be seen leaping at the glass doors that faced the intersection of Bryant and Boardman Place.

A network reporter said to the camera, "Chet, I'm hearing that there was an explosion inside the lobby."

I couldn't take this anymore. I texted Brady. He was rushed. He typed, *Security is checking in with me up and down the line. Don't come in, Boxer.*

Then, as suddenly as they had gone out, the lights in the Hall came back on.

My laptop was on the coffee table and I switched it on. I punched in the address for the SFPD site, and I was watching when a title appeared on our own front page: *This was a test.*

It was signed *Mala Sangre.*

Kingfisher's cartel.

This had been their test for what? For shutting down our video surveillance? For sending out threatening messages? For disabling our electronic locks inside the jail? For smuggling bombs into the Hall?

It would have been a laughable threat if Kingfisher hadn't killed two people from the confines of his windowless cell. How had he pulled that off? What else could he do?

I called Cat. She said, "Lindsay, she's fine. She was in sleepy land when the phone rang."

I heard Julie crying and Joe's voice in the background saying, "Julie-Bug, I'm here."

"Sorry. Sorry," I said. "I'll call you in the morning. Thanks for everything, Cat."

I called Jacobi. His voice was steady. I liked that.

"I was just going to call you," he said. "The bomb was stuck under the lip of the sign-in desk. It was small, but if it had gone off during the daytime…" After a pause Jacobi began again. "Hounds and the bomb squad are going through the building. The trial is postponed until further notice."

"Good," I said. But I didn't feel good. It felt like anything could happen. That Kingfisher was in charge of it all.

My intercom buzzed. It was half past one.

Cerrutti, my designated security guard, said, "Sergeant, Dr. Washburn is here."

Tears of relief filled my eyes and no one had to see them. I buzzed my friend in.

CHAPTER 25

CLAIRE CAME THROUGH MY door bringing hope, love, warmth, and the scent of tea roses. All good things.

She said, "I have to crash here, Lindsay. I drove to the office. It's closed off from both the street and the back door to the Hall. It's too late to drive all the way home."

I hugged her. I needed that hug and I thought she did, too. I pointed her to Joe's big chair, with the best view of the TV. On-screen now, a live report from Bryant Street.

Wind whipped through the reporter's hair, turning her scarf into a pennant, making her microphone crackle.

She squinted at the camera and said, "I've just gotten off the phone with the mayor's office and can confirm reports that there are no fatalities from the bomb. The prisoner, Jorge Sierra, also known as Kingfisher, remains locked in his cell.

"The mayor has also confirmed that Sierra's trial has been postponed until the Hall is cleared. If you work at 850 Bryant, please check our website to see if your office is open."

When the segment ended, Claire talked to me about the

chaos outside the Hall. She couldn't get to her computer and she needed to reach her staff.

Yuki called at two. "You're watching?"

"Yes. Is Brady with you?"

"No," she said. "But three cruisers are outside our apartment building. And I have a gun. Nothing like this has ever happened around a trial in San Francisco. Protesters? Yes. Bombs? No."

I asked her, "Do you know Kingfisher's new attorney?"

"Jake Penney. I don't know him. But this I do know. He's got balls."

Claire made soup from leftovers and defrosted a pound cake. I unscrewed a bottle of chilled cheap Chardonnay. Claire took off her shoes and reclined in the chair. I gave her a pair of socks and we settled into half a night of TV together.

I must have slept for a few minutes, because I woke to my cell phone buzzing on the floor beside the sofa.

Who was it now? Joe? Cat? Jacobi?

"Sergeant Boxer, it's Elena."

It took me a moment to put a face to a name. It came to me. Elena, a.k.a. Maura Steele, was Jorge Sierra's reluctant wife.

I bolted into an upright position. Had we thought to protect her? *No.*

"Are you okay?"

"I'm fine. I have an idea."

"I'm listening," I said.

CHAPTER 26

WHEN I'D MET WITH Elena Sierra, she had let me know that she wanted nothing to do with her husband. I had given her my card but never expected to hear from her.

What had changed her mind?

I listened hard as she laid out her plan. It was brilliant and simple. I had made this *same* offer to Sierra and utterly failed to close the deal. But Kingfisher didn't love *me*.

Now I had reason to hope that Elena could help put this nightmare to bed.

The meeting between Elena and her husband was arranged quickly. By late afternoon the next day our cameras were rolling upstairs in a barred room reserved for prisoners and their attorneys.

Elena wore a belted vibrant-purple sweaterdress and designer boots and looked like a cover girl. She sat across the table from Sierra. He wore orange and was chained so that he couldn't stand or move his hands. He looked amused.

I stood in a viewing room with Conklin and Brady, watching live video of Elena's meeting with Sierra, and heard him suggest several things he would like to do with her. It was creepy, but she cut him off by saying, "I'm not here for your pleasure, Jorge. I'm trying to help you."

Sierra leaned forward and said, "You don't want to help me. You want only money and power. How do I know? Because I created you."

"Jorge. We only have a few more minutes. I'm offering you the chance to see your children—"

"Mine? I'm not so sure."

"All you have to do is to plead guilty."

"That's all? Whose payroll are you on, Elena? Who are you working for, bitch whore?"

Elena got to her feet and slapped her husband hard across the face.

Joy surged through my body. I could almost feel my right palm stinging as if I had slapped him myself.

The King laughed at his wife, then turned his head and called out through the bars, "Take me back."

Two guards appeared at the cage door and the King was led out. When he was gone, Elena looked at the camera and shrugged. She looked embarrassed. She said, "I lost my temper."

I pressed the intercom. "You did fine. Thank you, Elena."

"Well, that was edifying," said Brady.

"She tried," I said to Brady. "I don't see what else she could have done."

I turned to Rich and said, "Let's drive her home."

CHAPTER 27

ELENA SIERRA HAD CURLED up in the backseat and leaned against the window. "He's subhuman," she said. "My father warned me, but I was eighteen. He was…I don't remember what the hell I was thinking. *If* I was thinking."

There was a long pause, as if she was trying to remember when she had fallen in love with Kingfisher.

"I'm coming to the trial," Elena said. "I want to see his face when he's found guilty. My father wants to be there, too."

Then she stared silently out the window until we pulled up to her deluxe apartment building on California Street. Conklin walked Elena into the lobby, and when he came back to the car, I was behind the wheel.

I switched on the car radio, which broke into a cacophony of bleats and static. I gave dispatch our coordinates as we left Nob Hill and said that we were heading back to the Hall.

At just about half past six we were on Race Street. We'd been stuck behind a FedEx truck for several blocks, until now, when it ran a yellow light, leaving us flat-footed at the red.

I cursed and the gray sedan behind us pulled out into the oncoming lane, its wheels jerking hard to the right, and the driver braked at an angle twenty-five feet ahead of our left front bumper.

I shouted, "What the hell?"

But by the time the word *hell* was out of my mouth, Conklin had his door open and was yelling to me, *"Out of the car. With me."*

I got it.

I snapped mental images as four men burst from the gray sedan into our headlight beams. One wore a black knit cap and bulky jacket. Another had a gold grille plating his teeth. The one coming out of the driver's side was holding an AK. One with a black scarf over half his face ducked out of view.

I dropped below the dash and pulled myself out the passenger side, slid down to the street. Conklin and I hunched behind the right front wheel, using the front of the car as a shield. We were both carrying large, high-capacity semiautomatics, uncomfortable as hell to wear, but my God, I was glad we had them.

A fusillade of bullets punched holes through the door that had been to my left just seconds before. Glass crazed and shattered.

I poked my head up during a pause in oncoming gunfire, and using the hood as a gun brace, Conklin and I let loose with a fury of return fire.

In that moment I saw the one with the AK drop his weapon. His gun or his hand had been hit, or the gun had slipped out of his grasp. When the shooter bent to retrieve it, Conklin and I fired and kept firing until the bastard was down.

For an eternal minute and a half curses flew, and shots punctured steel, exploded the shop windows behind us, and smacked into the front end of our car. If these men worked for the King, they could not let us get away.

Conklin and I alternately rose from behind the car just enough to brace our guns and return fire, ducking as our attackers unloaded on us with the fury of hell.

We reloaded and kept shooting. My partner took out the guy with the glittering teeth, and I wasn't sure, but I might have winged the one with the scarf.

The light turned green.

Traffic resumed, and while some vehicles streamed past, others balked, blocking cars behind them, leaving them in the line of fire.

There was a lull in the shooting, and when I peeked above our car, I saw the driver of the gray Ford backing up, turning the wheel into traffic, gunning the engine, then careening across the intersection at N17th.

I took a stance and emptied my Glock into the rear of the Ford, hoping to hit the gas tank. A tire blew, but the car kept going. I looked down at the two dead men in the street as Conklin kicked their guns away and looked for ID.

I got into the car, grabbed the mic, shouted my badge number, and reported to dispatch.

"Shots fired. Two men down. Send patrol cars and a bus to Race and N17th. BOLO for a gray Ford four-door with shot-out windows and flat right rear tire heading east on Race at high speed. Nevada plates, partial number Whiskey Four Niner."

Within minutes the empty, shot-riddled Ford was found ditched a few blocks away on 17th Street. Conklin and I sat for a while in our shot-to-shit squad car, listening to the radio snap, crackle, and pop while waiting for a ride back to the Hall. My right hand was numb and the aftershock of my gun's recoil still resonated through my bones.

I was glad to feel it.

I said to Richie, as if he didn't already know, "We're damned lucky to be alive."

CHAPTER 28

TWO HOURS AFTER THE shoot-out Conklin and I learned that the Ford had been stolen. The guns were untraceable. The only ID found on the two dead men were their Mala Sangre tats. Had to be that Kingfisher's men had been following us or following Elena.

We turned in our guns and went directly down the street to McBain's, a cross between a place where everyone knows your name and the *Star Wars* cantina. It was fully packed now with cops, lawyers, bail bondsmen, and a variety of clerks and administrators. The ball game was blaring loudly on the tube, competing with some old tune coming from the ancient Wurlitzer in the back.

Rich and I found two seats at the bar, ordered beer, toasted the portrait of Captain McBain hanging over the backbar, and proceeded to drink. We had to process the bloodcurdling firefight and there was no better place than here.

Conklin sat beside me shaking his head, probably having thoughts like my own, which were so vivid that I could still hear the *rat-a-tat-tat* of lead punching through steel and see the faces of the bangers we'd just "put down like dogs." I stank of gunpowder and fear.

We were alive not just because of what we knew about bad guys with guns, or because Conklin and I worked so well together that we were like two halves of a whole.

That had contributed to it, but mostly, we were alive and drinking because of the guy who'd dropped his AK and given us a two-second advantage.

After I'd downed half of my second beer, I told Conklin, "We weren't wearing vests, for Christ's sake. This is so unfair to Julie."

"Cut it out," he said. "Don't make me say she's lucky to have you as a mom."

"Fine."

"Two dirtbags are dead," he said. "We did that. We won't feel bad about that."

"That guy with the AK."

"He's in hell," said Rich, "kicking his own ass."

Oates, the bartender, asked if I was ready for another, but I shook my head and covered the top of my glass. Just then I felt an arm go around my shoulders. I started. It was Brady behind us, all white blond and blue-eyed, and he had an arm around Conklin, too.

He gave my shoulder a squeeze, his way of saying, *Thanks. You did good. I'm proud of you.*

"Come back to the house," Brady said. "I've got your new weapons and rides home for both of y'all."

"I've only had one beer," Rich lied.

"I've got rides home for *both* of y'all," Brady repeated.

He put some bills down on the bar. Malcolm, the tipsy dude on my left, pointed to the dregs of my beer and asked, "You done with that, Lindsay?"

I passed him my glass.

It was ten fifteen when I got to Cat's. I took a scalding shower, washed my hair, and buffed myself dry. Martha sat with her head in my lap while I ate chicken and noodles à la Gloria Rose. I was scraping the plate when the phone rang.

"I heard about what happened today," Joe said.

"Yeah. It was over so fast. In two minutes I'd pulled my gun and there were men lying dead in the street."

"Good result. Are you okay?"

"Never better," I said, sounding a little hysterical to my own ears. I'm sure Joe heard it, too.

"Okay. Good. Do you need anything?"

"No, but thanks. Thanks for calling."

I slept with Martha and Julie that night, one arm around each of my girls. I slept hard and I dreamed hard and I was still holding on to Julie when she woke me up in the morning.

I blinked away the dream fragments and remembered that Kingfisher would be facing the judge and jury today.

I had to move fast so that I wasn't late to court.

CHAPTER 29

CONKLIN AND I WERE at our desks at eight, filling out the incident report and watching the time.

Kingfisher's trial was due to start at nine, but would the trial actually begin? I thought about the power outage that had occurred two days ago, followed by the bomb explosion and the threatening message that had read *This was a test. Mala Sangre.* And I wondered if Kingfisher had already left the Hall through the drain in his shower, El Chapo style.

His trial had been postponed three times so far, but I had dressed for court nonetheless. I was wearing my good charcoal-gray pants, my V-neck silk sweater under a Ralph Lauren blazer, and my flat-heeled Cole Haan shoes. My hair gleamed and I'd even put on lipstick. *That's for you, Mr. Kingfisher.*

Conklin had just dunked his empty coffee container into the trash can when Len Parisi's name lit up on my console.

I said to Conklin, "What now?" and grabbed the phone.

Parisi said, "Boxer, you and Conklin got a second?"

"Sure. What's up?"

"Counsel for the defense is in my office."

"Be right there." I hung up, then said to Conklin, "I'm guessing Sierra wants to change his plea to insanity."

He said, "From your lips to God's ears."

It was a grim thought. In the unlikely event that Kingfisher could be found guilty because of mental disease or defect, he would be institutionalized and one day might be set free.

"There's just no way," said Conklin.

"Wanna bet?"

Conklin dug into his wallet and tossed a single onto the desk. I topped his dollar bill with one of mine and weighed down our bet with a stapler.

Then we booked it down the stairs and along the second-floor corridor at a good pace, before entering the maze of cubicles outside the DA's office. Parisi's office door was open. He signaled for us to come in.

Jake Penney, the King's new attorney, sat in the chair beside Parisi's oversized desk. He was about thirty-five and was good-looking in a flawless, *The Bachelor* kind of way. Because Cindy researched him and reported back, I knew he was on the fast track at a topflight law firm.

Kingfisher had hired one of the best.

Conklin and I took the sofa opposite Parisi, and Penney angled his chair toward us.

He said, "I want to ask my client to take Elena's offer. He changes his plea to guilty, and he goes to a maximum-security prison within a few hours' drive of his wife's residence. That's win-win. Saves the people the cost of a trial. Keeps Mr. Sierra in the USA with no death penalty and a chance to see his kids every now and again. It's worth another try."

Parisi said to Conklin and me, "I'm okay with this, but I wanted to run it by you before I gave Mr. Penney an okay to offer this deal to Sierra."

I said, "You'll be in the room with them, Len?"

"Absolutely."

"Mr. Penney should go through metal detection and agree to be patted down before and after his meeting."

"Okay, Mr. Penney?"

"Of course."

There was a clock on the wall, the face a hand-drawn illustration of a red bulldog.

The time was 8:21.

If the King's attorney could make a deal for his client, it had to be now or never.

CHAPTER 30

CONKLIN AND I WAITED in Parisi's office as the second hand swiped the bulldog's face and time whizzed around the dial.

What was taking so long? Deal? Or no deal?

I was ready to go up to the seventh floor and crash the conference when Parisi and Penney came through the door.

"He wouldn't buy it," Parisi said. He went to his closet and took out his blue suit jacket.

Penney said, "He maintains his innocence. He wants to walk out of court a free man."

It took massive willpower for me not to roll my eyes and shout, *Yeah, right. Of course he's innocent!*

Parisi shrugged into his jacket, tightened the knot in his tie, glanced at the clock. Then he said, "I told Sierra about the attack on you two by Mala Sangre thugs. I said that if the violence stops now, and if he is convicted, I will arrange for him to do his time at the prison of his choice, Pelican Bay. He said, 'Okay. I agree. No more violence.' We shook on it. For whatever that's worth."

Pelican Bay was a supermax-security prison in Del Norte

County, at the very northwest tip of California, about fifteen miles south of the Oregon border. It was a good six-and-a-half-hour drive from here. The prison population was made up of the state's most violent criminals and rated number one for most gangs and murders inside its walls. The King would feel right at home there.

"I'll see you in court," Parisi said to Penney.

The two men shook hands. Conklin and I wished Parisi luck, then headed down to the courtroom.

Kingfisher had agreed to the safety of all involved in his trial, but entering Courtroom 2C, I felt as frightened as I had when I woke up this morning with a nightmare in my mind.

An AK had chattered in the King's hands.

And then he'd gotten me.

CHAPTER 31

KINGFISHER'S DAY IN COURT had dawned again.

All stood when Judge Crispin, looking irritated from his virtual house arrest, took the bench. The gallery sat down with a collective *whoosh,* and the judge delivered his rules of decorum to a new set of spectators. No one could doubt him when he said, "Outbursts will be dealt with by immediate removal from this courtroom."

I sat in a middle row between two strangers. Richie was seated a few rows ahead to my right. Elena Sierra sat behind the defense table, where she had a good view of the back of her husband's head. A white-haired man sat beside her and whispered to her. He had to be her father.

The jurors entered the box and were sworn in.

There were five women and nine men, including the remaining alternates. It was a diverse group in age and ethnicity. I saw a range of emotion in their faces: stolid fury, relief, curiosity, and a high level of excitement.

I felt all those emotions, too.

During the judge's address to the jurors every one of them took a long look at the defendant. In fact, it was hard to look away from Kingfisher. The last time he was at the defense table, he'd cleaned up and appeared almost respectable. Today the King was patchily shaven and had flecks of blood on his collar. He seemed dazed and subdued.

To my eye, he looked as though he'd used up all his tricks and couldn't believe he was actually on trial. By contrast, his attorney, Jake Penney, wore his pin-striped suit with aplomb. DA Leonard Parisi looked indomitable.

All stood to recite the Pledge of Allegiance, and then there was a prolonged rustle as seats were retaken. Someone coughed. A cell phone clattered to the floor. Conklin turned his head and we exchanged looks.

Kingfisher had threatened us since the nasty Finders Keepers case last year—and *still* he haunted my dreams. Would the jury find him guilty of killing Stone and Whittaker? Would this monstrous killer spend the rest of his life inside the high, razor-wired walls of Pelican Bay State Prison?

The bailiff called the court to order, and Judge Crispin asked Len Parisi if he was ready to present his case.

I felt pride in the big man as he walked out into the well. I could almost feel the floor shake. He welcomed the jury and thanked them for bearing down under unusually trying conditions in the interest of justice.

Then he launched into his opening statement.

CHAPTER 32

I'D NEVER BEFORE SEEN Len Parisi present a case to a jury. He was an intimidating man and a powerful one. As district attorney, he was responsible for investigating and prosecuting crime in this city and was at the head of three divisions: Operations, Victims Services, and Special Operations.

But he was never more impressive than he was today, standing in for our murdered friend and colleague, ADA Barry Schein.

Parisi held the jury's attention with his presence and his intensity, and then he spoke.

"Ladies and Gentlemen, the defendant, Jorge Sierra, is a merciless killer. In the course of this trial you will hear witness testimony and see video evidence of the defendant in the act of shooting two innocent women to death."

Parisi paused, but I didn't think it was for effect. It seemed to me that he was inside the crime now, seeing the photos of the victims' bloodied bodies at the Vault. He cleared his throat and began again.

"One of those women was Lucille Stone, twenty-eight years old. She worked in marketing, and for a long time she was one of Mr. Sierra's girlfriends. She was unarmed when she was killed. Never carried a gun, and she had done nothing to Mr. Sierra. But, according to Lucy's friends, she had decisively ended the relationship.

"Cameron Whittaker was Lucy's friend. She was a substitute teacher, volunteered at a food bank, and had nothing whatsoever to do with Mr. Sierra or his associates. She was what is called collateral damage. She was in the wrong place at the wrong time."

I turned my eyes to the jury and they were with Len all the way. He walked along the railing that separated the jury box from the well of the courtroom.

He said, "One minute these friends were enjoying a girls' night out in an upscale nightclub, sitting together at the bar. And the next minute they were shot to death by the defendant, who thought he could get away with murder in full sight of 150 people, some of whom aimed their cell phones and took damning videos of this classic example of premeditated murder.

"I say 'premeditated' because the shooting was conceived before the night in question when Lucy Stone rejected Mr. Sierra's advances. He followed her. He found her. He taunted her and he menaced her. And then he put two bullet holes in her body and even more in the body of her friend.

"Lucy Stone didn't know that when she refused to open her door to him, he immediately planned to enact his revenge—"

Parisi had his hands on the railing when an explosion cracked through the air inside the courtroom.

It was a stunning, deafening blast. I dove for the floor and covered the back of my neck with my hands. Screams followed the report. Chairs scraped back and toppled. I looked up and saw that the bomb had gone off behind me and had blown open the main doors.

Smoke filled the courtroom, obscuring my vision. The spectators panicked. They swarmed forward, away from the blast and toward the judge's bench.

Someone yelled, "Your Honor, can you hear me?"

I heard shots coming from the well; one, then two more.

I was on my feet, but the shots sent the freaked-out spectators in the opposite direction, away from the bench, toward me and through the doors out into the hallway.

Who had fired those shots? The only guns that could have passed through metal detection into the Hall had to belong to law enforcement. Had anyone been hit?

As the room cleared and the smoke lifted, I took stock of the damage. The double main doors were nearly unhinged, but the destruction was slight. The bomb seemed more like a diversion than a forceful explosion meant to kill, maim, or destroy property.

A bailiff helped Parisi to his feet. Judge Crispin pulled himself up from behind the bench, and the jury was led out the side doorway. Conklin headed toward me as the last of the spectators flowed out the main doors and cops ran in.

"EMTs are on the way," he said.

That's when I saw that the defense table, where the King had been sitting with his attorney, had flipped onto its side.

Penney looked around and called out, "Help! I need help here!"

My ears still rang from the blast. I made my way around overturned chairs to where Kingfisher lay on his side in a puddle of blood. He reached out his hand and beckoned to me.

"I'm here," I said. "Talk to me."

The King had been shot. There was a ragged bullet hole in his shoulder, blood pumping from his belly, and more blood pouring from a wound at the back of his head. There were shell casings on the floor.

He was in pain and maybe going into shock, but he was conscious.

His voice sounded like a whisper to my deafened ears. But I read him, loud and clear.

"Elena did this," he said. "Elena, my little Elena."

Then his face relaxed. His hand dropped. His eyes closed and he died.

CHAPTER 33

JORGE SIERRA'S FUNERAL WAS held at a Catholic cemetery in Crescent City, a small northwest California town on the ocean named for the crescent-shaped bay that defined it.

Among the seventy-five hundred people included in the census were the fifteen hundred inmates of nearby Pelican Bay State Prison.

It was either irony or payback, but Elena had picked this spot because her husband had asked to be imprisoned at Pelican Bay and now he would be within eight miles of it—forever.

The graveyard had been virtually abandoned. The ground was flat, bleak, with several old headstones that had been tipped over by vandals or by weather. The chapel needed paint, and just beyond the chapel was a potholed parking lot.

Several black cars, all government property, were parked there, and a dozen FBI agents stood in a loose perimeter around the grave site and beside the chapel within the parking lot with a view of the road.

I was with Conklin and Parisi. My partner and I had been

told that Sierra was dead and buried once before. This time I had looked into the coffin. The King was cold and dead, but I still wanted to see the box go into the ground.

Conklin had suffered along with me when Sierra had terrorized me last year, and even though justice had been cheated, we were both relieved it was over.

The FBI had sent agents to the funeral to see who showed up. The King's murder inside the courthouse was an unsolved mystery. The smoke and the surging crowd had blocked the camera's view of the defense table. Elena Sierra and her father, Pedro Quintana, had been questioned separately within twelve hours of the shooting and had said that they had hit the floor after the blast, eyes down when the bullets were fired. They hadn't seen the shooting.

So they said.

Both had come for Sierra's send-off, and Elena had brought her children to say good-bye to their father.

Elena looked lovely in black. Eight-year-old Javier and six-year-old Alexa bowed their heads as the priest spoke over their father's covered coffin at graveside. The little girl cried.

I studied this tableau.

Elena had many reasons to want her husband dead. But she had no military background, nothing that convinced me that she could lean over the railing and shoot her husband point-blank in the back of the head.

Her father, however, was a different story.

I'd done some research into Mexican gangsters and learned that Pedro Quintana was the retired head of Los Toros, the original gang that had raised and trained Sierra on his path to becoming the mightiest drug kingpin of them all.

Sierra had famously disposed of Quintana after he split off from Los Toros and formed Mala Sangre, the new and more powerful drug and crime cartel.

Both Elena and her father had motive to put Sierra down, but how had one or both of them pulled off this shooting in open court?

I'd called Joe last night to brainstorm with him. Despite the state of our marriage, Joe Molinari had background to spare as an agent in USA clandestine services, as well as from his stint as deputy to the director of Homeland Security.

He theorized that during the power outage in the Hall, a C-4 explosive charge had been slapped onto the hinges of Judge Crispin's courtroom doors. It was plausible that one of the hundreds of law enforcement personnel prowling the Hall that night had been paid to set this charge, and it was possible for a lump of plastic explosive to go unnoticed.

A package containing a small gun, ammo, and a remote-controlled detonator could have been smuggled in at the same time, left where only Sierra's killer could find it. It could even have been passed to the killer or killers the morning of the trial.

Had Elena and her father orchestrated this perfect act of retribution? If so, I thought they were going to get away with it.

These were my thoughts as I stood with Conklin and Parisi in the windswept and barren cemetery watching the lowering of the coffin, Elena throwing flowers into the grave, the first shovel of dirt, her children clinging to their mother's skirt.

The moment ended when a limo pulled around a circular drive and Elena Sierra's family went to it and got inside.

Rich said to me, "I'm going to hitch a ride back with Red Dog. Okay with you?"

I said it was. We hugged good-bye.

Another car, an aging Mercedes, swung around the circle of dead grass and stone. It stopped for me. I opened the back door and reached out to my baby girl in her car seat. She was wearing a pink sweater and matching hat knit for her by her lovely nanny. I gave Julie a big smooch and what we call a huggy-wuffle.

Then I got into the front passenger seat.

Joe was driving.

"Zoo?" he said.

"Zooooooooo," came from behind.

"It's unanimous," I said. "The zoos have it."

Joe put his hand behind my neck and pulled me toward him. I hadn't kissed him in a long time. But I kissed him then.

There'd be plenty of time to talk later.

EPILOGUE

CHAPTER 34

THE LIMO DRIVER WHO was bringing Elena Sierra and the children back from a shopping trip couldn't park at the entrance to her apartment building. A long-used family car was stopped right in front of the walkway, where an elderly man was helping his wife out of the car with her walker. The doorman ran outside to help the old couple with their cumbersome luggage.

Elena told her driver, "Leave us right here, Harlan. Thanks. See you in the morning."

After opening the doors for herself and her children, Elena took the two shopping bags from her driver, saying, "I've got it. Thanks."

Doors closed with solid thunks, the limo pulled away, and the kids surrounded their mother, asking her for money to buy churros from the ice cream shop down the block at the corner.

She said, "We don't need churros. We have milk and granola cookies." But she finally relented, set down the groceries, found a five-dollar bill in her purse, and gave it to Javier.

"Please get me one, too," she called after her little boy.

Elena picked up her grocery bags, and as she stood up, she saw two men in bulky jackets—one with a black scarf covering the bottom of his face and the other with a knit cap—crossing the street toward her.

She recognized them as Jorge's men and knew without a doubt that they were coming to kill her. Mercifully, the children were running and were now far down the block.

The one with the scarf, Alejandro, aimed his gun at the doorman and fired. The gun had a suppressor, and the sound of the discharge was so soft the old man hadn't heard it, didn't understand what had happened. He tried to attend to the fallen doorman, while Elena said to the soldier wearing the cap, "Not out here. Please."

Invoking what residual status she might have as the King's widow, Elena turned and walked into the modern, beautifully appointed lobby, her back prickling with expectation of a bullet to her spine.

She walked past the young couple sitting on a love seat, past the young man leashing his dog, and pressed the elevator button. The doors instantly slid open and the two men followed her inside.

The doors closed.

Elena stood at the rear with one armed man standing to her left and the other to her right. She looked straight ahead, thinking about the next few minutes as the elevator rose upward, then chimed as it opened directly into her living room.

Esteban, the shooter with the knit cap, had the words *Mala*

Sangre inked on the side of his neck. He stepped ahead of her into the room, looked around at the antiques, the books, the art on the walls. He went to the plate-glass window overlooking the Transamerica Pyramid and the great bay.

"Nice view, Mrs. Sierra," he said with a booming voice. "Maybe you'd like to be looking out the window now. That would be easiest."

"Don't hurt my children," she said. "They are Jorge's. His blood."

She went to the window and placed her hands on the glass. She heard a door open inside the apartment. A familiar voice said loudly, "Drop your guns. Do it now."

Alejandro whipped around, but before he could fire, Elena's father cut him down with a shot to the throat, two more to the chest as he fell.

Pedro Quintana said to the man with the cap, who was holding his hands above his head, "Esteban, get down on your knees while I am deciding what to do with you."

Esteban obeyed, dropping to his knees, keeping his hands up while facing Elena's father, and beseeching him in Spanish.

"Pedro, please. I have known you for twenty years. I named my oldest son for you. I was loyal, but Jorge, he threatened my family. I can prove myself. Elena, I'm sorry. *Por favor.*"

Elena walked around the dead man, who was bleeding on her fine Persian carpet where her children liked to play, and took the gun from her father's hand.

She aimed at Esteban and fired into his chest. He fell sideways, grabbed at his wound, and grunted, *"Dios."*

Elena shot him three more times.

When her husband's soldiers were dead, Elena made calls: First to Harlan to pick up the children immediately and keep them in the car. "Papa will meet you on the corner in five minutes. Wait for him. Take directions from him."

Then she called the police and told them that she had shot two intruders who had attempted to murder her.

Her father stretched out his arms and Elena went in for a hug. Her father said, "Finish what we started. It's yours now, Elena."

"Thank you, Papa."

She went to the bar and poured out two drinks, gave one glass to her father.

They toasted. "Viva Los Toros."

Their cartel would be at the top again.

This was the way it was always meant to be.

BOOKS BY JAMES PATTERSON

Featuring Alex Cross

Cross the Line • *Cross Justice* • *Hope to Die* • *Cross My Heart* • *Alex Cross, Run* • *Merry Christmas, Alex Cross* • *Kill Alex Cross* • *Cross Fire* • *I, Alex Cross* • *Alex Cross's* Trial (with Richard DiLallo) • *Cross Country* • *Double Cross* • *Cross* (also published as *Alex Cross*) • *Mary, Mary* • *London Bridges* • *The Big Bad Wolf* • *Four Blind Mice* • *Violets Are Blue* • *Roses Are Red* • *Pop Goes the Weasel* • *Cat & Mouse* • *Jack & Jill* • *Kiss the Girls* • *Along Came a Spider*

The Women's Murder Club

15th Affair (with Maxine Paetro) • *14th Deadly Sin* (with Maxine Paetro) • *Unlucky 13* (with Maxine Paetro) • *12th of Never* (with Maxine Paetro) • *11th Hour* (with Maxine Paetro) • *10th Anniversary* (with Maxine Paetro) • *The 9th Judgment* (with Maxine Paetro) • *The 8th Confession* (with Maxine Paetro) • *7th Heaven* (with Maxine Paetro) • *The 6th Target* (with Maxine Paetro) • *The 5th Horseman* (with Maxine Paetro) • *4th of July* (with Maxine Paetro) • *3rd Degree* (with Andrew Gross) • *2nd Chance* (with Andrew Gross) • *1st to Die*

Featuring Michael Bennett

Bullseye (with Michael Ledwidge) • *Alert* (with Michael Ledwidge) • *Burn* (with Michael Ledwidge) • *Gone* (with Michael Ledwidge) • *I, Michael Bennett* (with Michael Ledwidge) • *Tick Tock* (with Michael Ledwidge) • *Worst Case* (with Michael Ledwidge) • *Run for Your Life* (with Michael Ledwidge) • *Step on a Crack* (with Michael Ledwidge)

The Private Novels

Missing (with Kathryn Fox) • *The Games* (with Mark Sullivan) • *Private Paris* (with Mark Sullivan) • *Private Vegas* (with Maxine Paetro) • *Private India: City on Fire* (with Ashwin Sanghi) • *Private Down Under* (with Michael White) • *Private L.A.* (with Mark Sullivan) • *Private Berlin* (with Mark Sullivan) • *Private London* (with Mark Pearson) • *Private Games* (with Mark Sullivan) • *Private: #1 Suspect* (with Maxine Paetro) • *Private* (with Maxine Paetro)

NYPD Red Novels

NYPD Red 4 (with Marshall Karp) • *NYPD Red 3* (with Marshall Karp) • *NYPD Red 2* (with Marshall Karp) • *NYPD Red* (with Marshall Karp)

Summer Novels

Second Honeymoon (with Howard Roughan) • *Now You See Her* (with Michael Ledwidge) • *Swimsuit* (with Maxine Paetro) • *Sail* (with Howard Roughan) • *Beach Road* (with Peter de Jonge) • *Lifeguard* (with Andrew Gross) • *Honeymoon* (with Howard Roughan) • *The Beach House* (with Peter de Jonge)

Stand-alone Books

Two from the Heart (with Frank Constantini, Emily Raymond, Brian Sitts) • *The Black Book* (with David Ellis) • *Humans, Bow Down* (with Emily Raymond) • *Never Never* (with Candice Fox) • *Woman of God* (with Maxine Paetro) • *Filthy Rich* (with John Connolly and Timothy Malloy) • *The Murder House* (with David Ellis) • *Truth or Die* (with Howard Roughan) • *Miracle at Augusta* (with Peter de Jonge) • *Invisible* (with David Ellis) • *First Love* (with Emily Raymond) • *Mistress* (with David Ellis) • *Zoo* (with Michael Ledwidge) • *Guilty Wives* (with David Ellis) • *The Christmas Wedding* (with Richard DiLallo) • *Kill Me If You Can* (with Marshall Karp) • *Toys* (with Neil McMahon) • *Don't Blink* (with Howard Roughan) • *The Postcard Killers* (with Liza Marklund) • *The Murder of King Tut* (with Martin Dugard) • *Against Medical Advice* (with Hal Friedman) • *Sundays at Tiffany's* (with Gabrielle Charbonnet) • *You've Been Warned* (with Howard Roughan) • *The Quickie* (with Michael Ledwidge) • *Judge & Jury* (with Andrew Gross) • *Sam's Letters to Jennifer* • *The Lake House* • *The Jester* (with Andrew Gross) • *Suzanne's Diary for Nicholas* • *Cradle and All* • *When the Wind Blows* • *Miracle on the 17th Green* (with Peter de Jonge) • *Hide & Seek* • *The Midnight Club* • *Black Friday* (originally published as *Black Market*) • *See How They Run* • *Season of the Machete* • *The Thomas Berryman Number*

BOOK**SHOTS**

Night Sniper (with Christopher Charles) • *Juror #3* (with Nancy Allen) • *The Shut-In* (with Duane Swierczynski) • *French Twist* (with Richard DiLallo) • *Malicious* (with James O. Born) • *Hidden* (with James O.

Born) • *The House Husband* (with Duane Swierczynski) • *The Christmas Mystery* (with Richard DiLallo) • *Black & Blue* (with Candice Fox) • *Come and Get Us* (with Shan Serafin) • *Private: The Royals* (with Rees Jones) • *Taking the Titanic* (with Scott Slaven) • *Killer Chef* (with Jeffrey J. Keyes) • *French Kiss* (with Richard DiLallo) • *$10,000,000 Marriage Proposal* (with Hilary Liftin) • *Hunted* (with Andrew Holmes) • *113 Minutes* (with Max DiLallo) • *Chase* (with Michael Ledwidge) • *Let's Play Make-Believe* (with James O. Born) • *The Trial* (with Maxine Paetro) • *Little Black Dress* (with Emily Raymond) • *Cross Kill* • *Zoo II* (with Max DiLallo)

Bedding the Highlander by Sabrina York • *The Wedding Florist* by T.J. Kline • *A Wedding in Maine* by Jen McLaughlin • *Radiant* by Elizabeth Hayley • *Hot Winter Nights* by Codi Gray • *Bodyguard* by Jessica Linden • *Dazzling* by Elizabeth Hayley • *The Mating Season* by Laurie Horowitz • *Sacking the Quarterback* by Samantha Towle • *Learning to Ride* by Erin Knightley • *The McCullagh Inn in Maine* by Jen McLaughlin

For Readers of All Ages
Maximum Ride

Maximum Ride Forever • *Nevermore: The Final Maximum Ride Adventure* • *Angel: A Maximum Ride Novel* • *Fang: A Maximum Ride Novel* • *Max: A Maximum Ride Novel* • *The Final Warning: A Maximum Ride Novel* • *Saving the World and Other Extreme Sports: A Maximum Ride Novel* • *School's Out—Forever: A Maximum Ride Novel* • *The Angel Experiment: A Maximum Ride Novel*

Daniel X

Daniel X: Lights Out (with Chris Grabenstein) • *Daniel X: Armageddon* (with Chris Grabenstein) • *Daniel X: Game Over* (with Ned Rust) • *Daniel X: Demons and Druids* (with Adam Sadler) • *Daniel X: Watch the Skies* (with Ned Rust) • *The Dangerous Days of Daniel X* (with Michael Ledwidge)

Witch & Wizard

Witch & Wizard: The Lost (with Emily Raymond) • *Witch & Wizard: The Kiss* (with Jill Dembowski) • *Witch & Wizard: The Fire* (with Jill Dembowski) • *Witch & Wizard: The Gift* (with Ned Rust) • *Witch & Wizard* (with Gabrielle Charbonnet)

Confessions

Confessions: The Murder of an Angel (with Maxine Paetro) • *Confessions: The Paris Mysteries* (with Maxine Paetro) • *Confessions: The Private School Murders* (with Maxine Paetro) • *Confessions of a Murder Suspect* (with Maxine Paetro)

Middle School

Middle School: Escape to Australia (with Martin Chatterton, illustrated by Daniel Griffo) • *Middle School: Dog's Best Friend* (with Chris Tebbetts, illustrated by Jomike Tejido) • *Middle School: Just My Rotten Luck* (with Chris Tebbetts, illustrated by Laura Park) • *Middle School: Save Rafe!* (with Chris Tebbetts, illustrated by Laura Park) • *Middle School: Ultimate Showdown* (with Julia Bergen, illustrated by Alec Longstreth) • *Middle School: How I Survived Bullies, Broccoli, and Snake Hill* (with Chris Tebbetts, illustrated by Laura Park) • *Middle School: My Brother Is a Big, Fat Liar* (with Lisa Papademetriou, illustrated by Neil Swaab) • *Middle School: Get Me Out of Here!* (with Chris Tebbetts, illustrated by Laura Park) • *Middle School, The Worst Years of My Life* (with Chris Tebbetts, illustrated by Laura Park)

I Funny

I Funny: School of Laughs (with Chris Grabenstein, illustrated by Jomike Tejido) • *I Funny TV* (with Chris Grabenstein, illustrated by Laura Park) • *I Totally Funniest: A Middle School Story* (with Chris Grabenstein, illustrated by Laura Park) • *I Even Funnier: A Middle School Story* (with Chris Grabenstein, illustrated by Laura Park) • *I Funny: A Middle School Story* (with Chris Grabenstein, illustrated by Laura Park)

Treasure Hunters

Treasure Hunters: Peril at the Top of the World (with Chris Grabenstein, illustrated by Juliana Neufeld) • *Treasure Hunters: Secret of the Forbidden City* (with Chris Grabenstein, illustrated by Juliana Neufeld) • *Treasure Hunters: Danger Down the Nile* (with Chris Grabenstein, illustrated by Juliana Neufeld) • *Treasure Hunters* (with Chris Grabenstein, illustrated by Juliana Neufeld)

Other Books for Readers of All Ages

House of Robots: Robot Revolution (with Chris Grabenstein, illustrated by Juliana Neufeld) • *Word of Mouse* (with Chris Grabenstein, illustrated by Joe Sutphin) • *Give Please a Chance* (with Bill O'Reilly) • *Jacky Ha-Ha* (with Chris Grabenstein, illustrated by Kerascoët) • *House of Robots: Robots Go Wild!* (with Chris Grabenstein, illustrated by Juliana Neufeld) • *Public School Superhero* (with Chris Tebbetts, illustrated by Cory Thomas) • *House of Robots* (with Chris Grabenstein, illustrated by Juliana Neufeld) • *Homeroom Diaries* (with Lisa Papademetriou, illustrated by Keino) • *Med Head* (with Hal Friedman) • *santaKid* (illustrated by Michael Garland)

For previews and information about the author, visit JamesPatterson.com or find him on Facebook or at your app store.